The
Serendipity

The
Serendipity
EMMA
ST. CLAIR

Chapter One
Archer

SOME MEN, when dealing with a not-quite-midlife crisis, might take an extended vacation. Maybe consider a complete career change. They might buy a new car. Start a new relationship. Take up a hobby, like juggling. Or BASE jumping.

Me? I buy a building in a town nowhere near the source of my crisis.

"And this is our basement." Galentine Valencia, the previous owner, does a little spin, arms outstretched as though she's in the middle of a flowering field rather than a dark, dusty basement. Her long floral dress flutters around her, and the costume jewelry jangles on her wrists like a jester's bells. Her bright red pouf of hair and sparkly green eyeshadow only add to the effect.

She has the look of a woman who grew up in musical theater.

I survey the large, low-ceilinged space where we're currently standing, which smells a little like sardines and musty newspapers. Thankfully, I see no sign of either.

"It *is* a basement," I agree. I don't have any other words to add.

The harder I frown, the wider Galentine smiles.

I've been trailing her around The Serendipity for the last half hour, getting a tour I didn't ask for filled with commentary as colorful as her outfit and personal stories—both of which I could do without. If Bellamy, the CEO of my company and my closest friend, had arrived on time, he would be the one listening as Galentine prattles on with her unamusing anecdotes. He'd probably even enjoy them. Then he'd fill me in on what I need to know without all the extra fluff I'm getting now.

But Bellamy isn't here, which means I'm trying to listen politely while fighting off my mounting frustration. I calm myself by making silent calculations about just how much work and time The Serendipity will require.

Because I didn't just buy a building—I bought a historic apartment building in need of a massive overhaul.

The Serendipity isn't in bad shape structurally. Honestly, that would be an easier fix. But the early-1900s college-dormitory-turned-apartment-building has great bones and has been exceptionally maintained. It is the embodiment of the cliché *they don't build them like they used to*.

I might prefer more modern, clean architecture, but even I can appreciate the brick exterior, elaborate scrollwork along the cornices, and the porch with wide cement steps reminiscent of a New York brownstone.

Inside, the building has been equally well-preserved, with original hardwood floors, high coffered ceilings, and thick crown molding. Even the renovations done years ago to transform the small dorm rooms into full-sized apartments were done almost seamlessly.

No, the overhaul isn't needed for the building itself but in terms of its general operation. *Overhaul* might be too small a word. The amount of work it will take to get this place profitable will require my entire focus in the coming months. Profit seems to be an unfamiliar word to Galentine.

For a few decades now, Galentine has been running The Serendipity less like an apartment building and more like a charity or nonprofit organization. Certainly, few—if any—profits are being made. I suspect when I actually dig into the books, which I opted not to do before making my hasty offer, I'll find that it's been operating at a significant loss.

My father would have called my deferred investigation a thoroughly *unconscionable* choice, the purchase itself *frivolous*, but thankfully, I only have echoes of his biting words in my head. No more surprise visits to my office with unsolicited performance reviews. And it's easy to avoid his phone calls since I changed my number. He still tries through his lawyers or through Bellamy, but he's also busy preparing his defense against the variety of financial crimes he apparently was committing for years.

So, no—I don't need my father's advice.

Even if what he'd say about this might ring true. This is a much bigger undertaking than I realized. On the plus side, its magnitude will provide maximum distraction for me at a time when I can really use it.

"The laundry room is this way," Galentine says. "Back in the dorm days, it used to be coin-operated, but I took care of that." She laughs.

Which I assume means now the use of the laundry facilities is completely free for residents at the expense of—well, now *me*.

"And over here, there's a large storage facility—"

"Storage for whom?" I ask.

"Residents, of course."

"And what do they store here?"

"Oh, you know." She waves a hand. "Odds and ends."

"Show me."

She leads me to a series of spaces separated by chain-link partitions and padlocked gates. Each numbered unit corresponds to one of the apartments in the four floors above our heads. Most are packed floor-to-ceiling with things better suited for a dumpster: boxes, bicycles, basketball hoops. I startle, thinking I see a person deep in the shadows of one unit, but when I squint, it's only a seamstress's dress form. I think.

So. Much. Junk.

"And how much does each storage unit cost per month?" I ask, fearing I already know the answer.

Galentine laughs again. "Oh, it's included in the rent. Did I mention I haven't raised the rent in the twenty-five years I've owned The Serendipity?"

"You did."

Twice.

"Commendable," I force myself to say.

Irrational, I think.

Galentine beams. "Thank you. The last area is the basement unit, and that's where John stays."

There's a basement unit?

"And John is...?"

"John is our full-time, live-in building manager," Galentine says.

"There's a building manager?" My best guess is that this is a fancy name for someone who sweeps the hallways and fixes plumbing issues.

"Yes. It's a salaried position—has been for the last seventeen years. He keeps this place running."

Salaried position.

I pull the tin of Barkley's Ginger Mints out of my pocket, shake three onto my palm, and pop them into my mouth. Numbers flash through my mind as the mints dissolve on my tongue, making my eyes water. I hope they settle my stomach. They certainly aren't helping settle my thoughts.

"I'd introduce you, but it's Wednesday afternoon. He's at Bingo."

"Bingo," I repeat, as though a standing weekly Bingo appointment before five o'clock is something relatable. I guess it's the kind of thing you do when you have the safety of a salaried position and a place to live.

She doesn't show me the inside of the unit—*For the sake of his privacy,* Galentine says—but tells me it's a roomy one bedroom with a full kitchen.

"And some natural light, which you don't usually get in a basement," she says. "There's a private exit leading to the pocket park next to our building." At my blank look, she adds, "It's not a full park, just a little space between buildings with a few benches and plants. You'll love it."

Will I? Other than running five miles a day, usually on sidewalks and not in parks, I don't spend much time outside.

"I'm sure it's lovely," I say.

I follow Galentine back into the elevator. It shudders and heaves a tired groan but manages to rise up to the fourth floor. The doors open to reveal a woman waiting for the elevator, with a large cat in her arms and a small dog on a leash. Galentine greets her with a hug as we step off, and I walk briskly away from the woman and her small zoo, sensing an imminent introduction I'd prefer to do without.

My people quota for the day has already been met ... and exceeded.

When Galentine catches up to me, I ask, "The building allows pets?"

"Oh, yes. We're one of the few places in the downtown area that do."

For now, I think, adding pet policy to the list in my mind of changes I'll be putting into place—starting tomorrow by eliminating John's salaried position, which apparently pays for Wednesday afternoon Bingo.

My lawyer is already looking at the leasing agreements to make sure the rent isn't fixed through contract. Because I will be ending Galentine's twenty-five years with no increase as soon as I'm legally able.

Then I'll eliminate wasted spaces, like the first-floor parlor, library, and commercial kitchen. These rooms might have had some functionality when this was a dormitory, but there's absolutely no need now. I'll start charging monthly fees for the storage units and figure out how to eliminate free laundry. If the units don't have washer and dryer hookups, the basement option might be a necessary evil. But there has to be a way for it to generate revenue.

A bigger undertaking will be filling in the pool and enclosing the courtyard to make more rentable units. Though construction in the courtyard may prove tricky. Perhaps there's a way to create a rental option for the outside area as well as the rooftop garden. Both would have event planners salivating.

Eventually, once I drive most of the tenants out through rent increases and policy changes, I'll renovate. The Serendipity will transition to luxury lofts. In a historic building like this, they'll bring in far more money.

We finally reach what is now my apartment door. Temporarily. At least until I feel safe returning to New York without the constant harassment of headlines and reporters following me around, shouting questions about my father's crimes and my alleged involvement. The lack of my name on any indictment should have been enough to silence their questions about me, but it's too juicy of a story.

Billionaire Father and Son Collude to Defraud Investors is more of a viral story than *Selfish Billionaire Businessmen Single-Hand-*

edly Defrauds Investors and Continues to Be a Complete Disappointment as a Father.

It didn't help that my father tried to throw me under the bus. You know, as fathers do.

"You don't mind if I take one last look around the apartment, do you?" Galentine asks. Her voice is a little hoarse, and I glance away when I see that her eyes are wet.

"Of course not," I tell her.

Because I'm not a monster, even if I don't relate to her need to see the spacious owner's apartment, which is where she's lived for the past twenty-five years.

When I walked out of my life two weeks ago, that's exactly what I did: I walked out. No tearful goodbyes with people or sentimental last looks at places.

Goodbye, New York. Hello, Serendipity Springs. As easy as that.

But I won't stand in the way or judge Galentine for seeking closure just because I don't need it in my own life.

The only furniture in the apartment to speak of right now is the desk in the second bedroom Galentine used as an office. There was an issue with the furniture company, but my things should arrive first thing tomorrow morning.

Galentine crosses the empty space and walks out on the balcony. She grips the railing, lifting her face to the sky, while I grab a bottle of water and chew another ginger mint.

The owner's apartment is The Serendipity's version of a penthouse. The unit encompasses the whole front width of the building's fourth floor, looking out onto the small city of Serendipity Springs.

And facing west, apparently, based on the intense sunlight beaming through the tall windows and almost straight into my eyes. Galentine doesn't seem bothered, though a moment later she comes back inside. She spins a slow circle in the living area, her heels echoing on the hardwoods.

"Thank you," she whispers.

I'm about to tell her *It's nothing* and drop a hint about the time when she continues speaking in the same hushed tone.

"Thank you for always giving me exactly what I needed when I needed it. You've been good to me over the years, just as I hope you'll be good to him."

She chuckles quietly. But given that this empty apartment is an acoustical nightmare at the moment, I can still hear every word as she talks to ... herself? Some long-dead relative?

To the building itself?

Based on the reverent way she speaks about The Serendipity, almost as though it's a sentient being—a character in her colorful life—I'd bet on the last option. Galentine is actually talking *to* the building.

In addition to giving me the Serendipity's whole history today, she prattled on, sharing stories about the building's legendary ability to bring luck and love to its tenants. A story in line with the silly tall tales I've heard about the city of Serendipity Springs itself.

Magical springs, good fortune, et cetera.

All nonsense, of course. About the town and the building. But clearly, some residents still hold these stories as true. Galentine being one.

"The Serendipity is the only building in town that's still spring-fed—that's where the magic comes from," she told me earlier with a wink as she gestured to the fountain in the courtyard. "It's why the town was named Serendipity Springs —because the spring water brings love and luck."

Whenever Galentine mentioned magic, I hoped she was speaking figuratively.

Like, wink, wink—*magic*.

But I'm more and more convinced that Galentine believes in the stories I only half listened to. Especially now, as she carries on a one-sided conversation with an inanimate object, now dropping her voice too low for me to hear.

I wonder if it would be rude to interrupt this imaginary conversation.

Don't get used to conversations, I silently warn the building.

Then realize what I've just done and silently chide myself: *Don't talk to buildings, Archer. And don't buy into anything Galentine Valencia is selling.*

"Even if he won't think he needs your help, don't give up on him," she says a little louder now. "Men like him are always the toughest nuts to crack, but they're the ones who most need a nudge. And love."

It would take more than a magical nudge to make me think about love right now.

Bright light suddenly beams directly into my eyes. The sun, dipping low, hits every window in the small downtown with blinding force.

For a moment, I can't see at all. I spin away from the windows, blinking until my vision returns to normal.

I add buying a set of blinds to my ever-growing to-do list.

But first—Galentine.

I clear my throat. She walks toward me, offering the kind of smile that makes concern rise in my chest. It's sincere, but with a small, knowing edge. Like there's a cosmic joke she's a part of—a joke on me.

No need to worry, I tell myself. *What can a woman who talks to buildings possibly know that I don't?*

I hold out a hand to shake, but Galentine launches herself at me in what's more of an assault than a hug. She smells like peaches and sentimentality as she pins my arms to my body with surprising strength.

"You're in good hands," she says, patting my back.

As much as I immediately want to break free, there's something comforting about her embrace. I can't remember the last time anyone hugged me. It feels ... motherly. Though I don't have any memories or personal experience to draw from there.

I find myself swallowing hard and blinking away ... are those *tears?*

Clearing my throat, I manage to grunt out a brusque *thank you.*

Giving me one last squeeze, Galentine releases me and steps back with a sniffle. I offer her a monogrammed handkerchief from my pocket. Her eyes light up as she takes it, dabbing at her eyes.

"I do like a man who carries a handkerchief," she says, then laughs. "Don't worry. You're too young for me. And I prefer blonds." She winks.

"Good to know." I wave her off when she tries to hand the handkerchief back. "Keep it. Please."

With a wide smile, Galentine tucks it away into her overstuffed purse. I wait to see if the bag's seams will hold. They do. If anything here is magical, it's her handbag.

"You'll find everything you need on the desk in the office, all in order," Galentine says, waving toward the closed door of the second bedroom, which has served as her work space. "Or ... somewhat in order. I have my own filing system."

She laughs, but I suspect I won't find it funny once I start going through her records. I only glanced inside the office and the clutter made my blood pressure immediately spike.

"Let me know if you have any questions—though I'll be on a cruise for the next month." She gives a little shimmy. "Can't wait."

"I'll be in touch if I need anything."

I won't. I can think of very few circumstances in which I would need help from a woman who speaks to buildings.

When I finally lock the door behind her, I lean against it for a moment, eyes closed. Waiting for the sense of relief I always feel when I transition from being around people to being alone.

One second, two, three.

But the constriction in my chest doesn't ease. If anything, it squeezes tighter. A fist, crushing coal into diamonds. Or just pulverizing stones into dust.

I work to breathe steadily through it, which is usually enough to help me pass through these moments of anxiety, most often brought on by spending too much time with unfamiliar people. Or too many people. Or just ... people. Normally, it's so manageable that it's hardly an issue. But I should have expected an uptick with so many changes all at once.

It takes me longer than it should to regain some sense of normalcy in my heart rate and breathing.

Eventually, I peel myself off the door, and I wander toward the windows and double doors leading to the balcony. With the sun now out of sight behind the small skyline of Serendipity Springs, a peaceful glow descends. The golden hour, I think photographers call it. And truly, it does soften everything, painting the city in the kindest light.

Serendipity Springs is no New York. Not even comparable. A few blocks of Manhattan could swallow up this small city. But there is something special here—something that drew me to this place.

And no—it wasn't magic.

I was drawn to the surprisingly robust economy of such a small city and the challenge of turning this historic building into something much greater and more profitable. A small task compared to the real estate empire I run in New York, but I *did* want a change. Something more hands-on. This will certainly be *that*.

Maybe a little too *hands on*, I think, my lip curling as I think of the air mattress I'll be sleeping on tonight. A hotel really would have been a better option. Even the basic establishments in this city at least have *beds*.

I'm lost in my thoughts when I hear a noise. A thud coming from the direction of my bedroom.

I frown. This unit doesn't share a wall with other apartments. The noise sounded much closer than it should. Almost as though it's coming from *inside* my apartment.

My nerves hum to life as I quietly walk through the open kitchen and living area toward the primary bedroom.

Another sound makes me stop in the doorway. This time, it's more of a shuffle. Followed by a mumble.

My skin prickles and my body tenses, flooding with adrenaline. These are *human* sounds.

And they seem to be coming from the closet.

Had I not watched Galentine leave, I might suspect she hid here, having second thoughts about leaving her magical building.

But I locked the door behind her. That's the only entrance, aside from the balcony, and certainly no one came in there.

I debate. Should I call the police? Grab the small lamp and brandish it as a weapon?

Another sound—a whisper.

"Who's there?" I call in the kind of sharp tone I usually reserve for boardrooms.

The stillness that follows is unnerving. Clearly, whoever is hiding inside my closet has frozen in place.

One way to fix that.

Striding forward, I throw open the door.

There's a woman.

In my closet.

From the sounds, logically, I could tell there was a person in there, but it's a different thing to see an actual woman crouched defensively on my closet floor.

With the way she's cowering, I can only make out wide eyes blinking up owlishly at me. Wisps of blond hair falling around her face. Full lips parted in what appears to be shock.

She's beautiful, in a messy, girl-next-door-on-a-bender kind of way. But that isn't my first thought.

My first thought is: "You're trespassing."

"What?"

I try a different approach. "Would you mind telling me who you are and why you're hiding in my closet?" I ask.

She hesitates for a moment, then rises to her feet. Standing, she barely reaches my shoulders. She's mid- to late-twenties, I suspect.

And beautiful, I catch myself thinking again, then force the errant and unwelcome thought away.

She's trespassing, I remind myself.

"I'm Willa," she says, barely above a whisper. "And I'm not sure why or how I got here." She pauses. "Where is *here*, exactly?"

"You're in my closet," I reply.

"Right. And you are?"

"The new owner of this building."

She frowns. "The Serendipity?"

"Yes. Are you a resident?"

She nods, and I'm not sure if I'm relieved or disappointed.

"So this would be Galentine's apartment?" she asks.

"Formerly. It was hers up until this morning, when we signed the paperwork. Now, it's mine. And again—I'd like to know why you're in my closet."

"So would I," she mutters, turning around and running her hands along the walls as though seeking a hidden door or passage.

It's a walk-in closet but barely meets the definition. It could possibly fit two people, though not comfortably.

The woman—*Willow, she said?*—is now pushing on the

back wall. She rattles the single rod with its two empty hangers, and for a moment, I wonder if she's going to test its strength by hanging from it.

I clear my throat before she can try. "So. You live in the building. And you're in *my* closet ... why?"

She turns to face me again, and again, I'm drawn to her blue eyes. They're suddenly guarded. Vulnerable. Once more, I force myself to glance away, then take a step back, not wanting to make her feel like a cornered animal. And because I need a bit of distance.

"I don't know," she says. "I walked into *my* closet in *my* apartment and then—*poof!*—now I'm in yours." She emerges from the closet, stepping closer to me, and the large bedroom suddenly feels small. "It was almost like ... magic."

Chapter Two
Archer

I REMEMBER one of my father's wives—the second or third?—reading to me exactly one time, and it just so happened to be *The Lion, the Witch, and the Wardrobe.*

After much begging on my part, she kicked off her heels with a heavy sigh and climbed into bed beside me. Her perfume made my eyes water, and the sequins on her dress dug into the bare skin of my arms, but I didn't dare complain. Having anyone but a nanny pay attention to me was a rarity.

In a somewhat bored tone, she read about half a chapter before my father called her name from downstairs. She scrambled away like she'd been caught, grabbing her heels and leaving the book face down on the floor.

I rescued it, reading for hours until I understood that Edmund—the character I most related to, perhaps because he also didn't seem to fit—turned into the bad guy. With my stomach feeling sour, I tiptoed downstairs, where the night nanny was drinking wine and watching television, and stuffed the book into the bottom of the kitchen trash.

Now, it's as though this woman with the wild blond hair and big blue eyes has metaphorically plucked the book out from under the empty wine bottle and coffee grounds and tried to shove it back in my hands.

A portal closet in the new building I own? Absolutely not.

I have filled my quota of magical talk for today—and beyond—with Galentine. She would probably be clapping her hands with glee and citing this as an answer to her earlier mutterings.

Not on my watch.

"Look, Willow—"

"Willa," she interrupts.

"Isn't that what I said?"

"No, you said *Willow*. Like the tree. I'm *Willa* like ... well, like me."

She brushes a strand of blond hair out of her face. Her hair looks unruly, like it's rebelling and plans to fall out of its ponytail and down around her shoulders any moment, just to prove a point.

"Right. Well, I don't know why you feel the need to lie—"

"I'm not lying," she says.

I pause. A long, dramatic one.

She crosses her arms, all traces of vulnerability gone from her flaming blue irises. The third time I've made direct eye contact. I pull out my tin of mints, this time crushing two between my teeth. The strong ginger makes my eyes burn.

"So, you want me to believe that you were in your closet somewhere in this building—"

"Second floor," she supplies.

"Okay. So, you walked into your closet on the second floor. And then you found yourself here, in *my* closet, which is on the *fourth* floor?"

"Yes."

I pause again, giving her plenty of time to hear how absurd this sounds and come up with some other kind of explanation. Or perhaps come clean and tell me the truth.

"Unexplained things can happen. They *do* happen," she says, but she sounds like she's trying to convince herself—and failing. Then she straightens and snaps her finger. "What's the branch of science dealing with wormholes?"

"I believe that's science *fiction*."

"This isn't fiction. It happened," she insists, sounding more firm now. "I may not be able to explain the physics of *how*, but it did." She glares. "And I'm not crazy."

"I would never presume to diagnose someone else's mental health issues for them."

"I don't *have* mental health issues. Not that there should be a stigma against anyone who does," she adds quickly. "But my mental health has nothing to do with... this." She gestures to the closet behind her.

"Again, I'm not jumping to any conclusions or making a judgment"—*I absolutely am*—"but I simply need you to consider the plausibility of what you're saying." I use the most reasonable tone I can muster for this absurd conversation. "Put yourself in my shoes."

She glances down at my Tom Ford oxfords. "From the look of it, I couldn't afford your shoes."

I pointedly stare at her bare feet. Then rip my gaze away when it starts to move up her likewise bare legs. I'm not sure how I didn't notice the moment she stood up, but she appears to be wearing some kind of silky blue pajama set. With *very* short shorts.

Why are we having this discussion, anyway?

What I need is to get this Willow person out of my apartment and my personal space. And then to change the locks.

"In case you're worried, I'm not going to press charges," I tell her, gesturing toward the bedroom door, hoping she'll take the hint and walk through it.

She doesn't. Her eyes narrow. "Press charges for *what?*"

"Breaking and entering. Trespassing."

I could also see her earning a resisting arrest charge. As I watch her boil like a kettle, I get the sense that she wouldn't go quietly. I can almost picture it.

"What are you smiling about?" she demands.

Am I smiling? I regain control of my features.

"Nothing. The point is—I'm not going to involve the authorities. But I would like you to leave."

She throws up her hands. "But we don't even know what happened!"

This absurd statement needs no response. There is no *we*. We are not a mystery-solving team. And I'm less interested in science fiction theories and more interested in finding a locksmith with availability ... now.

The best explanation for Willow appearing in my closet is that Galentine gave out copies of her key. It would certainly fit with her bleeding-heart sentimentality toward this building and its residents.

Though if this Willow woman did use a key to enter and then forgot how she got here, she has bigger problems to worry about.

Because she seems very sincere and coherent.

But that's not my problem.

"Perhaps an MRI might be a good place to look for answers?" I suggest mildly.

Willow gasps. "I told you I'm not crazy!"

"An MRI would be to detect whether there might be anomalies causing atypical brain function. The kind that might result in memory loss or confusion."

"You think I'm in your apartment because I have a *brain tumor?*" Her hands ball into fists and she blinks rapidly, looking both furious and like she's about to burst into tears.

"I'm just seeking more rational explanations than you magically or science-fictionally portaling your way into my closet from yours. I don't think you're here because of—how did you put it?—*wormholes*."

I turn on my heel and stride out of the bedroom and toward the front door. The air is starting to feel thin, and the tightness in my chest from earlier has returned.

Thankfully, Willow follows me out of the room, scurrying to catch up.

"Aren't you the least bit curious?" she asks.

"No." The sooner I get her out of my space and forget how distracting her blue eyes are, the better.

"This could be newsworthy."

"Definitely not." The last thing I need is rumors spreading about The Serendipity's delusional tenants. Or magical wormhole closets in the building.

She scoffs. "Clearly, no matter what I say, you won't believe me."

"What's more believable—that you literally defied the basic laws of physics to transport two floors, or ..." I trail off.

"Go on. Or *what?*"

"Or ... that you had some kind of blackout or have memory loss or wandered up here sleepwalking—"

"I do not sleepwalk."

"Narcolepsy?"

"I don't suffer from narcolepsy!"

The other options are worse. But she doesn't look like she's on any kind of substance. Her blue eyes are too clear, too lucid, too—

I catch my errant thoughts and halt them in place.

If there is no other medical explanation, we're left with lying. Which is, to me, the worst option of all. And, considering how she's doubling down on her story, the most likely.

"Whatever the case, I think it's time for you to go."

She's quiet for a long moment, and I clutch the doorknob

leading out into the hall like it is the last shred of my good sense.

Still, something keeps me from actually opening the door.

Maybe it's watching Willow, who seems to be vacillating between self-righteous anger and what she finally slips into—resigned defeat.

But then she takes a step closer, and before I can back away, she brushes her fingers against my hand. The touch ignites something—not a spark or flame but a shock of cold, crackling up my arm like electric frost. I'm frozen, my eyes locked on hers.

"What if it happens again?" she whispers.

I don't like the slump of her shoulders and the vulnerable look in her eyes—the same one she had when I threw open my closet door a few minutes ago.

I prefer her fiery anger.

Not that I should prefer *any* version of this woman—only the version that is out of my apartment and banished from my memory.

But something about her fingertips on my hand, something about the rawness in her voice and the pleading look in her blue eyes, has protectiveness rising up in me. Willow seems to remember she's still touching me and drops her hand, blinking and stepping back.

I swing open the door and step back, allowing her space to exit. "I don't think we need to worry about it happening again."

Her fire returns. Throwing me one last glare, Willow stomps out of my apartment and toward the grand staircase. I step into the hallway, needing to be sure she goes.

Not because I want to watch her walk away.

"It was so *lovely* to meet you," she calls over her shoulder in a tone generally reserved for people who club baby seals. "I guess the rumors weren't far-off after all."

Rumors? I wonder what she or any other residents could possibly have heard about me. And from whom? The back of my neck heats.

As Willow reaches the top step, a familiar face appears on the stairwell, climbing up. I groan. *Oh, the timing.*

Bellamy presses himself against the wall to avoid being flattened as Willow stomps past him. His manicured white eyebrows shoot up as he looks from Willow—specifically her bare legs—and back to me. His grin is infuriating.

"Good evening," he says cheerfully.

Willow grumbles a response but does not pause, her blond head disappearing from view as Bellamy crests the top of the stairs. He's impeccably dressed, as always, in a gray tailored suit, his white hair slicked back and his grin wide and highly amused. Though he'll turn fifty-nine this year, I swear, he possesses a youthful energy I've never had.

"Looks like I missed more than the grand tour," he says.

"It was nothing," I mutter.

"Sure." He glances back toward the stairs, still smiling. "Already making friends, I see."

"Hardly."

"Making enemies?" he suggests as he waltzes into my apartment.

A surprisingly clear mental image of Willow glaring pops up, and I shake my head to clear it. "Enemies would be more accurate."

I close the door, double-checking the lock and making a mental note to call a locksmith tomorrow.

Bellamy's assessing gaze turns appreciative, and he lets out a low whistle. "The pictures didn't do it justice. This building is gorgeous," he says, then turns away from the windows. It's now dark, the winking lights of the city offering a comforting view, reminding me of New York. Only ... far less bright and noisy.

"The architecture, the details—all of it. And I'm sad I missed out on all the fun."

My closing of the door is more of a slam. "I wouldn't call my interaction with that woman—or the guided tour Galentine Valencia gave me—fun."

I pause by the large marble island, gripping the edge so tightly, my fingers start to tingle. It takes some effort to slow my breathing, and spots dance across my vision, even after I close my eyes. Now, against my dark lids, they're more like sparks. Tension coils in my chest.

A gentle hand falls between my shoulder blades. "I'm sorry I was delayed," Bellamy says quietly.

Almost instantly, his voice soothes me. Just the way it always has, from the very first time he found me like this when I was a young boy and he was my father's assistant, sent to find out why I wasn't dressed for some event I was being forced to attend. Bellamy had been on the verge of being fired, though neither of us knew that then. The fact that he had been sent looking for me should have been an indication of how things were going for him. I was always lowest on my father's priority list.

When Bellamy found me sitting in an empty bathtub, he took the time to help calm me down. Which turned out, in some ways, to save us both. My father didn't fire him, but did give him a new title: *my* assistant. It was more like glorified nanny, and I'm not sure why Bellamy didn't take the insult and quit.

But he stayed. He moved from being more of a glorified babysitter to an actual executive assistant and now is the acting CEO of Archway Investments. I'm very involved, but Bellamy runs the day-to-day and lets me pass off a lot of the things I don't want to do. Like dealing with people.

"I get more done and learn more from people when they think of me as an assistant," he liked to say. I think he misses it now that he's CEO. It's a little harder to joke about. "You can call me your executive *assassin*. Without all the murder, of course."

I take a slow breath and open my eyes, nodding my thanks to Bellamy, who steps back.

"It's fine."

"*You* are fine, Archer," he corrects. "But I wish I'd been here. I know it wasn't ideal, and I truly am sorry."

He does know. Probably the only person in the world who knows.

"It's fine," I repeat, the words a little more true now than when I said them a moment ago.

I straighten and find a bottle of water on the counter. I didn't see him pull one out of the otherwise empty fridge, but he must have. He's resourceful like that. Uncapping the bottle, I swallow most of it down in a few quick gulps.

"I'm also sorry your furniture did not arrive today. I'd hoped for a smoother transition for you all around, though it is nice to see the bones of this place." Bellamy glances around again. "Truly remarkable. I can see why you took an interest."

"If only the building came with less people," I mutter, setting the nearly empty bottle back down.

Bellamy turns back with a smile, but before he can utter whatever remark is on his tongue, there's a knock.

I know it's Willow again before Bellamy even opens the door—there's something irritating in the rap of knuckles against wood.

"Hello again," Bellamy says, grinning.

Willow's gaze flicks to me. "Um, hello."

"I'm Bellamy. You can call me Bellamy. Or Bell. I also answer to Alfred."

I groan. "That's not your name. Stop telling people that. You're not my assistant anymore and were never my butler."

"It might as well be." Bellamy leans toward Willow and, in

a stage whisper, says "It's a long-running joke, though an apt one. I'm the Alfred to his reclusive and eccentric billionaire Bruce Wayne."

"Billionaire?" Her eyes widen, and now I really want to toss Bellamy from the rooftop.

"He doesn't like to talk about his money," Bellamy whispers dramatically.

"O-kay..." Willow looks between us again, and her hair—finally—comes tumbling down. She quickly twists it up again, securing it with a hair tie from her wrist without bothering to look for the one that must have fallen out.

"This is Willow," I say.

She glares. "It's Will*a*. With an A."

Willow's—Will*a*'s—voice is icy. Deservedly so.

I hate that I forgot. Again. Names are simple. But names are one thing that do not stick in my brain, especially when meeting people for the first time or if I'm in a new or uncomfortable situation.

There's a pause, probably one in which I could easily fit an apology, but my throat feels too tight to speak.

"I'm sorry, Willa," Bellamy says cheerfully, perhaps sensing my vocal freeze. "Can we help you with something? Did you, perhaps, leave your shoes here?"

"No, I ..." Willow glances down at her bare feet, and when she looks up again, this time at me, her cheeks are flushed pink. "I have a little problem."

I step forward, edging Bellamy out of the way as I regain my composure. With an arch of an eyebrow, he steps back but hovers close enough to be part of the conversation. Unfortunately.

Despite his many redeeming qualities, the man consumes gossip like some people drink coffee.

"*Another* little problem?"

She frowns. "I'd hardly call"—Willow frowns at Bellamy

like she also doesn't want to explain earlier events—"what happened earlier a *little* problem."

"More of a legal problem," I mutter. "Or it would be if I weren't in such a forgiving mood."

"*This* is you in a forgiving mood?"

"Archie missed nap time today, I'm afraid," Bellamy says, shifting forward again to reinsert himself into the conversation. "It has quite the impact on his mood."

"Archie?" she asks, looking at me with the slightest upturn of a smile.

"Archer," I correct.

"See? *Grumpy*," Bellamy whispers.

At this, Willow smiles, and a flash of irritation moves through me at the way Bellamy has already won her over. It's one of his special skills—one that makes him indispensable to me. He's the charmer; I'm the curmudgeon.

Right now, I wish he'd be a little less charming.

I wonder if he'd be so friendly if he knew I found Willow in my closet. Likely not. Eventually, he will find out. He always does. And though Bellamy loves people, he is extremely protective of me. A stranger hiding in my closet would have him on high alert, thinking of security measures, not flirting with the intruder.

So, why don't I tell him? It would be the fastest way to ensure I don't have to deal with Willow. But I decide to keep this to myself.

"What is your little problem?" I ask, again stepping between her and Bellamy.

Willow clears her throat. "I'm locked out of my apartment."

"You didn't bring a key with you?"

"I never left—" Willow stops herself just before she insists she never left her apartment. "I never *had* my key. Or my purse. Or my shoes." She directs this last bit at Bellamy.

"Are you sure the key isn't in your pocket?" I ask.

"No pockets. See?"

She gestures to her shorts. Which, I realize now that she's forcing me to look, have llamas on them.

Llama pajamas.

I almost laugh, and the urge to do so stuns me into silence.

When was the last time I laughed?

"I didn't realize we were having a pajama party tonight or I would have dressed accordingly," Bellamy says.

I ignore him. Willow offers him another smile. "It wasn't exactly a plan." Turning back to me, her smile falls. "In any case, no pockets. No key."

"And this is my problem *how*?" I ask.

Willow crosses her arms. "Because you're my new land-lord, and that makes *me* your problem."

She most certainly is.

Chapter Three

Willa

"OKAY," I tell my closet. More precisely, my closet door.

Which is closed and looks exactly as a normal closet door should. Sturdy. Wooden. Door-like.

I marched straight to it the moment the new building owner unlocked my door. More precisely, the moment after I slammed the door on his handsome but grumpy face—the one I'm struggling to banish from my memory.

My closet and I need to have words.

"You," I say, "are a closet. You store clothes and shoes. You tend to attract moths. That is your sole purpose." I pause. "The clothes storing, I mean, not the moths."

The closet, being just a closet, does not respond.

"You are not a T.A.R.D.I.S. or a portal. You aren't even a Narnian wardrobe. There is no Mr. Tumnus or Turkish delight inside you." I shake a finger at it. "Remember your place. You have one job, and it is not to somehow transport me into the closet of a very attractive man who now thinks I'm some kind of stalker *and* who also has the power to evict me. Do we understand each other?"

I didn't really expect the closet to react in any way. But I still pause and wait a few long seconds while the closet continues doing its normal closet thing.

Exactly as it was doing earlier when whatever happened *happened*.

Depositing me in the closet of the most intimidating—and attractive—man I've ever met. When he threw open the door, I felt a mix of terror and *hel-lo, nurse*.

Not that there was anything at all nurse-like about him. From his tailored suit to his fierce eyes and tense jaw, he is not the kind of person you'd want at your bedside. His manner is far too severe.

Plus, I think he'd cause swooning rather than cure it, with those steely eyes, broad shoulders, and deep, rumbly voice.

Even though he was, at best, dismissive and, at worst, downright rude to me, there was something commanding about his presence. Commanding *and* alluring. Like, he could bark out an order that would have me responding with a crisp salute and a quick *yes, sir*, but then I'd find myself swaying into his orbit rather than standing at attention.

Archer Gaines.

The new building owner. On whom I've made a horrible first impression.

"He thinks I'm either a cat burglar or a woman with narcolepsy. Or worse," I tell the closet. Normally, I don't speak to inanimate objects. But normal flew out the window thirty minutes ago. "He suggested I might have a brain tumor. And it's all your fault."

I'm still trying to wrap my brain around it. There were no voices at the time. No weird sounds, no flash of light. I just opened the door—*I open the door now just as a test*—stepped inside—*I step inside*—and started rummaging through the hanging clothes—*I start to rummage*. I remember blinking a few times, like I'd gotten dust in my eye or something, and then I was suddenly not in my very overfull closet but a very empty one in an apartment two floors up and on the other side of the building.

I blink now.

Open my eyes.

And ... I'm still in my closet.

I shouldn't be disappointed. Because this? *This* is normal. Closets should just be closets. Not teleportation devices or wormholes. Or whatever.

But now, I think I might be losing it. Or whatever *it* I had left to lose.

I sink down to the floor and sit cross-legged next to a pair of high heels I haven't worn in at least a year. Not since I quit my office job. Work is the last thing I want to think about right now—even less than a magical closet that transported me into the apartment of a man who seemed to hate me on sight.

Not that I can blame him. I mean, if some stranger showed up in my closet saying they teleported there?

Ugh! What a way to make a first impression! Archer was right not to believe me. Though I'm loath to do so just because of his attitude, I have to agree with his assessment, which is that what I said happened couldn't have happened.

It *couldn't* have.

The problem is that it *did*.

I throw my head back and laugh, the absurdity of it all hitting me anew. I'm honestly lucky the man didn't call the cops.

The thought sobers me right up. Why *didn't* he call the cops?

Maybe he'll just evict me. Icy panic zips through me at the thought. But then, he didn't seem eager to say anything about it to Bellamy either. This surprises me, though maybe the moment I left, they had a meeting about upping security measures and kicking me out of the building.

Grasping at possibly the final straw of my sanity, I stretch out my legs in the cramped space and click my heels together three times.

"There's no place like home?"

Nope.

Now, I'm just a woman sitting in a dark closet.

Alone.

Possibly demented.

What other explanation is there for me having somehow moved through space and time? Oh, no ... what if I time-traveled too? I scramble to my feet and stumble out of the closet to find my phone.

The screen lights up, showing today's date on top of a photo of Sophie and me.

I'm not sure why I'm so relieved about the time. I guess if I have to handle an event so absurdly ridiculous, it needs to be one thing at a time.

Closet that transports me across the building? Not great, but somewhat manageable. Closet that transports me across the building and also makes me jump forward or backward in time? Too much.

Since the phone is already in my hand, I call Sophie.

"Hey," she says distractedly after the first ring. From the windblown background noises, I can picture exactly where she is.

"You still up there, planting flowers in the dark?"

The rooftop garden of The Serendipity is as much Sophie's place as the commercial kitchen downstairs is mine.

She snorts. "Where else would I be?"

"I don't know—maybe your apartment? Or hanging out with Peter?"

Peter is Sophie's other best friend. I'm not sure why *just* a friend since he's super cute and a really decent guy, but both of them are insistent on the platonic thing. There's a muffled sound, and I imagine her shoulder pressing the phone to her ear while she drags a trowel through fresh dirt. Since winter is just releasing its clutches to make room for spring, Sophie is more likely covering the flower beds with sheets, whispering sweet nothings to her baby buds.

"You should pitch a tent and live up there with your plant friends," I suggest.

"Now you're making me sound ridiculous. Crazy Plant Lady, living on the roof with all my babies."

Her joking words strike a little too close to my current situation of Crazy Closet Lady, teleporting through the building.

"Wait—do you think I'm a Crazy Plant Lady?" Sophie asks.

"No! Absolutely not."

"Then why are you so quiet?"

"I just had an incident."

"An incident, huh? Sounds serious. I'll come down. Do you have any icing?"

"Duh."

"Be right there." And without a goodbye or waiting for a response, she hangs up.

In an age when most people treat phone calls like venomous snakes, I'm so glad I still have Sophie, who, like me, prefers to use the phone for its primary function. But when the conversation is done, she sees no need to put the frilly bow of a goodbye on it. She just ends the call. I admire that about her. She's the most decisive person I've ever known.

I tend to land on the other side. *Far* on the other side. While Sophie's decisions fall as swiftly as a guillotine blade, I tend to let things go on and on, hoping conflicts and things I don't like will just resolve on their own.

A perfect example is my last relationship. Which I should

have ended months before my latest failure of a dating experiment, Paul, finally got exasperated with my complete passivity and put us both out of our misery.

I keep hoping Sophie's decisiveness will rub off on me. So far, no luck.

I unlock my door and leave it cracked for Soph, then root around in my fridge. I almost always have a container of royal icing on hand, along with broken sugar cookie pieces. They are helpful if I want to practice technique—or to feed my best friend.

Sophie and I first met almost exactly two years ago in The Serendipity's courtyard. It was the kind of early spring day so sunny and so glorious that residents came stumbling out of the building like bears awakening from hibernation. In our case, it was more like human beings to a swimming pool.

The weather wasn't quite warm enough to swim, but the lounge chairs quickly filled up with people savoring the weather.

Sophie took the chair beside me and asked if I liked the book I was reading. It was historical fiction—the kind showing a woman's back on the cover with planes flying overhead. Award-winning, from the gold seal on the cover. I'm sure it was a lovely book. But every time I picked it up, I hated reading just a little bit more. On the plus side, it was more helpful than melatonin for falling asleep at night.

"It's well-written," I answered after a moment of trying to remember which war the book was even about.

Sophie rolled her eyes, snatched the book from my hands, and rooted around in her bag until she pulled out one with a sword and shiny gold lettering on the front.

"Try this."

I frowned. "I don't read fantasy."

She only hummed. "Just read the first chapter. If you don't

like it, I'll give back the book that's clearly boring you to tears."

I read the first chapter. And I didn't come up for air until almost an hour later to see Sophie grinning at me. "Told you."

"Can I borrow this?" I asked. "It's ... wow."

She gave me her apartment number and contact info, then headed out, taking my historical fiction with her.

I texted her for the first time that night at three a.m. like some kind of addict.

WILLA

Is book two out yet?

She immediately called, sounding like she, too, had been up. She also sounded smug. Like she'd just been up *waiting* for my call.

And friendship was born. Over dragons and epic romance and my admiration for her decisiveness and my willingness to ply her with royal icing.

"Hey!" Sophie bursts in, her greeting breathless, like she ran down the stairs to my apartment.

She and I avoid the elevator, which is toward the front of the building and groans, like any moment it's going to give up on life. Neither of us want to be inside it when it finally dies.

"Icing's on the counter, and I'm working on your tea."

While I put on the kettle, she hangs her coat on the hook by the door and fluffs out her dark curls. A smear of dirt is on her cheek.

Settling onto a stool, she drags the broken head of a unicorn cookie through the bowl of royal icing I set out. Her eyes roll back in her head as she takes a bite.

"You're the best," she mumbles around the mouthful. "I swear, these should be illegal."

"Thank you." I wish her endorsement was enough to keep my fledgling cookie business afloat.

But alas, Sophie's love of my cookies, and my own skill at baking and decorating, is not enough to bring in the wild success I hoped for when I quit my job to start Serendipitous Sweets.

Mostly because I'm as bad at marketing and the business side of things as I am at making firm decisions. I set Sophie's tea in front of her. I'm a steadfast coffee drinker but keep Lady Grey just for her. As best friends do.

"Nice pajamas," she says around another bite.

I glance down, then groan, reminded that not only did I defy the laws of space, time, and probably physics tonight by appearing in my new landlord's closet, but I did so wearing my favorite llama pajamas.

With shorts that feel indecently short, considering I wore them in front of him. And Bellamy too. I groan again, louder, then drop my head into my hands.

"That bad, huh?"

"Worse."

"So, tell me about this incident that has you looking like you've seen the Ghost of Christmas Past."

The Ghost of Christmas Future would be the scary one. Especially now that I can imagine not just my inability to ever pay back my small business loan but also ending up evicted.

I drag a stool around to my usual spot on the other side of the island. My knees knock into the lower cabinets this way, but I like sitting across from Sophie. I take a piece of a broken daisy and twirl it between my fingertips.

"You're going to think I'm delusional."

Sophie gasps. "I would never."

"The alternative is that you'll think I'm lying."

"I would *also* never. Now, spill."

Drawing in a steadying breath, I explain what happened, watching her green eyes grow rounder and rounder as I explain being in my closet one minute, searching for my favorite soft blue sweater, and then upstairs in a totally different apartment the next.

I stop just short of saying how hot our new building owner is. And how good he smelled. The way I wanted to keep arguing with him just to hear him growl out answers in that gravelly voice.

Irrelevant, I tell myself. *Too old. Too grumpy. Too much the owner of the building you live in.*

I skip over the parts of Archer that make my stomach flip even now. Instead, I focus on how cold and stiff he was, how he marched me silently back down to unlock my apartment like he was my prison warden.

Which somehow *really* worked for him. Something—besides my closet—is clearly wrong with me.

"Well—say something."

Sophie hasn't spoken a word but *has* polished off most of the broken cookie pieces.

"It's my fault," she says miserably.

"What? Did you enchant my closet somehow?"

"No. I have your blue sweater. I borrowed it and didn't give it back yet. It's so *soft*," she says in a reverent whisper.

"It is the very best sweater," I agree. "But this didn't happen because you haven't returned it. Wait—what about the rest of it? You don't think I've lost my mind or my marbles?"

I hate how my voice wobbles a little at the question. My mental health is something of a touchy subject for me.

Sophie gives me a fierce look. "Like I said—never." She drags a finger through the icing and pops it in her mouth, her expression turning thoughtful. "I do have some thoughts, but first—I have questions."

"Shoot," I say, straightening on my stool and preparing to talk her through how it happened.

"What was the new owner like, aside from grumpy? Is he

anything like Galentine? Did you get the sense he's going to come in and change everything? Do we need to start looking for a new place to live?"

Not the questions I anticipated, but o*kay*.

I do get it. Ever since Galentine mentioned selling The Serendipity, rumors have swirled among the residents. Mostly because we live in a gorgeous historic building in a fantastic downtown location with relatively low rent. Securing an apartment here is like winning the lottery.

Galentine announcing her retirement and subsequent selling of the building sent many residents into a mild panic. Though she loves to talk, she was tight-lipped about the person who purchased The Serendipity. Rumors spread anyway about the new owner being a filthy rich recluse— seems pretty close to accurate.

Galentine could not have picked a more different person to carry on her legacy. But maybe she was more concerned with retirement money?

Doesn't quite seem in character, but then, she was never someone who made predictable decisions.

"He is absolutely nothing like Galentine. And we probably should be worried. Especially me, now that he thinks I either lied about sneaking into his apartment or that I'm totally unstable."

Sophie eats the last cookie. "Unrelated but also critical info—is he hot?"

"I didn't notice," I lie, already feeling a blush rising in my cheeks.

Sophie doesn't miss my reaction, and she smirks. "Right. Clearly, he *is* hot. And you haven't shown any interest in a guy since—"

"I'm *not* interested in him," I say, but it comes out a little too defensive.

Because despite Archer Gaines being hot, I'm *not* interested. And, based on the cool way he assessed me, neither is he.

In case I need any more reasons to *not* be interested, Archer is older. Maybe ten years or so? There was no sign of gray in his hair, but the one time he smiled, he had those little lines around his eyes that have a way of making men somehow look more attractive.

Also, unless Bellamy was kidding about the billionaire thing, Archer is ridiculously wealthy. Polished and poised in his suit and shoes, which simply reeked of not only money but status and class. Sophisticated and serious to my ... well, neither of those things.

I'm the broke, disheveled failed baker who apparently teleports in llama pajamas.

Even if he weren't probably a hair too old and a lot too classy for me, there's no chance he saw me and thought, *Now, there's a woman I'd like to take out on a date!*

So, I can stop thinking about him and his hotness right now.

Sophie's playful expression disappears. "For real, though—do you seriously think we need to start apartment hunting?"

Slumping against the counter, I say, "Maybe. He seems like he'd come in with a wrecking ball. After he found me *trespassing* in his apartment, he'll probably evict me. Or at least remove my access to the kitchen. I mean, I couldn't explain how I got there. Sophie—how did that even happen?"

"Here's what I know." She holds up a finger at each point. "I know you're not a liar, and you're clearly coherent. This event was witnessed by one other person, so it wasn't in your head. You actually ended up in his apartment somehow, right?"

"Right."

"That's wild." Sophie leans back a little, smiling a little.

"You ... believe me?"

"Of course. I can't explain it and you can't explain it, but it happened."

"Yes," I say, feeling confident. Even if I have no idea how my closet managed to bend the space-time continuum.

"I mean, we both know the town history," Sophie says slowly.

"Tall tales, not history," I argue.

"We've heard about the building being magical."

"And I didn't think either of us believed those stories."

Sophie and I don't discuss it often, but it's impossible to grow up in Serendipity Springs and not hear the whimsical tales about its good fortune. Or, depending on who you talk to, *magic*. Our building, specifically, has a lot of lore connected to it. It was impossible to have a conversation with Galentine when she *didn't* mention it. Sophie has always found this fascinating, while I prefer magic to stay between the pages of the fantasy novels we trade back and forth.

Right now, I should be jumping on the town magic train. But despite what I experienced earlier, I'm still struggling with this explanation. Even if I don't have a better one.

"Clearly, I'm more open to possibilities than you are," Sophie says. "Which is ironic since you're the one who experienced something supernatural."

"It wasn't supernatural. And the only magical thing about this place is the price of rent." I pause, then add, "For now, anyway."

Archer's face comes to mind again. His hot, rent-increasing face.

"I mean, you know I'm not a firm believer in magic or whatever, but if it's the best explanation, then why fight it?" Sophie shrugs.

"*Is* it the best explanation, though?"

"Have you got a better one?"

I don't. But that doesn't mean I want to suddenly decide I

believe in supernatural or magical events. Even if I might have been part of one.

"No. Could we change the subject, please? I'm starting to get a headache."

"Fine." Sophie gives me a devilish grin. "New subject. On a scale of Clooney to Hemsworth, how hot is the new building owner?"

Chapter Four
Archer

BY SIX O'CLOCK THE next morning, I already have regrets in taking on The Serendipity. Or, at least, in staying here. When we realized the furniture wouldn't be here, Bellamy suggested he book me a suite at the hotel a few blocks away where he's staying.

I couldn't articulate my reasons, but it somehow felt *significant* that I stay here. The kind of gut instinct I don't ignore.

Now, waking up aching and exhausted, I'd like to fire my gut instinct.

My air mattress leaked slowly through the night, which required me to add more air. Twice. A few hours later, it had almost fully deflated, leaving me like a human hot dog in the center of a floppy air mattress bun.

Physical discomfort aside, my ability to sleep was also hindered by the events of the evening. Specifically, the woman who appeared in my closet with her ridiculous story. I was thrown by the whole encounter, and her face kept popping up in my mind, along with paranoid and intrusive thoughts about someone being in my closet.

I checked the space both times I got up to refill the air mattress. Empty. Thankfully.

But I can't help but wonder if there could be some secret passage—another way for Willow to have entered. The Serendipity is old, and if any building were to have hidden features like that, this would be it. I feel around for hidden cracks, knock and listen for hollow sounds, and run my fingers up the wall searching for hinges.

I find nothing.

But I do make a note to contact Galentine to ask if she has blueprints of the building. Just to double-check.

After a cup of coffee—thankfully, I brought my Jura machine from the city—I find a hair tie by the front door, one Willow must have lost last night. Though I intend to throw it away, I slip it into my pocket instead, next to my mints.

I haven't been intrigued by a woman in a long time. Maybe ever? My relationships have never been particularly engaging. They've been more about finding someone suitable who isn't *only* interested in my money.

Patricia, the last woman I dated, wasn't intriguing so much as a woman who made sense. I was wrong, but that's beside the point.

Willow makes *no* sense.

Not her appearance in my apartment. Not her flimsy explanation—or her lie. A woman who can't be honest or who had some kind of strange temporary amnesia—another idea I had while listening to the slow hiss of air leaving my mattress—is not someone I should be thinking about.

And yet, I struggle to banish thoughts of her from my mind. The memory of the way her fingertips brushed over the back of my hand—and the reaction it elicited—makes me shiver now.

Work. Work should help. Especially when I consider the

mountain of tasks at hand, starting with forging some semblance of organization out of the mess in Galentine's office. My office now.

Though she cleared out most of her personal items, the clutter on the large wooden desk and on every other surface makes me twitchy. The filing cabinets might as well be tables, as manila folders are stacked haphazardly on top. Galentine's version of organization could best be described as chaotic, and it takes me an hour just to sort things into somewhat organized piles.

No order. Hardly any labels. No rhyme or reason to what I find.

One folder contains nothing but movie ticket stubs.

Another: receipts so old, the paper is soft and the ink has faded too much to read.

Yet a different folder holds a collection of *Serendipity Star* newspaper articles from the 1990s, clipped seemingly at random.

I should throw them all away, but it's hard when I don't know if there is some secret significance to the articles and movie stubs—perhaps something Galentine might have forgotten? I toss the unreadable receipts in the trash and place the other two folders in the very back of the bottom drawer, the tabs labeled with a series of question marks.

One of the very first major tasks will be to shift everything from physical to digital. Not only did Galentine not change the rent in the twenty-five years she owned The Serendipity, it appears she was also still using the original paper application and taking payment primarily by check.

Shudder.

Bellamy will help with organization, of course, putting systems in place here, but he'll be heading back to New York soon. After talking with the board, we decided it would be better to have me out of sight. Bellamy will go back soon to man the ship. Which means this disaster of an office falls squarely on my shoulders.

Hire someone.

I should. I will. The little voice in my head is wise, but the louder voice is stubborn, telling me to do as much of the work myself as I can. I need to learn the operations so I can improve them. It would be harder to manage someone at this point when I'm still getting my bearings. Once things are in a more manageable working order, *then* I'll hire someone.

There is another, deeper reason why I feel compelled to do the kinds of tasks I'd usually hire out. The headlines were hard to read but easier to ignore: *Illegal Gaines: Like Father, Like Son?* Credit to them for creative use of our last name.

But the accusations flung from reporters anytime they could get at me ... those were different. One man slipped past my security as I was mobbed leaving a lunch meeting.

Before he was yanked away, he managed to spit on my tie and say, "You might still be walking free, but don't think for a minute you're any different from your old man."

As I ducked into the waiting car, Bellamy squeezed my shoulder and said, "They're just trying to get a reaction out of you."

I knew that and still know it, but the words struck and landed.

Now, I carry them with me, less like a haunting weight and more like a torch. I refuse to be like my father. Not as a businessman; not as a man.

And if that means I sometimes make choices like this—to acquire and then be hands-on with something like The Serendipity—then I'll dig in and do the minutiae and the hard work. Even if it's not typical for someone like me and I'm in over my head.

I can only spend so much time in the office before it starts to feel like the walls are closing in on me. The antique desk is too large for the room, making it feel smaller than it is. It must have been assembled inside. I might have to chop it into pieces to remove it.

With my furniture delivery set for later this afternoon and an hour before Bellamy is set to arrive, I head down to the lobby alone. I'd like to assess the parlor and the library spaces to see how they might be repurposed into more functional—and profitable—areas.

A waste of space, I think as I march down the grand circular staircase at the front of the building. Tearing it out to replace it with a regular set of stairs would free up a little bit of square footage on every floor. For storage or bumping out the apartments next to them for added space. Anything would be more useful than a dramatic staircase taking up unnecessary square footage.

I make a note to ask the engineer when we talk next week about other structural changes. I can see how, at one time, this stairway might have made for grand entrances. Perhaps when The Serendipity was a women's dormitory, at a time when men would have been banned from rooms and waited here for their dates or girlfriends.

The tiniest twinge of *something* tugs at my chest, and I shake it off.

Galentine's influence is lingering a little too much in my head.

"Good morning, Mr. Gaines. Hope you're settling in well."

I'm startled by the voice and almost stumble down the last step. An older woman I'm sure I haven't met stands at the wall of mailboxes, a few envelopes in hand. She has a bright smile, wild white curls, and jangly bracelets on both arms.

"Hello. Yes. Thank you."

My words come out stiffly, and my mind spins, trying to make a connection. Have we met? Should I know her name? Willow mentioned rumors last night, so clearly, Galentine spoke to at least some of the residents about me. Anyone could have googled the sale of the building to find out my name.

"I'm Sylvia," she says. "Fourth floor, toward the back. I made an educated guess that you're the new owner based on Galentine's description. I think she said well-dressed but not fully because he never smiles. It's a reference to the movie *Annie*."

This is a lot of information to take in. "Happy to meet you."

"Are you?" she asks, the smile on her lips turning sly. "Happy?"

I don't get a chance to answer as another woman barrels down the hallway, being dragged by a monstrously large, hairy dog who shoves his head right into my hand and starts bathing it with a proportionally large tongue.

"I'm so sorry!" the woman says breathlessly, brushing her dark hair from her face and tugging on the leash. "Archibald, no!"

I freeze at the sound of my full name, then realize she's talking to this beast with overactive salivary glands. My entire hand is slimy by the time the woman manages to pull him back.

"Your dog's name is Archibald?" I ask.

"Yes. And he's still learning his manners. He's just a puppy."

"A *puppy*?"

The beast is sitting now, his city-block sized tongue hanging out of his mouth, drool puddling on the hardwoods.

"He's a Bernese Mountain Dog. This is one of the few apartment buildings in town without a weight limit on dogs."

Not for long.

Needing an immediate escape and a hand-washing, I make

a beeline for the kitchen—one more useless room that's a vestige of the building's past.

But I open the door to the kitchen and find it already occupied—by the woman who has been residing in my thoughts since last night.

"Willow," I say.

She startles, dropping a cup of flour. A white cloud rises around her face.

My mouth tightens, unsure if it wants to grimace or smile. "Sorry—I didn't mean to startle you."

Coughing, Willow waves a hand through the air, stepping back from the stainless-steel prep table, which, even aside from the flour, is already a mess. Mixing bowls, bins of flour and sugar, and a variety of other baking paraphernalia litter every surface in the room. It makes Galentine's office look tidy.

"Will*a*," she corrects, coughing once more. "Remember? I'm a person, not a tree."

"Right."

*Willa—not a tree. Will*a.

"What's happening in here?" I ask, glancing at the stainless steel worktable littered with baking supplies.

The urge to reach for my mints is strong, but I remember my saliva-covered hand and curl it into a fist at my side, itching to push past Willa and wash it off.

"Oh," Willa says, seemingly surprised at the question. "I use the kitchen for my business."

"Which is?"

Her cheeks flush, turning the same rosy pink as the frilly apron she wears. "I'm a baker." Her tone of voice is defensive.

"And you bake what, exactly?"

"Cookies," she says, sounding even more defensive. She's even clutching a rolling pin now, like she's prepared in case she needs to use it as a weapon.

I hold back from any remarks I might otherwise make about cookies as a business, not wanting to risk her taking a swing at me.

Instead, I cross the kitchen to the sink, washing away the remnants of my canine namesake. While I'm scrubbing, I make note of the cookie cutters, bowls, and baking sheets piled high in the deep sink.

Cookie baking, indeed.

I turn off the water, only to realize there are no towels of any kind. With dripping hands, I glance around the kitchen.

"Here." Willa thrusts a towel at me. It's white with pink cursive writing which reads, *Let's Get Our Bake On!*

"Thank you," I say, drying my hands. "I had an ... encounter with a large dog who greeted me with his mouth."

"Let me guess—Archibald?" Willa smirks. "He's very cute, but his bad manners won't be cute when he's a hundred and fifty pounds of untrained, hairy beast."

One hundred and fifty pounds?

The horror must be evident on my face because she says, "Don't worry—Sara just enrolled him in obedience school."

"Let's hope he makes the honor roll."

Willa laughs. "Wow. You just made a joke. I didn't think you were the type."

Neither did I. Without thinking, I've folded the towel into a neat square. "Here." I hold it out. "Thanks, Willa the Person."

She laughs again, and our fingers brush. The same icy zip I felt last night moves up my arm. My pulse quickens, far too much for such a small touch. I walk away, putting the crowded prep counter between us. Apparently, I need the barrier.

Willa stares at the neat square like it's the first time she's ever seen a folded towel. I get the sneaking suspicion she's the kind of woman who keeps all her clothes shoved into drawers. Or maybe lives out of her laundry basket and never puts anything away.

As though to prove my point, Willa rumples the towel a little before tossing it on the counter. I can feel her gaze on me and need somewhere to look. But everywhere, there is just *mess*.

"Does this kitchen hold the necessary permits for commercial baking?" I ask, reaching out to push a cookie cutter back into line with others.

"Yes. See for yourself." Willa's tone is clipped as she points to the wall, where an official looking document is hanging in a cheap frame. Indeed, it's a city of Serendipity Springs inspection for the kitchen.

And, I can't help but notice, it expires in exactly ten days.

"Did you and Galentine have a contract for you to rent this space?"

There is a long moment of silence, which is at least a partial answer to my question.

"I had an agreement with Galentine to use the space." Willa shifts. "But we didn't—she didn't ask me to sign anything. We had a verbal agreement. A verbal *contract* about the appropriate use of the space."

Clearly, she's grasping for legal terms. Trying to justify the free use of this kitchen for her business without a written contract or rental agreement. Unless it's in writing, it won't hold up in court. As I consider how to explain this to Willa, she sighs and picks up the measuring cup she dropped earlier.

"Want to help?" she asks, not looking up as she levels what I realize is powdered sugar, not flour, into the cup.

"What?"

"You're standing here, doing nothing. Make yourself useful. Grab that little container of meringue powder."

I have no idea what meringue powder is, nor did I have any

urge to help with baking this or any other morning, yet I find myself instantly responding to Willa's bossy tone. The meringue powder isn't hard to locate; it's in a small white container near the stand mixer Willa is dumping her sugar into. I move next to her, our arms nearly brushing, and hold it out.

When she takes the container from me, a light dusting of powdered sugar covers the lapels of my suit. Frowning, Willa tries to brush them away, only making it worse.

"I'm messing up your nice suit," she says, dismayed.

"It's fine. I have more suits."

But Willa is already untying the apron strings at her back, and before I can protest, she pulls it off. Standing on tiptoes, she tries to drop it over my head but can't reach.

"You're a giant," she says with a giggle. "Duck down."

Again with that bossy tone. No one speaks to me like this, not even Bellamy, and I find I really like it. At least, coming from her. It makes no logical sense, and yet I find myself obeying her order.

I dip my head, and Willa drops the loop around my neck. "There."

Her gaze flicks to mine, and only then does she seem to realize how close our faces are. There's the smallest intake of breath, a tiny gasp, but Willa doesn't move away. Neither do I. Instead, she leans in and reaches around my waist.

I stop breathing.

For a moment, I think it's my second hug in twenty-four hours, though this is nothing like Galentine's embrace. Willa's cheek presses to my chest and her arms link around my lower back. My muscles tense like over-coiled springs as the scent of her—sugary almond and vanilla—hit my bloodstream like a drug. I swear, I can feel my pupils dilating.

Should I ... hug her back? Do I put my arms around her back or her waist or—

It is at this humiliating moment I realize she's simply tying the apron strings.

"There we go." She takes a step back and pats my chest, now covered by a pink, frilly apron. Unaware of how impacted I am by her proximity or my embarrassment for thinking she was hugging me, Willa grins. "I like your business attire, but this suits you."

"Does it?" My voice sounds rougher than usual, a low growl.

Willa runs her hand over a ridge of ruffles along the top of the apron. She's not making contact with any part of my skin, yet I feel her touch everywhere.

"Not every man can pull this off, you know. Consider yourself lucky. Now." Her brisk, businesslike tone returns. "Hand me a clean tablespoon. I need to finish this batch of icing."

Before I can discern which of the half-dozen measuring spoons is the correct one, the kitchen door swings open.

"Well, good morning!" Bellamy strides into the kitchen, grinning when he sees me standing next to Willa, wearing her apron. "Isn't this a delightful surprise. Nice to see you again, Willa. Good morning, Archer."

I am caught, a boy elbow-deep in the cookie jar. Or a man who has better things to do than search for a tablespoon while wearing a pink apron.

"Archer is helping me make royal icing," Willa says. "I'll give you a job too, if you'd like one."

Bellamy waves her off. "I won't get in the way. Too many cooks in the kitchen and all that. I'll happily watch."

I'm keenly aware of Bellamy watching, a smirk on his face. I pointedly ignore him as Willa directs me to add six tablespoons of meringue powder to the stand mixer. She finishes up with water, then attaches a clear plastic shield to the top and turns on the mixer.

"You didn't measure the water," I say, hoping my tone comes across how I intend, which is curious, not critical. But with the powdered sugar and meringue powder, she insisted on things being precise. For water, she used a larger measuring cup with a handle and didn't use it all.

Willa lightly—but very intentionally—steps on my toe before beaming up at me. She explains that royal icing is tricky and there are different consistencies she needs depending on if she's flooding or piping. I have no idea what the terms she's using actually mean, but find myself listening raptly anyway, my attention darting between her eyes and her mouth.

"You don't know what I'm talking about, do you?" Willa asks, mouth slightly upturned.

"I ... no."

But I'm intrigued all the same. More interested than I've ever been in cookies, which I rarely eat. Though it's the baker, not the baked goods, who has me standing here in a frilly pink apron, playing sous chef.

I've forgotten Bellamy is in the room at all until he says, "Did you see these, Archer? Wow, they are exquisite, Willa. Well done."

"Oh, thank you."

I step away from Willa, needing but not wanting a respite from her closeness. Somehow, I've spent nearly half an hour now in this kitchen and missed the fully decorated cookies drying on a rack. There is a whole cookie zoo, each animal with tiny, expressive faces and the kind of detail I've never seen on anything edible. It's shocking how perfect they are, given the chaos surrounding them and the decidedly messy nature of the one who made them. This kind of detail must take hours and a steady hand. Plus a kind of creative vision I don't possess.

I'm unable to find words that adequately convey how

impressed I am. Words that apparently come so easily to Bellamy.

"Remarkable," he's saying now, and I want to elbow him in the side to stop the effusive show of praise. Even though I agree. "You have a gift."

"Thank you, Bellamy."

Willa's cheeks flush, and she fidgets, dragging a finger through a little pile of powdered sugar. Her smile is shy, and another flicker of irritation moves through me at Bellamy's easy way with people.

Before he walked in, I had no problem speaking with Willa. I forgot to be self-conscious in the way I sometimes can be.

But now I'm far too aware of myself. Overthinking my words. Distracted by my hands and feet. Feeling stupid in this pink apron as Bellamy tugs at the ruffles.

I nudge him away and then untie the strings and pull it over my head.

"I need to get back to work." I briefly consider putting the apron on Willa the same way she did me, but I can't with Bellamy here. Instead, I fold it and set it on the edge of the counter.

"Before we go, might you have any samples? I'd die for a bite." Bellamy smiles mischievously like a naughty schoolboy.

"You don't need to give him anything," I tell Willa, glaring at him. "It's barely breakfast."

"Well, you're in luck," Willa says. "I always have a few rejects and broken pieces."

Bellamy grins. "As long as the old adage isn't true about how you are what you eat."

Willa laughs. "I make no promises. Here." She holds out a tin she procured from somewhere behind her on the counter.

Bellamy eagerly takes a few pieces, and Willa steps toward me. "You can try them too, if you ask nicely."

"I'll take his," Bellamy says, trying to block me from taking one. "He's not really a cookies-in-the-morning kind of person. Or a cookies-at-all person. He likes a strict, no-fun meal plan that doesn't include treats."

"Give me that."

I grab for the tin, my hand closing over Willa's in the process. Though I could shift my grip, I don't, leaving my fingers over hers as I take my time looking through the messy, misshapen pieces. I'll be honest: it's more about holding onto Willa than being selective about which broken piece I choose. Finally, I pick a larger piece covered in vivid pink icing.

"It was part of a hippo," she says.

"What?"

When I glance up, once again, I find my gaze clashing with hers. She's the first to look away, nodding down at the cookie in my hand.

"You looked like you were trying to figure out what it was supposed to be. It was a hippo, but I broke it."

"It's pink. Hippos aren't pink."

"Hippos are a grayish brown in real life, which doesn't make a particularly cute cookie for a child's birthday party."

"People buy these for children? At how much per cookie?"

The flush in Willa's cheeks is more of a red fire now, and I realize too late how rude my question sounds. I'm not saying what I mean, which is that her cookies are far too beautiful to waste on children who probably wouldn't appreciate the difference between something hand-decorated and a factory-produced cookie in a package.

Willa turns away without answering, putting away the tin of broken cookies.

"I'm pretty sure your father paid outrageous prices to cater your birthday parties," Bellamy says drily.

Then he grimaces and shoots me an apologetic look. Those parties were never really for me, and he knows it. I made it through my entire childhood without blowing out a candle. Somewhere, I've amassed a whole collection of unused birthday wishes.

If I could use one now, I'd wish to take back my foolish words.

"These are absolutely delicious," Bellamy says quickly, grabbing another rejected cookie. "What's the minimum number of cookies to purchase?" he asks. "I might need to place a standing weekly order."

Of course he would. His love of sugary treats rivals his love of people.

As Bellamy and Willa discuss details, I lift the cookie to my nose and take a deep inhale. Sweet vanilla and something else … almond, maybe?

My mouth waters. I can almost taste it. When was the last time I allowed myself to eat processed sugar? Bellamy tells me I'm too regimented—though he uses a less polite term—about my daily five-mile runs and my refusal to eat sweets.

I realize the room has grown quiet, and both Bellamy and Willa are watching me expectantly to see my reaction.

Immediately, I drop my hand, palming the cookie, feeling a flush work its way up my neck at their attention. This small moment has become too significant.

"We should let you get back to baking," I say without looking at Willa.

"Right," Bellamy says. "I'll be in touch about my orders. Do you have a website?"

Willa pulls a card from a pocket I hadn't seen in her apron. "All my information is here, and you can place orders online."

"Wonderful." Bellamy tucks the card into his pocket. "One more cookie for the road?" he asks, batting his lashes at Willa.

I know he's not genuinely flirting, but it still bothers me.

I'm not sure if it's his ability to build familiarity so quickly. Or if it's because he's turning his charms on Willa.

"You're incorrigible, aren't you," Willa says, swatting at him with the dish towel I used earlier.

"I'm not sure you should insult future long-term customers," Bellamy says.

"Here," I say, holding out my piece of cookie. "You can have mine."

Again, I've upset Willa. I can see it in the way her lips purse as she walks back to the stand mixer, testing out the icing consistency and pretending we've already gone. She looks hurt, like rejecting a cookie is rejecting her.

It makes me want to grab the tin of broken pieces and shovel them into my mouth.

I try to remind myself that it shouldn't matter as we say quick goodbyes and leave Willa to her work. This is the same woman who appeared in my closet just last night and is either confused or lying about how she got there.

But already, something has shifted in the way I see her. Which shouldn't happen. Can't happen.

She's a resident here, and I don't need to make friends. I certainly won't be making any once I announce the first round of changes I intend to make. One of which needs to be ending the free use of spaces like this.

The thought of telling Willa that has me pulling out my tin of mints and popping one in my mouth. It's fine. I need the separation and the space. A firm boundary between us.

But all day long, the smell of sweet almond sugar cookies lingers around me, just like thoughts of the woman who baked them. And for the first time in years, I find myself truly longing for something sweet.

Chapter Five
Willa

As though someone has pressed a giant red button, my brain devolves into panic mode over the next few days. Mostly because I can't stop thinking about Archer.

One part of my brain keeps circling back to his interest in my arrangement with Galentine regarding the commercial kitchen. I *know* she should have charged me to use the space. The person I hired to do my taxes last year was shocked I didn't have more overhead costs, especially in terms of my baking space. But here's the thing: my profit margins are so close (read: nonexistent) that if I *did* have to pay for the kitchen, it would be the thing that puts me out of business.

I've been lucky. And I think Archer Gaines is the physical embodiment of my luck running out.

Then there's the *other* part of my brain. It's not worried about kitchens or rent or businesses. That part of my three-pound thinking organ is consumed with things like the way Archer smells and his response to me bossing him around. How good it felt to stand with my cheek pressed to his chest as I tied apron strings behind his back.

What possessed me to do that?!?

No idea. But I started to see another side to the man I'd written off as stuffy and grumpy and too old—even if very attractive.

Now, I am a little girl plucking daisies and getting a different answer with each petal that flutters to the ground. Only instead of *he loves me, he loves me not*, I'm vacillating between *I despise him* and *I'd like to tie his apron strings once more*.

When I need my feet to come back to earth, I remind myself that he wouldn't try my cookies.

And can you really trust a man who refuses a cookie? No. You can't.

I'm so distracted that I walk into the wrong office building to deliver a cookie order and have to backtrack a whole block.

Then I almost drop the box as I hand it off to the woman who placed the order. She's wearing a pale blue sundress, an odd choice considering the crisp weather outside. But then, my wardrobe has been a revolving door of yoga pants and pajamas for what feels like months, so I have no room to judge.

She must see me eyeing her bare shoulders because she smiles. "I dress for the weather I want," she says with a shrug. "And I'm ready for spring."

"Good philosophy. Another few weeks and hopefully we'll start to see it."

When she finally glances down at the box, her mouth falls open as she sees the cookies through the viewing window. "These are beautiful. Better than the pictures on your website. *Wow*."

A surge of pride fills me—mixed with something a whole lot uglier.

These aren't the zoo cookies Archer and Bellamy saw. This order is to celebrate a coworker's newborn baby boy, and they were maybe the hardest ones I've ever had to decorate.

Not as far as skill goes—they were pretty standard, with blue and white bottles, onesies, and rattles. Very little detail work needed, aside from writing monogrammed initials and the name Bronson.

The hard part was thinking about babies for the hours it took me to finish. I always wanted to be a young mom. I thought I would be. Until those hopes came smash-crashing down—along with the relationship I thought would be *it* for me.

The cookies were a very tactile reminder of the hopes I lost and how quickly time is zipping by me. I swear, I could practically feel my ovaries turning to dust while I piped the name *Bronson* in white. It didn't help that Bronson is one of my favorite baby names.

With no relationship—or even potential relationship—on the horizon, motherhood seems to grow farther and farther out of my reach. It makes me angry with Trey all over again. Not because I want to be having *his* babies, but because I invested almost four years in our relationship. Our breakup was like hitting reset on my whole timeline. My whole life, really.

I'm right back at the starting line. If I met someone today—Archer comes to mind, and I briefly wonder if a lobotomy would effectively remove him—and we dated, got engaged, then married in a normal amount of time, I'd be pushing thirty by the time we had kids.

Which isn't old! It's fine! My ovaries and my eggs will still be fine! Women have children into their forties now. I know this. I've googled.

I just thought my life would be different by now.

I almost had it all. Until I didn't.

And as I decorated each sweet onesie cookie with Bronson's monogrammed initials, my loss was all I could think about.

I'd almost prefer making naughty adult cookies for a bachelorette party. *Almost*.

"Honestly," says the woman in the sundress, shaking her head, "I'm not sure you're charging enough for these."

She's right—I'm not charging enough, despite Archer's shock about my prices. *Definitely* not enough. But with a fledgling business, I need any sales I can get, hoping they'll bring reviews and word-of-mouth recommendations.

Speaking of…

I force a smile. "There's a card inside the box with information on how to leave a review—those really help—and a few flyers with coupon codes for you and your friends."

I try to say this cheerfully, not allowing the edge of desperation I feel to creep into my voice.

I hate selling. The word—along with the *marketing* and *promotion*—triggers my gag reflex. When I quit my office job to do this full-time, I was floating on the compliments of people who had raved about my cookies for years, not thinking about taxes and LLCs vs S-corps and things like brand awareness.

Or having to be the one to actually *sell* my cookies to people. Shouldn't they just sell themselves by virtue of how pretty they are?

Apparently not.

Some people, I think to myself, a certain suit-wearing billionaire coming to mind, *won't even try them*.

"There's my little baker!" Mom says, beaming as she opens the door and envelops me into a hug.

My relief is instant, a full-body sigh as I press into her warm embrace. The familiar scent of home, today mixed with something deliciously savory that Mom must be cooking, adds to the comforting effect.

"Hi, Mom."

At least once a week I make the twenty-minute drive to my parents' house for dinner or to say hello. Just walking through the front door makes my day better.

Unless I think about moving back here if things don't pick up with my business. Or if Archer Gaines decides to make me pay to use the kitchen space. Then, this house would stop feeling like a comfort and start feeling like a real-life metaphor symbolizing my failure to *adult*.

"What's wrong?" Mom asks. "You just tensed up."

She pulls back to examine me, her silver-threaded blond hair falling into her eyes.

I brush it away and offer her the best smile I can muster. "Just the same old. Nothing new." Which is mostly true.

Mom and Dad are very aware of my struggle to get Serendipitous Sweets off the ground. They've been supportive in every way they can be, including financially. Mostly, their support comes by way of cheerleading and telling everyone they know about my cookies.

As far as business advice, they're both lifelong teachers and know more about their respective subjects—history for Dad and English for Mom—than they do about business and finance.

In fact, just last year Dad got taken by some kind of random phone scam. Maybe a Ponzi scheme? I don't know what that is, exactly, or how he got tricked. All I know is that he lost a chunk of their retirement. Now, when telemarketers or scammers call the home phone my parents insist on keeping, he finds creative ways to mess with them.

So, yeah—our family is all in the same boat when it comes to the ins and outs of money and business stuff.

"What's wrong with my Willa?" Dad bellows, lumbering into the hall.

While I'm average height like my mom, Dad is a staggering six-foot-four and built like a one-man wrecking crew. He looks like some kind of retired sports hero, or maybe even a lumberjack, what with his propensity for flannel.

People are surprised whenever they find out that he never played a sport in his life. He spends most of his time on the model train set in the basement, wearing an Optivisor to help him see the tiny pieces. I like to take pictures of him wearing it, especially when I catch him looking up, his eyes distorted through the magnifying glasses. He's an adorable nerd trapped in the body of a linebacker.

Now, Dad lifts me off my feet in a hug so tight, I can feel my back snapping into alignment. His beard scrapes pleasantly against my forehead.

"Who do I need to pummel?" he growls.

I giggle. "No one, Daddy."

"Oh, George. What have we said about you fighting people?"

"That I should leave it to the experts," he says, setting me back down and giving me a wink. "Like you."

Mom swats at him, and he bends down to plant a kiss right on her lips. The two of them are disgustingly adorable. I love it, even if it makes my heart ache with longing for the same thing.

"You're just in time for dinner," Mom says. "Your favorite—chicken and dumplings."

"It's like she magically knew you were coming and made dinner just for you," Dad says.

I roll my eyes. "Or, like you have it at least once a week, so my chances are one in seven."

"I prefer my explanation." Dad chuckles and wraps an arm around my shoulders, guiding me downstairs before dinner to show me the latest updates to the whole little world of model trains he's created.

The tracks are just part of what he's built over the years. There are buildings and people and roads with cars that drive. Tiny houses with lampposts and sidewalks, bushes and trees. Most recently, he added a lake with sunbathers and a power boat. One year for Christmas, I got him a tiny dog with his leg lifted. I didn't think he'd really put it up, but he likes to move it around to "water" different shrubs.

"Do you want to blow the whistle?" he asks with a grin. Dad has the tiniest gap between his front teeth, and it makes his smile all the more endearing. "You can make a wish when the train goes through the tunnel, just like old times."

"Sure, Daddy." The sound of the engine humming and clacking over the tracks is familiar, reminding me of being so little I'd have to stand on a chair to see. Back then, his display was a tiny fraction of its current size, but it brought him every bit as much joy.

I press the button to make the little whistle blow, a sound that leaves me feeling both nostalgic and sad, even though Dad winks at me when the train enters the tunnel, its tiny engine light cutting through the dark.

Not unlike Sophie, Dad is always looking for signs and magic in average daily events. I have no doubts that if I told him about my closet experience, he would light up and insist on driving to my place right now so he could test it out.

Which is exactly why I don't tell him.

It's been a few days, and I've already started convincing myself that I somehow wandered up into Archer's closet in some kind of stupor.

Or something.

Maybe a stress-induced waking sleepwalking kind of thing?

I've never heard of that, but people come up with new ailments and disorders daily, it seems.

Whatever actually happened, I'd prefer not to think of it again. Time can soften the edges of the memory until it's more a foggy *Did that even happen?* and less a solid reality.

That's my plan. That—and to avoid my closet.

And to stop all my thoughts that keep boomeranging back to Archer.

Which is even harder after the run-in we just had. On my way to the parking garage, I saw Archer jogging toward me on the sidewalk. I didn't recognize him at first because he was in running clothes. Correction: running shorts.

And that is all.

Yes, he had on shoes and socks, but I wasn't paying attention to those. Totally irrelevant. No—my full focus was on Archer's bare, muscly, sweaty chest.

So, that's what he's hiding under those suits.

I had my cheek pressed right ... there.

That's not a body built by cookies.

As he saw me, he slowed to a stop, and then all my focus shifted to not tripping or falling over or saying something stupid.

The good news: I did not trip or fall or say something stupid.

The bad news: I couldn't locate words at all.

And when Archer stopped right in front of me and ran a hand through his dark, sweaty hair, making his biceps pop, it only got worse. I stood there, staring stupidly. I think I was even smiling a dreamy, goofy smile, but I'm not certain what my face was doing. At that point, my entire body was running on a backup generator.

"Hello, Willa the Person," Archer said in that low, rough voice of his, the tiniest of smiles lifting one corner of his lips.

At which point I lifted a hand and waved. Not a full wave

either. One of those little finger waves, the kind you'd expect from some vapid socialite with a purse dog and a spray tan.

Archer frowned, perhaps wondering if I was sleepwalking again, and before he could ask, I walked right around him and hoofed it to my car like I was being chased by the boogeyman. An over six-foot, very well-built boogeyman who doesn't like cookies but also is now into calling me by a cute nickname.

I'm startled when Dad's hand drops over mine. "What?" I ask.

Gently, he lifts my hand away. "You've been jamming your finger into the button forever. I think the whistle's about to give out."

"Oh ... sorry."

"Everything okay?" he asks, even as he's directing the train back to its resting spot at the station with the controls. He could probably do this in his sleep.

"Totally!" I respond a little too brightly.

But he seems to buy it, and Mom calls us up for dinner before I have to flat-out lie about catching feelings for a man I really shouldn't. Or about the still lingering melancholy brought on by the baby cookies.

Over dinner, the ache in my chest grows as I sit across the table from my parents. Mom and Dad weren't just high school sweethearts; they've been dating since junior high. Or, *going out*, which is what they tell me people called it back then.

That's their favorite running joke: "Where were we even going?" Mom likes to ask.

"Eventually, to the altar," Dad will answer, and then it devolves into laughter and, inevitably, kissing.

Again, they are adorably gross.

A weird kind of silence falls when I'm taking the last bite of dumpling, the one I'd been saving to the very end. I've tried this dish in a number of restaurants before, but nothing beats Mom's dumplings, even if they're made from a box of Bisquick.

I look up, the pillowy softness melting on my tongue, and both Mom and Dad have pinched expressions.

"What?" When neither one answers and, instead, they exchange a heavy glance, the last bite of dumpling suddenly feels stuck in my mouth. I swallow and take a sip of water. "Whatever it is, just tell me. Are you retiring and moving to Miami? Did you get scammed by a telemarketer again? Did they discontinue your favorite kind of train track?"

"Trey is moving back," Mom blurts.

I am immensely glad I already swallowed my bite of dumpling because I think I would have choked.

Though we both grew up in Serendipity Springs, Trey and I didn't meet until freshman year of college. We both went to Boston and met when a friend of a friend mentioned they had another friend driving back to Serendipity Springs for fall break. Mom and Dad didn't let me take a car my freshman year because parking was such a nightmare, but they hated coming to get me because driving in Boston is also a nightmare. Mom and Dad suggested I take the train to Worcester, but I'm a little bit of a baby and don't love doing public transportation alone.

I jumped on the chance to ride back home with Trey, sight unseen. If I had seen him ahead of time, I would have jumped even faster.

The instant I saw him, I got that fluttery crush feeling. It wasn't just his perfectly tousled dirty blond hair and deep brown eyes but the warmth in his smile and the way he immediately took my bags and loaded them in the back before opening my car door. When he told me I got to choose the music, I was already half-smitten.

After an hour and a half that felt like ten minutes, he was pulling up in front of my house, and I was fighting off disappointment. I didn't want to get out of the car. Or say good-bye. But Trey felt the same way and asked if he could take me to dinner rather than dropping me off.

I ended up getting home—finally—after midnight and after we'd made plans to hang out the next day.

Both of my parents waited up. Not because they were worried, but because my dad said once they got my texts that I was going to hang out with the boy who drove me home, they just knew.

Like magic, Dad said.

So, yeah. I've got some real-world reasons not to like the idea of magic. Because our ending was not so magical.

"He's moving back from Paris? To Serendipity Springs?"

"Yes," Dad says, looking warily at me, as though he expects me to spring out of my seat and run away. Or perhaps he's thinking I might spontaneously combust.

I will *not* burst into flames. Or bolt from the table.

Mostly because I hate few things more than I hate running.

Which brings unwelcome thoughts of shirtless, sweaty Archer to mind.

Ugh—not now! I can't manage thoughts about Trey and Archer at the same time.

"Trey, as in, *the* Trey?"

What I mean, of course, is *my* Trey.

Only, he isn't that now. Hasn't been for close to five years. Not since he got a job offer right out of college and moved to France without me.

Let me rephrase that: Not since he accepted a job offer overseas without telling me, proposed, and made my acceptance contingent on moving to Paris with him. *Then* he moved to France without me.

I said no. For … reasons. Multiple.

The main reason, though, at least in the moment, was that

I *couldn't* go to France. Trey knew it. And he knew why. But he took the job and asked me to come anyway, like my reasons would just disappear.

Or like they weren't valid in the first place. It's a really sad feeling when you realize a person you love doesn't believe things you tell them.

"Actually, he's already here," Mom says, and I swallow down the urge to vomit.

"So, Trey is back in Serendipity Springs," I say, testing out the idea and nodding like it's the kind of thing I can handle. Like I'm talking about a new tire shop opening around the corner.

Like my favorite meal wasn't just ruined—possibly forever —by the thought of Trey somewhere nearby, like a ticking timebomb I could run into at any given time.

Serendipity Springs isn't a tiny town. It's a small city. Even so, it's inevitable that you see people you know almost everywhere. Especially when you don't want to.

And because I'd rather not have to face Trey again, like, *ever*, it probably means he'll start working in an office building on the street where I live.

Or, worse—he'll move into The Serendipity.

Another fun fact: while we were dating, our moms became best friends. They stayed best friends, despite the circumstances. I think they secretly hoped we'd get back together. That I'd change my mind and, in grand gesture fashion, hop on a plane to Paris and tell Trey I made a huge mistake, the Eiffel Tower a glittering backdrop to my apology.

Though I sometimes regretted my decision early on, I did not change my mind. I did not get on a plane.

Did I hope Trey would give up the job and come back for me? At first, yes. Yes, I did.

But the longer time went on, the more I realized that our breakup was a gift. Because the way Trey handled not only the decision about his job but the proposal showed me something I had missed about his character.

I wouldn't want to marry a man who would make a choice to take a job halfway across the world without consulting me. Where's the partnership in that? My dad consults my mom before downloading a new app on his phone. Which might be a little *too much* togetherness, but it works for them.

And though Trey was, according to *his* mother, who told *my* mother, crushed, *he's* the one who put me in an impossible position. Leave home for Paris to be together. Or ... lose everything.

I wouldn't want to marry a man who turns proposals into ultimatums.

His love had limits. Even if most people—particularly his parents and our mutual friends—didn't understand it.

My parents *mostly* did, once I finally admitted my reasons for saying no.

But I think they were still deeply saddened and, at first, held me responsible rather than seeing Trey's proposal as what it was: a test.

I wasn't the one who failed. *He* did—by giving me a test in the first place.

Still. Knowing that Trey was in the wrong didn't stop it from breaking my heart. Maybe it broke it even *more*. The betrayal ran deeper than I could ever express in words.

I think only Sophie truly understands. I hope I have enough leftover icing for *this* discussion when I get back to The Serendipity.

"I'll be fine. I *am* fine," I say loudly, as though volume will give my words more weight. "It's been almost five years. I've moved on."

In theory, anyway. Because I haven't moved on in terms of a relationship.

Before boring Paul, my most recent attempt at dating, I

went out with a handful of guys whose faces and names are largely forgettable or, at the least, interchangeable.

Not memorable, not serious.

Not Trey.

Which, I remind myself now, is a *good* thing. I've had years to perform an extensive post-mortem on our relationship and finally saw the proposal as a pattern. Trey didn't just make that one choice without me.

We somehow slipped into a dynamic where he made all the choices, all the time, and I went along with them, all the time. I think I told myself in those moments I was being easy-going and low-conflict, when really I was stifling things I wanted and letting Trey's opinions eclipse mine. Until I had none of my own.

Again, our breakup was a good thing.

"And he's engaged," Mom says.

I can't help it. I gasp.

I know her intention was to rip the Band-Aid off, but Band-Aids shouldn't always be ripped off. Sometimes, they should be left until all the painful sticky residue disappears and it slips off on its own, revealing a perfectly healed wound underneath.

"I told you not to do it that way," Dad says. "You can't just blurt out something like that about the love of her life being engaged."

Mom reaches over to pat my hand while directing her words at Dad. "And *you* can't still call him the love of her life!"

He throws up his hands. "I'm just speaking the truth!"

"So am I!"

The thing about my parents being ridiculously in love is that the same passion carries over into their fights. Mom and Dad both have a *lot* of feelings. Good and bad. Ones they like to express at full volume.

"He's not the love of my life," I whisper, but they're yelling too loudly at each other to hear me. "He never was."

This argument might continue, but the home phone attached to the kitchen wall rings. All three of us sigh in relief.

My dad leaps out of his chair, almost knocking it over in the process, and answers the phone with an excited, "Hello?"

Mom watches with hearts in her eyes and a smile on her face.

Me? I'm still frozen in my chair, iced over by the knowledge that Trey is engaged. To someone else.

He (presumably) bought another ring and (in all likelihood) got down on one knee for someone else.

It's okay. You didn't want him. You made the right call, I tell myself.

And while this might very well be true, the thought of Trey proposing to someone else and—this is the real kicker— is moving here with *her* leaves me feeling bruised and vulnerable.

Yeah, my very favorite home-cooked meal is definitely ruined.

Goodbye, chicken and dumplings. You have been spoiled because I got blindsided with news about an ex I don't even have feelings for. It's not you, it's me—and it's complicated.

"Oh, is that right?" Dad's saying into the phone. "You're selling solar panels? That's great. I'm definitely interested. And I have questions. A lot of them." Dad drags his chair closer to the wall and sits down, wrapping the curly phone cord around his arm. He almost looks like he's deep-sea fishing, settling in to battle some big catch on the end of his line.

Which isn't all that far off from what he's actually doing.

"His latest thing is timing how long he can keep them on the line," Mom says, giving my hand a squeeze. I'd forgotten she was holding it, and my hand has lost all feeling. "His current record is forty-seven minutes. I think he's going for an hour."

"Tell me about your silicon production in the panels," Dad says. "Is it ethically sourced?"

I pull my hand away from Mom's and start clearing the table. I need to move, and I don't particularly want to be touched right now.

Dad's really picking up steam now. "Do you only install them on human houses? What about henhouses?" A pause. "I see. Outhouses? Doghouses?"

I hold back a snort. He's referencing a Tommy Lee Jones quote from one of Dad's favorite movies, *The Fugitive*. I've watched it enough times with him that I think I could quote most of it at this point.

Mom joins me, taking Dad's empty bowl and stacking it on top of hers. "At least he's creative. And never rude."

"The argument could be made that wasting someone's time is rude," I say, placing my bowl in the sink and taking the dishes from her hands.

"But if these are scammers, not just salespeople, he's saving someone else from making his mistake," Mom points out. It doesn't make me feel any better, though, because it reminds me that I *also* took my parents' money. And if Serendipitous Sweets fails, they may never see it again.

I know they'd tell me it's fine and not to worry, but I also know how hard they've worked year after year for teachers' salaries. It's why Dad's train set took literal decades to build—he has to scrimp and save for every piece.

Now I'm almost as bad as a scammer. I had such high hopes for my business, promising to pay them back with interest. Then, promising to pay them back in full.

Now, I make no more promises. The money is a subject we don't talk about, I think because they know it's been slow, even if I try to avoid the subject.

"I've got this," I tell Mom, shooing her away. "Go watch *Wheel of Fortune*."

She kisses me on the cheek before darting in to watch her favorite show. I never thought she'd survive Pat Sajak leaving the show, but as much as she moaned and groaned about his replacement, I think she has a burgeoning crush on Ryan Seacrest.

With the wheel spinning in the other room and my dad asking ten million questions about solar panels he won't buy, I get to work on the dishes. There's always been something therapeutic to me about washing up after a meal or after making a big batch of cookies. The warm water and the smell of dish soap make me happy.

Good thing considering the sheer number of dishes and utensils I have to wash almost daily.

"I'm sorry for surprising you about Trey. Are you okay?" Mom asks, coming into the kitchen as I'm starting in on the pots and pans. Ryan Seacrest must be on commercial break.

"I mean, I'm not sure how you can ever prepare for that kind of news. It shocked me. But I'm fine. It's not like I'm still in love with him."

"Mm-hm," Mom says.

I really need to find a guy I like enough to bring home so maybe she'll finally start to believe me.

"I dodged a bullet," I tell her, scrubbing a bowl a little harder than necessary. "Trust me. More like dodging a cannonball."

"What about bird poop?" Dad is asking, and Mom and I both chuckle.

I wonder if Dad is coming up with these on the fly or if he has some kind of script memorized. Either way, he's pretty amazing. Too bad this isn't a skill he could monetize.

"We have a lot of crows around here. If there's a buildup

of bird poop, how does that impact the functionality, the ability of the panels to gather solar rays?"

"Should we stop him at some point?" I ask.

"Oh, Willa. Let him have his fun. We all need something to spark joy in life, even if it's being a complete and utter pest to telemarketers."

Honestly, I don't disagree with her there.

But the sad thing, I realize as I rinse out bowls and spoons, is that I don't even know if I have something as silly as messing with telemarketers to spark joy in my own life.

Chapter Six
Archer

"Maybe firing the building manager wasn't the best starting move," Bellamy says, propping his feet up on my coffee table.

I frown. My new furniture has only been set up a few days, and he's already putting his shoes on it. I clear my throat pointedly, and Bellamy rolls his eyes and lets his feet drop to the floor dramatically.

"I didn't mean to *fire* him," I say, returning to the argument Bellamy and I have rehashed several times over the last two days. "He could have stayed on, just not with housing included in his package. It was a renegotiation of terms."

"With no negotiating," Bellamy points out.

My father started entrusting me with his various businesses and investments when I was in my early twenties. I've handled mergers. Acquisitions. Market expansions. Weathered (attempted) hostile takeovers. Those kinds of stressful, high stakes situations are where I thrive.

And yet, so far I'm drowning in the details of managing one little apartment building.

Not that The Serendipity is necessarily little. With four

floors and sixty-one apartments, it houses just over one hundred people. And it's the people who are the problem.

"The least he could have done was give notice before disappearing."

Bellamy doesn't argue further, but he doesn't need to. He's made it clear multiple times that he disagreed with my decision.

Who else would want to rent a basement apartment, anyway? he asked. *Now you'll have an almost unusable space and no building manager.*

He's right, of course. But as unhappy as John was to hear that his apartment would no longer be included as part of his salary package, I didn't expect the quiet older man to simply *disappear*. When I went down to find him after he stopped answering his phone, the basement apartment was completely devoid of any signs of life. John left nothing but the furnishings. Which may have belonged to The Serendipity in the first place. I have no way of knowing without calling Galentine to ask, which, less than a full week into my tenure as the new owner, would feel like some kind of failure. A concession of defeat.

Plus, I doubt she's reachable on her cruise.

I can handle this. I *can*. I just need to find someone (or *someones*) to fill John's role. And fast. It would be easier if I could find a previous job application or a full description of the building manager position. But the only resource I have for knowing what John's job entailed (besides a general Google search) is from the complaints I'm now receiving.

Because it appears that before leaving, John gave out my phone number. To the entire building. Now, I'm going to have to get a new phone.

But first, I need to get a new person to handle all of this.

Because I certainly don't have the time or the ability to unclog a kitchen sink on the third floor, fix the hissing radiator, and empty the various trash cans around the building into ... wherever trash is emptied. I tug at my collar.

"Can you blame him?" Bellamy asks, popping a cookie into his smiling mouth.

Those cookies.

All week long as we've plowed through my task list together, I've had to suffer through watching Bellamy scarf down Willa's cookies. Listening to him chew and make happy little moans. Having my apartment infused with the scent of almond and vanilla, which lingers even after he heads back to his hotel each night.

He just finished his second dozen, and it's Friday. Willa is probably thrilled with the extra business.

I haven't seen Willa when she's dropped off the cookies, only heard her voice. And felt strangely jealous over the sound of her laughter at something Bellamy said. I'm not sure what it is about Willa that has burrowed under my skin.

I want to see her at my door rather than strain to hear the sound of her voice from the safety of my office.

I also want her to move out of the building.

Possibly *because* I want to see more of her. Distance from a woman who intrigues me for no good reason seems like a safe bet.

But it's hard to get distance when Bellamy keeps ordering the stupid cookies, bringing her to my door. Even just him eating the cookies is a constant and unwelcome reminder of her. She might as well have been sitting next to me on the couch, tapping a foot impatiently, those blue eyes fixed on me.

"Don't get crumbs on my new couch," I say.

Bellamy grins and continues chewing. "Are you sure you want me back in New York? I could stay another week until you've got things settled," Bellamy says, his voice kinder now.

I frown.

Why do I prefer it when he argues with me?

Probably because in my life, kindness always seems to go hand in hand with pity, and there's nothing I hate more. Except maybe people who clip their fingernails in public places.

"I'm settled."

"Or at least until you find another building manager."

"I have a list of prospects right here." I tap my phone. It's a slim list, but it's a start.

"And how many have responded to our inquiries?" he asks.

He knows the answer. It's none.

"Have any of the plumbers returned our calls?"

"No."

It's been crickets. Or what's worse than crickets—roaches?

Apparently, we have those too, in one of the first-floor apartments.

But as with the plumbers, no exterminators have answered their phones or called back. Same with electricians to help figure out why the lights on the left side of the first floor keep blinking.

If I believed in Galentine's magic, I'd say I've been cursed. A very specific curse, foiling every effort I make to do anything with The Serendipity.

"At the very least, you now have a larger list of local services you can contact since you've struck out so far," Bellamy says. "I created a full spreadsheet with all the electricians, plumbers, exterminators, and handypersons I could find in the greater Serendipity Springs area."

"Handy*persons*?"

He shrugs. "Several on the list are women. So, yes ... handypersons. Though it does sound odd. The S on the end makes me think of *handsy*, not *handy*, for some reason. Maybe it should be handypeople? In any case, you have a list."

"Thank you. That should suffice."

"Do you want me to call anyone else today?"

What I would like is for Bellamy to call all the people—handy and otherwise. I'd like to get back to an office that isn't filled with years of someone else's inability to set up a filing system. A job in which I have several layers of protection against having to deal with people. In New York, I always had Bellamy and several administrative assistants acting as my defense.

Here, I have no defenses. No protections. Every resident knows where I live—and they're all *right here*. They now also have my phone number.

But going back to New York isn't possible. And even if it were, it wouldn't be a respite. I would be walking back into the same dumpster fire I left. Better to send Bellamy back. He needs to be running Archway Investments, not making phone calls to plumbers. And it's the best thing for me not to show my face until some other scandal eclipses mine.

Plus, I remind myself, this project is about more. It's about me being different from my father. More down-to-earth. Less pampered and stuck in some kind of wealthy person's tower with my silver spoon and my Amex Black.

Right now, though, I sort of miss the tower and spoon.

"I don't need to go back right away. I could put it off until Sunday night," Bellamy says, and the idea that he thinks I need hand-holding is the only thing worse than knowing I do, in fact, need hand-holding.

"That won't be necessary."

"Well, then, I'd better head on to catch the last Boston train from Worcester. If you're sure," he adds. "Would you like me to at least do something about the trash situation before I go?"

Bellamy's nose wrinkles when he says this, as though the very idea of emptying trash bins causes the reflex. It probably does. He probably hasn't emptied a trash can since he was a child, if at all.

He and I have this in common.

"Wouldn't want you to sully your suit," I tell him.

The only thing Bellamy might love more than sweets is his wardrobe. I suspect his suit collection is more expensive than mine. I don't care about brands or labels, only the fit and whether I can get dressed while making as few decisions as possible. But Bellamy religiously attends Fashion Week. I wouldn't know the difference between an Armani and anything else. Especially since Armani is the only designer I can think of right now.

"Do I have any Armani suits?" I ask, and Bellamy's mouth curves into a smile.

"No. You prefer the look and cut of Tom Ford, and I've always loved that you don't know that." He tilts his head, examining me with an amused smile. "Are you suddenly interested in fashion?"

"Definitely not. And please—go to New York. I don't trust anyone else, and I assume you're prepared to handle the board."

"You know what they say about assuming."

"That it's better to assume the worst in order to avoid the worst outcome," I say firmly, and Bellamy laughs.

"Not quite, though I like your version better." He pauses. "Are you sure about all this? Leaving the city, not being the face of the company?"

"Positive. At least, for now."

"Because you shouldn't have to run away to avoid your father's crimes. They're his, not yours."

"I know. And I'm not running."

Not *only* running. Maybe I am running ... a little bit. But even the idea of returning to New York has my stomach feeling like a pit of acid. I pull out my mints and let one dissolve on my tongue. The potent ginger makes my eyes water.

"Because," Bellamy continues in a lighter tone, "I'll happily stay here and eat cookies and round up handypeople and manage the buildingpeople ... this is fun, actually, just adding *people* to the ends of words—"

"*Bellamy*."

"Fine, fine." He stands, brushing crumbs from his suit pants. "I'll be back in a few days. Want me to call you after the meeting Monday?" I must make some kind of horrified face, because he chuckles and says, "Got it. No phone calls. I'll send an email or text."

"Goodbye."

He pauses in the doorway, frowning. "You're sure I can't help with the trash before I go? It seems like the most pressing of all the menial tasks."

"I have everything I need. Including someone to deal with the trash."

―――――

I am the someone.

Although taking out trash has never once been something I've been asked to do in my life, it can't be a complex task.

Remove overly full trash bags from the various cans in public areas around the building. Locate where trash should be deposited. Place it there. Replace bags.

Consider eliminating all trash cans in The Serendipity's public spaces.

Once again, reconsider my recent life choices.

It's the location issue I'm focused on as I carry the first two bags toward the rear exit of the building where I hope to find dumpsters. This was, unfortunately, one area of the tour Galentine neglected.

If I were a dumpster—*a ridiculous statement*—this is where I'd be.

I'm not sure who is using the various trash cans in public spaces around the building, but this seems to be where people deposit the things deemed too disgusting for their own personal trash. I'm trying to breathe through my mouth while holding these two particular bags away from my body. One smells like raw onions mixed with raw sewage, and the other one is worse because I can't even attach a guess to the sickly-sweet odor of rot.

It's too light for a dead body, so at least there's that.

"Only two more," I mutter to myself as I reach the rear exit where, thankfully, I do find three dumpsters along the back of the building.

I ignore the sounds of something scuttling around back there. Serendipity Springs is no New York, with its massive rat overpopulation, but a city is a city, a dumpster is a dumpster, and rats are rats.

Hurrying back inside, I try to think about my reward once I'm done. Running might be a punishment, not a reward for many, but it's the one activity that's never failed to make me feel energized—a reset for my body and my brain.

What probably would have been smart, I think, noting some kind of unidentifiable stain on my shoe, *is to have changed into running clothes before doing this.*

At least it's late enough that the building is fairly quiet. I didn't want to risk running into any other people, having any more conversations, or, most especially, being seen taking out the building trash. Nothing screams *I'm in charge* like carting stinking garbage bags around a building.

The only person I wouldn't mind seeing is—

Nope.

I don't want to run into Willa. Especially not with a trash bag in each hand and unidentifiable sludge on my shoes.

Though I've already made a terrible impression on her, and I'm not sure how it could be worse.

In any case, it shouldn't be so hard to think about Willa. Especially when I remind myself about her appearance in my closet—and her ludicrous explanation. She is—with her trespassing and penchant for leaving ponytail holders all over the building and hard-to-banish sugar cookie scent—an embodiment of the kind of chaos I don't need in my life right now.

But telling myself this doesn't seem to have the effect it should, especially not when, as I'm emptying the kitchen trash, the scent of vanilla rises to greet me.

Chapter Seven

Willa

I AM WHOLLY unprepared to be transported across the building again.

One second, I'm reaching in for a sweater to put on over my tank top. Then I trip. And because I must protect the cookies at all costs, I awkwardly fall inside my closet, shielding the box against my chest.

And now, here I am. It's dark, and I'm surrounded by a scent I would describe as Sexy Man Who Wears Expensive Cologne.

"Ouch!" I whisper-shout, clutching the box of cookies to my chest with one hand as I rub my eye with the other. "Who even uses wire hangers?"

Archer Gaines, that's who.

If I had any question about whether I was transported to his or some other random closet in the building, the smell of Archer—heady, rich, masculine, *expensive*—assures me I'm back at the scene of the original crime against nature. It's like the man has somehow infected my nostrils.

Why should I remember his smell? And why does he have to smell good?

If his scent matched his personality, it would be sour grapes. Or sour milk. Just ... sour. And dour.

Okay, that's not *fully* true. He has a tiny sense of humor I've seen glimpses of, like when he calls me Willa the Person. He also happens to look as good in only running shorts as he does in a fitted suit.

So it's not fair that he *also* has an intoxicating smell that's currently going straight to my head.

Speaking of my head, it's surprisingly calm about the whole transportation thing. Or maybe I'm just resigned?

The reality—strange and unbelievable as it may be—is that my closet seems to inexplicably shoot me across the building and into Archer's closet.

Against my will, I might add.

Is it possible to charge an inanimate object with time-travel assault?

Probably not.

But now, I'm fairly convinced that Sophie is right and the building does have some kind of magic.

I would have preferred a genie granting wishes or a cloak of invisibility.

Basically, just about *anything at all* instead of being transported to the closet of a man who disliked me on sight.

Probably because I appeared in his apartment unexpectedly. Just like right now.

Gee, thanks, building. Tell me you don't like me without telling me you don't like me.

As soon as I'm sure I did not, in fact, blind myself on Archer's blasted wire hanger, I readjust my grip on the box of cookies and listen.

If I'm lucky, the apartment will be empty. It's after nine o'clock on a Friday night when most people—those who haven't been decorating cookies all night—are out. Though I don't see Archer as a night owl or a party animal. He seems like the kind of man who has a very specific sleep schedule and probably gets up at some ungodly hour, like four in the morning, to run or, at the least, go to work.

Oh, no ... what if he's asleep?

The idea of running into Archer *awake* isn't a prospect I'm thrilled with, but the idea of exiting this closet to find him in bed has my stomach tensing.

I wonder if he sleeps shirtless...

NOT RELEVANT, I tell my brain, which has clearly taken up residence in the gutter.

But it's especially hard to fight off speculation now that I can picture him shirtless.

One more time for the Willa in back: NOT. RELEVANT.

Honestly, it's a little concerning that my thoughts are occupied more with thoughts of Archer and his potential shirtlessness than the fact that I once again somehow transported magically from one closet to another. I'm not sure what this says about me or about the human brain's ability to adapt—or maybe compartmentalize.

I'll worry about that later. Once I'm safely out of here—if possible, without being detected.

As I press my ear to the door, I hear nothing. Not the sound of footsteps or voices or snores or even breathing. Nothing to indicate a (definitely hot) man is sleeping (possibly shirtless) a few feet away.

When I slowly emerge from the closet, there is still only silence, accompanied by the potently eerie feeling of being completely alone.

Archer is not here.

Which means if I hurry, I can get out before he knows I have once again appeared in his closet.

This time, he probably *would* call the police, and I don't want to test my theory.

I mean, the man wouldn't even try one of my cookies! He's a fun hater. Or a sugar hater.

Possibly—probably—a Willa hater.

Bellamy, on the other hand, just might keep me in business a little longer if he maintains his current ordering frequency. That man knows how to wear an expensive suit but also eat a sugar cookie.

Their good cop/bad cop dynamic is fascinating to me. Archer is younger but is also Bellamy's boss. And yet the vibe is less boss-employee and more like that of a fun older uncle with his fun-hating adult nephew. Or something.

But I don't need to ponder their odd relationship right now. What I need to do is to sneak out of this apartment and deliver these cookies.

Though if the apartment is empty, that means Bellamy isn't here either. I'm not sure where else I'd find him. He had me deliver them to Archer's apartment the other two times. By way of the front door, not a stupid portal closet with a mean streak.

Tonight, I lost track of time—not an unusual circumstance—so I'm delivering them later than I'd like.

Though I'm fairly confident I'm alone in the apartment, I still creep out of the closet as quietly as I can. Archer's furniture has arrived, giving the bedroom a very different look today.

Unsurprisingly, his furnishings are spartan and masculine, with only a few necessary items: bed, side tables, dresser. All dark, heavy wood with a plush area rug. No paintings or pictures on the wall. Nothing personal. Nothing out of place.

The perfection of it makes me want to go untuck his bedspread and rumple his sheets or leave a few drawers askew. Disrupt his order just the tiniest bit.

But I also don't want to leave any evidence behind.

Hurrying out to the main room, I draw in a sharp breath.

The furnishings are still heavy and masculine, but here, there's a much homier feel than his bedroom. Warmer. Almost cozy.

The couch is leather, but it's the supple kind that looks like you'd sink comfortably when you sit. A navy chenille throw blanket is tossed casually over the back of it. A newspaper sits folded on the seat of an armchair upholstered in a plush blue patterned fabric.

A number of potted plants, the kind I can't afford and probably wouldn't be able to keep alive anyway, enhance the hominess of the space. Sophie could tell me their names, but I'm going to assume most are the only indoor plant whose name I know: the fiddle leaf fig.

Rather than a giant television like I'd expect to see, on the wall across from the couch hangs a large painting of what appears to be a western landscape: fields with scattered cows and snow-capped mountains in the background. It's the kind of picture you could stare at for hours and dream about climbing into it.

A few other smaller, abstract paintings adorn the walls. Not the weird kind of abstract that makes me question art and whether it's really a big inside joke and preschoolers are the ones actually making it. But attractive swaths of color that look intentional and balanced and really liven up the large room.

The space looks warm and inviting. There's even a half-full glass of water on the coffee table.

Gasp! A glass left on the table without a coaster?

Perhaps Archer Gaines is human, after all.

But I don't have time to test out how comfy his couch is or relish in confirmation of his humanity.

I need to get out before he returns.

At the front door, I hesitate.

What about the cookies? I could just leave them in the

hallway and text Bellamy to say that no one answered the door. While I like the residents of The Serendipity and think it's a safe place, I don't trust people, as a general rule. Especially not when it comes to something tempting like a box of delicious—unless you're Archer—cookies left in the hall.

What's the likelihood the cookies will still be here when Bellamy returns to the apartment?

I'd feel safer leaving them on the marble island in the kitchen—a counter so gorgeous I'd like to climb up and lie down on just to feel the cool marble on my skin. But that would be evidence I've been inside Archer's apartment. Again.

Debating, I set the cookies down and slide my phone out of my pocket, sending Bellamy a text.

WILLA

> Sorry it's so late, but I've got your cookies!
> Can I bring them up?

I try not to wince at the lie. I mean, *technically* it's not a lie. My text makes no false statements. But it does imply I'm in my apartment asking this question. Not standing inside Archer's kitchen, lusting over his glorious island and considering pulling a Goldilocks on his leather couch.

BELLAMY

> Unfortunately, you missed me. I'm on a train
> to Boston, then back to New York until late
> next week.

WILLA

> I'm so sorry! I should have come earlier.

BELLAMY

> It's fine. I didn't let you know when I was
> leaving. Just leave them with Archer. If for
> some reason he's not there, put a note on
> the box saying they're from me.

88

I chuckle. The man really does love his sweets. I thought, at first, maybe Bellamy just felt sorry for me. That he was trying to make up for Archer's coldness by ordering dozens of cookies.

Or maybe that he sensed my desperation for more business.

But when I dropped off the last box, Bellamy shoved one in his mouth immediately, eyes rolling back in his head. I can't say I mind the encouragement and enthusiasm.

My conclusion is that Bellamy just really loves my cookies.

And I will refuse to be offended that Archer wouldn't even try them. Or I'll tell myself not to be offended. My phone buzzes with another text.

Archer—lonely? This gives me an unwanted squeeze of something a little too like empathy. Loneliness is something I understand. After I rejected Trey's proposal and before I met Sophie, I had some lean, lonely years.

I had a handful of high school friends who moved back after college. But our friendships weren't the same as before, and Mel, the one I'd been closest to back in the day, totally ghosted me. It was an extra vulnerable time in my life, and even thinking back to it makes me feel a little ill.

As much as I haven't enjoyed my interactions with Archer, moving to Serendipity Springs from New York would be a transition. And he doesn't quite fit here, what with his fancy suits and his whole cranky vibe.

Archer seems like an incredibly self-sufficient person. Confident, capable, and cool ... but could he be lonely?

And why should I care if he is?

BELLAMY

I'm sure he'd love company.

WILLA

Not mine.

BELLAMY

Especially yours.

WILLA

Most especially NOT mine.

BELLAMY

Between the two of us, I'm the Archer Gaines expert, and I'm telling you he'd be happy to see YOU.

He might think he's an expert, but Bellamy is wrong. At least in this regard.

The fact that he's arguing with me about it makes me think Archer still hasn't told him about finding me in his closet.

Which makes me wonder ... *why?*

Why would Archer keep this a secret?

And why is Bellamy insisting Archer would be happy to see me?

It doesn't matter. I'm not coming back here another time, especially now that I know Bellamy won't be back until next week. Everything in my body is screaming for me to get out of this apartment *now* before Archer finds me here.

There's a pen in a neatly organized drawer, and I add the word "from" above Bellamy's name on the box.

If I leave the cookies here on the island, hopefully Archer will assume Bellamy left them here before he went.

The only issue is leaving Archer's door unlocked as I exit. But I don't have much choice. So I leave, furtively glancing around the hallway, grateful when I don't run into anyone on the fourth floor.

I had the foresight to give Sophie a key to my place after the original closet incident.

Just in case.

I head down the back stairs to her apartment, hoping she's there when she doesn't respond to my text.

What I *don't* expect is to be bowled over the moment I exit the stairwell by someone running.

"Oof!"

My back hits the wall, and I almost go down, but a large body pins me in place. A large body and ... trash bags?

"Archer?"

He jumps back, dropping one of the bags in the process. His eyes flash to mine, then quickly away. He bends to grab the trash bag he dropped, and when he straightens, his cheeks are red.

The whole thing is a strange look—a man in a very expensive suit with a blush on his cheeks and an overflowing garbage bag in each hand.

It's almost like one of those *Celebrities—They're Just Like Us!* moments.

Grumpy billionaires ... they're taking out their trash—just like us!

But does Archer *really* take out his own trash? If I didn't see it with my own eyes, I wouldn't believe it. I also can't really see Bellamy, with his tailored suits and perfectly coiffed hair, being that person either. He might have joked about being the Alfred to Archer's Bruce Wayne, but Bellamy is no butler.

"I didn't see you," Archer says in a clipped tone, which I guess is as close to an apology as I can expect.

Based on how he smashed into me, it appears he was running away from the back doors.

But that doesn't make sense—running *or* bringing trash bags inside when the dumpster is just outside the doors.

"Is everything okay?" It definitely doesn't *look* okay.

Besides the trash, his dark hair is rumpled, and his suit jacket looks like it popped a button and is hanging open, his tie askew.

He looks better this way, and it reminds me of how I wanted to mess up his bedroom just a little bit.

And now *I'm* also blushing. Because I was just in this man's bedroom, and he has no idea. I'm also in my pajamas in front of Archer. Again. I hope he can't look at me and tell that I just crept out of his apartment like a cookie-leaving criminal.

"There's an opossum out there," he says through clenched teeth. "Or a whole family of opossums. I'm not sure. It's— they're—guarding the dumpster."

I do my very best not to laugh, but the mental image of this scenario is too potent. "I see."

He glares. Guess I'm not hiding my amusement as well as I'd like. "They gave chase," he says.

"*Gave chase?*" I repeat. Even the man's words sound like rich-person speak.

He ignores me. "They're probably rabid."

"Possums play dead. They don't typically chase people. And they almost never get rabies—something about their body temperature."

I typically don't store up random animal facts, but Sophie started sending me Instagram reels of cute puppies and kittens that soon shifted to raccoons, possums, and capybaras, which I didn't know existed before this year. A two-hundred-pound rodent sounds like something out of a movie.

Actually, it is—an R.O.U.S. from *The Princess Bride*. Though capybaras are much cuter and less likely to eat you in a fire swamp.

The point is: my entire Instagram feed is now nothing but animals, and I have amassed a random collection of facts.

"It's why possums are so good for the environment," I continue, though it's immediately clear Archer doesn't care. "They eat ticks and other icky pests and are less likely to carry rabies than raccoons."

"And guard dumpsters," Archer mutters.

"Are you sure they were possums?"

"*O*possums, and yes."

I know it's childish, but I can't stop myself from rolling my eyes. "It's possum. Opossum is the slang word for them. The one little kids use."

"Incorrect. The technical name is opossum." Archer seems so sure that now I'm questioning myself, even though I'm the one with the possum-filled Instagram feed. "Look it up if you don't believe me," he says.

We stand there, glaring, until it dawns on me that for a person who avoids conflict like it's an infectious disease, I can't seem to stop diving headfirst into it with Archer. It's like his personality unlocks some basement level in me.

I don't like the transformation.

And yet, it clearly energizes some part of me, which isn't something I want to admit, even to myself.

"We can save this debate for later," I say, fully intending to walk away, find Sophie and my spare key, and then place caution tape across my closet so I never go in there again.

But then Archer glances toward the back doors with clear trepidation on his face, and my steps slow.

He's lonely, Bellamy told me earlier, and I wish he hadn't.

Because if there's one thing I can't resist, it's helping people who need it. Before those texts, Archer seemed like the kind of man who needed nothing.

Now, he's standing here in a fancy suit holding a trash bag in each hand, still breathing a little hard from being chased—allegedly—by possums.

I frown. "*You* were taking out the building trash?"

I wish I'd done a little better job of hiding the disbelief in my voice.

He hesitates. "Yes."

Then I remember that this week, Archer fired John, the building manager. Gloria from 3G told me when I ran into her getting mail this week. She stores juicy tidbits about people in the building like some people doomsday prep. But somehow, it's not in an unkind way. More like she's The Serendipity's version of a gossip column.

I didn't particularly *love* John—he was slow to respond if residents had any issues and a grumbly crank about most things—but he did work here *forever*.

If Archer can kick someone like him to the curb, what other changes will he make?

I think of the kitchen and Archer's questions about my agreement with Galentine. If I have any hope of keeping my baking space, maybe I need a different approach than sparring with Archer at every turn.

And it's thoughts of my business—and *mostly* my business—not an unwelcome spark of pity for how lost Archer seems right now that has me asking, "Can I help?"

Archer blinks at me, looking a little stunned. "With the trash?"

I bite back a few remarks about things I think he could use help with. Like his personality. And his apparent lack of a heart, as evidenced by firing John. Despite all my reasons not to help him, my sense of compassion has mixed with my sense of self preservation.

We are doing this thing.

I hold out my hand. "Give me a bag. We can go together. Safety in numbers."

I want to add, *Don't worry, I'll keep you safe from the big, bad attack possum*, but Archer looks so flustered, I hold back.

Flustered is a state of being I'm very familiar with. I'd guess for a man like him, it's more like an out-of-body experience.

He hesitates but then hands me one of the bags. "Fine. But I warned you."

He *did* warn me.

So when we step outside and immediately there is a hissing gray creature hurtling toward us, all jagged teeth and pointy snout, I should be prepared.

But I'm not really sure words can be enough to warn someone about an attack possum. Or *o*possum.

There's only one, but it seems much too large and far too angry and somehow gives the impression of being a possum army rather than one rather oversized rodent.

Mammal?

Marsupial!

Instagram possum facts zip through my addled brain at the speed of light before I take hold of my limbs and *move*.

With a shriek probably heard three states away, I hurl the garbage bag at the creature and dart back into the building. Unfortunately, Archer is a step ahead of me but stopped, like he suddenly remembered he was probably supposed to be chivalrous and let me go first.

I plow into him, knocking us both to the ground. His bag of garbage goes flying and, unfortunately, lands in exactly the right spot to block the door from closing.

And then the attack possum leaps over the garbage bag and bolts inside The Serendipity.

Acting completely on impulse and instinct, I grab Archer by his fancy suit lapels and roll. We're a tangle of limbs and chaos of grunts, ending when I hit the wall. Archer's broad back is the only thing shielding us from certain possum doom.

The creature bolts past us in a streak of dirty gray fur, scamper-sprinting toward the front of the building like it's on some kind of mission.

Only once it's halfway down the hall do I turn my attention back to Archer and realize I'm still clutching his jacket with a certain-death grip, holding him inches away. We are practically nose to nose, our breaths mingling.

I realize I'm staring at his mouth, which has the tiniest white scar through his cupid's bow, and my gaze snaps up to his. Archer is already looking into my eyes, and unlike so many times before, he doesn't glance away.

His eyes are lovely, actually, a dark blue-gray that's softer than I'd thought, almost like the color of sky at twilight after the golds and pinks have faded. A warm, fluttery feeling moves through my middle. His gaze is heavy, weighted with something I cannot read.

But there's an openness and vulnerability to him right now, as though crashing to the ground knocked loose whatever tight shell he keeps wrapped around himself. What's revealed underneath has left me stunned and breathless.

Or maybe I just knocked the wind out of myself while rolling.

"Sorry," I say in a breathy whisper, not even sure what I'm apologizing for.

Knocking him over?

Not taking him seriously about the possum?

Or maybe for not making any move to put a reasonable distance between us?

Right now, the distance between us is highly *un*reasonable. We're *end of a first date about to kiss* close.

You may kiss the bride close.

Soldier back from war close.

Or, in our case, *possum frightened into panic mode* close.

"For what?" Archer says, his voice just as unsteady as mine.

"What?" I parrot back. My thoughts are syrupy and slow.

"You're sorry for which part—for not believing me about the attack opossum, tackling me, or ensuring my suit will need to be dry-cleaned and pressed?"

I swear, I see a hint of amusement in his eyes. I didn't think Archer had the ability to *be* amused.

I release my grip on his lapels. But pressed this close together, my hands have nowhere to go except to what I have confirmed is a muscular chest. Because it's not enough that Archer Gaines smells good and has really lovely eyes—when he's not glaring at me. He has to pack a bunch of muscles underneath his fancy suits too.

There's a crash and clatter at the end of the hall, startling me out of whatever sorcery has left me feeling a whole new set of emotions for Archer Gaines.

He scrambles to his feet and reaches down, tugging me up in a swift motion—more evidence of his enviable fitness level. I'm so startled, I just stand there, gaping.

Until barking at the front of the building has both our heads whipping that way.

Before my feet can move, Archer is jogging down the hall. He turns his head and calls, "Considering this is your fault, are you going to help?"

I chase after him. "This isn't my fault! For the record, it's the possum who's to blame. Not me. And you're the one who threw the trash bag right in the doorway."

"Sure," Archer says as I catch him. The edge of his mouth lifts in a smile. "Because you tackled me."

We round the corner at the end of the hallway and enter the front lobby. Where Sara's massive puppy—already larger than most full grown dogs—is barking at the possum, which is lying belly-up on the floor, motionless.

Sara is barely able to hold back Archibald, who has his butt in the air, tail wagging wildly like he is hoping the possum will decide to be his new best friend.

"Oh, now you play dead," I say, glaring at the possum, who's doing a very convincing job.

"Maybe it *is* dead?" Sara says, struggling with Archibald's leash. "It keeled over and hasn't moved an inch. But could someone get it out of here?"

Archer looks to me, and I shrug. "I'm not the one who owns the building."

With a sigh, he steps forward and nudges the possum with the now-scuffed toe of his dress shoe.

With a deeper frown and a bit more force, Archer pushes the possum again. Still no movement. No reaction. Is it even breathing? I see no sign that it is.

Archibald sits back on his haunches and whines, the very literal picture of puppy-dog eyes.

"I think," Archer says with a frown, "it's actually dead."

"Do you think Archibald scared it ... to death?" Sara whispers. With a heavy sigh, the dog in question drops his head to his paws.

I shouldn't feel anything remotely sad for this overgrown creature, with its wicked teeth, rat tail, and its propensity to chase humans. But I *do* feel bad.

Perhaps because I was at least partly responsible for the whole situation. Though I would argue that Archer shares equal responsibility for its demise. I certainly can't blame Archibald. Puppies get a pass on scaring possums to an early demise.

"Maybe he was already dying?" I suggest. "He was behaving oddly. I mean, he chased us, then ran into the building."

"You said opossums don't get rabies," Archer says.

"I'm not saying it was rabid. Just maybe ... sick."

"What do we do with it?" Sara asks.

"I suppose put it in the dumpster," Archer says, nudging it once more. I watch hopefully for any movement, but there's nothing.

Archer gives a firm nod, like he's decided something, then bends and reaches for the possum's tail.

"You can't pick him up by his tail!" I say.

He pauses, still bent over the animal. "Why not? And how do you know it's a *him*?"

"I guess I don't. And it just feels ... wrong. Be respectful. He *died*."

I expect an argument or at least resistance. But Archer's soft twilight eyes meet mine again, and he offers me a grim smile. Crouching down, he flexes his fingers, then starts to slide them underneath the creature's midsection, much like you might pick up a cat.

In a hiss and a flash of pointy teeth, the possum miraculously revives and launches itself at Archer.

With a very girlish scream Archer shoots to his feet, flailing his arms as the possum climbs him like a tree.

Not to be left out, Archibald leaps, Sara loses her grip on the leash, and the billionaire, the dog, and the marsupial crash to the floor in a flash of fur, teeth, and an expensive suit that will most *definitely* require dry cleaning. Or perhaps a funeral pyre.

Chapter Eight
Archer

LIMPING INSIDE MY APARTMENT, I close the door and slump against it, wincing at the contact as I recognize a new bruise forming on my back. I'm exhausted. Being tackled to evade an opossum attack will do that to a person.

So will being unintentionally mauled by a dog who's trying to play with—or eat?—the opossum climbing your body.

And then there's everything that happened after: Sara wrangling her dog back upstairs. Willa driving the opossum out. Me blurting out words to her I already regret.

The whole situation was a disaster.

Tomorrow, the first thing I will do is send out an email telling all residents that effective in thirty days, there will be no more pets. None. No dogs, no cats, no fish. No puppies that almost outweigh me.

No animals of any kind.

Then I'll find some kind of pest control company that deals with opossums—and will actually call me back—to do whatever is necessary to eradicate them.

I shudder, then make my way to the sink, where I remove my suit jacket, dumping it unceremoniously on the floor.

Why not? It's already spent a good deal of time on the ground tonight.

Rolling up my shirtsleeves, I scrub my arms up to my elbows with hot water until my skin turns pink. Until I'm sure I have no more animal hair or germs—or possible rabies. Then I turn the water as cold as it can get and splash it on my face.

Did that really just happen?

The opossum. The dog. *Willa.*

And then the words I blurted to her after the opossum was outside. I wince, remembering what I said. Upon further examination, it was probably timed poorly.

No—timed *horribly.*

The more I think about it, the more I think I shouldn't have said what I said at all. Ever.

Is it too late to go downstairs and take them back? I'm not sure Willa would let me in if I knocked right now.

My phone buzzes in my pocket, startling me. By the time I've dried my hands, it's stopped. A text pops up before I can unlock it.

BELLAMY

Are you okay?

BELLAMY

I leave you alone for a few hours and what happens? Disaster.

BELLAMY

Should I come back? Do we need to order a rabies test?

BELLAMY

Do they have tests for rabies?

BELLAMY

Do possums carry rabies?

How could he possibly have heard what happened already? The man is always attentive, always intuitive. But so far as I know, he's not surveilling the building with cameras and a live feed.

ARCHER

First, it's opossum, not possum. Second, they don't carry rabies.

ARCHER

Third, how do you already know?

BELLAMY

Willa texted me.

Guess that answers the question of whether she's up.

Why does it bother me that Willa and Bellamy are texting buddies? It really shouldn't.

But it does.

Especially when I remember the blaze of her blue eyes just before she stormed off a few minutes ago. My gut twists, and as the phone screen darkens, I catch sight of my scowl in the reflection. I text Bellamy again.

ARCHER

You and Willa are texting now?

BELLAMY

Your jealousy is showing. Usually it's just about cookies.

BELLAMY

USUALLY.

That makes me feel only slightly better. Not that I suspected there would be anything romantic between them. I mean, it's not outrageous for men Bellamy's age to date women as young as Willa. My father certainly did.

But Bellamy has never expressed romantic interest in anyone *ever*. Back when I was just a boy and Bellamy had taken over what was my father's job in essentially raising me, my father told me Bellamy had reasons for being alone—and that it would be rude to ask.

Slowly, I stopped being curious. And I never broached the subject with him, even years later.

I find, suddenly, that I want to know why he doesn't date. Why he's never dated, why he seems so content and self-sufficient as he is.

Why someone so warm and so drawn to people would remain alone.

A pang of guilt shoots through me, that after so many years of being an adult and Bellamy being as much of a close friend as I've ever had, I never thought to ask him why.

Even so, I don't like the thought of him being buddy-buddy with Willa. Especially when I basically ruined any chances for *me* to be close with her.

BELLAMY

Kidding about the jealousy. Unless, that is,
you ARE jealous.

BELLAMY

Are you?

ARCHER

I'm not.

ARCHER

But I don't like the idea of you and Willa
having conversations about me.

I wonder if she told him what I said. The fact that Bellamy didn't start there seems to indicate that she didn't.

For some reason, this only makes me feel worse about my

careless words, uttered while my nerves were still screaming after the opossum incident.

Though it was more like the opossum was using me as an escape route and the dog was going after the creature. If anything, I was collateral damage—an extreme case of wrong place, wrong time.

Though I may have been in some way complicit, as the entire reason the opossum was inside the building was because of my attempt to empty the trash.

A mistake I won't make again. If only I can successfully contact people tomorrow, I can hire personnel for everything The Serendipity needs right now.

BELLAMY

Any chance we have CCTV set up in the
building?

ARCHER

No.

BELLAMY

Opportunity missed. Once again, I'm happy
to come back if you need me. I'm still
waiting on my flight. I could always rent a
car and drive back? Or wait until the
morning?

ARCHER

That won't be necessary.

Though I'm honestly tempted to say yes. To *beg* him to return.

Because if tonight was any indication, I'm apparently incapable of doing the bare minimum on my own. I can't even take out the trash, and I have no plans to try to do so again. Ever. I'm realizing my limits as to how "down-to-earth" I want to be.

Clearly, the day-to-day of running a building is not in my wheelhouse. I need someone with a different skill set than the one I possess.

The prospect of spending my Saturday trying to hire a building manager is gloomy. I'm used to working on weekends, but not *this* kind of work.

BELLAMY

I do think I might have an idea of someone
who could help you.

ARCHER

Do go on.

With a heavy sigh, I squeeze my eyes closed. Willa—the woman I can't seem to escape.

Even on the days I don't see her, she lingers in my thoughts. She fills my apartment through the scent of Bellamy's cookies. And anytime I use my closet, I can't help but think of finding her inside.

There's still a nagging discomfort when I think of that situation. That night, I saw Willa as some confused person, or perhaps someone suffering from a delusion. A very pretty compulsive liar.

But after our other interactions, none of those explanations seem to fit.

I may not understand how a sugar cookie business works, but the detail in her confections speaks to a meticulous person. Focused. Attentive and good with details. Not to mention the creativity and the artistry in her work.

Then there was tonight. She offered to help me with the trash, something she didn't need to do.

And it was Willa who managed to wrangle Archibald off me and back to Sara, ordering them upstairs until we'd taken care of the opossum.

It was Willa who propped open the door and shooed the opossum—which had taken refuge behind what used to be the building's front desk—outside.

All while I sat stunned on the floor.

Willa helped me up.

And it was Willa who ended up taking out the trash. Though her eyes practically incinerated me after I said what I said, she didn't tell me to do it myself.

None of these characterize a woman who would fabricate

a story to gain access to my closet, at least not for any reason I can think of.

And if that's not enough, she's had numerous interactions with Bellamy now—including texts, apparently—and his radar hasn't gone off once.

In fact, I'm sure if I were to tell him what happened that first night, he wouldn't believe it. I don't really believe it either.

Which leaves me confused.

But whatever would explain the appearance in my closet is irrelevant.

Willa is the last person who would want to work for me after what I said tonight.

Even for a paycheck.

ARCHER

Why Willa?

Bellamy appears to be typing a lengthy message, dots blinking as I wait impatiently. Then they disappear altogether, and I toss the phone onto the island in frustration. It skids across and stops when it hits a familiar box. One of Willa's.

And yet again, here she is.

I have a hard time believing Bellamy would have left his trash on the counter—he's the only person neater than I am—but when I peer through the box's clear plastic window, it's full of cookies.

There's a sticky note that reads *From Bellamy*.

He must have left them ... for me?

My phone lights up. Bellamy has sent an audio message. Still eyeing the box of cookies, I press play.

"Sorry. This is easier to say, and I didn't want to type it out. As to why Willa, she's lived at The Serendipity for a few years and grew up in town, so she'd be a good asset as far as connections.

107

She's also a hard worker and makes me laugh. I think you could use a little more of that. Also, I suspect her business is struggling. She hasn't said as much, but a few comments indicate orders are slow. I suspect that if you offered her a position, she would jump at the chance." He chuckles. "The only real downside is having to work with you. But I've managed for years, so it *is* possible."

Though Bellamy is teasing, it's true that I've been called hard to work with. I can be focused to the point of prioritizing tasks over people—especially people's feelings.

What I said to Willa tonight is a perfect example.

Emotions are, in general, tricky waters for me to navigate. Dark. Murky. Full of unseen hazards.

Often, it's more of me thinking about how I am *supposed* to feel than actually feeling anything at all. Probably because I don't *feel* a lot of anything. Kids at school called me Robot for years. Which didn't sting the way they wanted it to because they weren't wrong.

My father prioritized feelings last on his list, if they even made the list at all. And though I never wanted to emulate him, this passed down to me either by example or genetics. Or both.

If I'm not the best at my own emotions, I am lost when it comes to reading or reacting to other people's.

Bellamy's voice is interrupted by a loudspeaker in the background calling for a flight to board. He pauses, and I can hear him shuffling, probably picking up his bags.

"Okay, that's my flight! Finally. Let me know if you need anything. Think about asking Willa to work for you—at least temporarily. And please, stay away from the wildlife."

I snort at his last sentence, then I set my phone face down on the counter.

This has all been a disaster. Maybe I should have stayed in New York and dealt with—no.

Even thinking of it gives me a visceral reaction. I couldn't have stayed. Leaving was the best option, given everything.

Maybe I should have just taken a vacation rather than choosing this particular challenge. Worked remotely from a luxury beach resort until the dust settled and the headlines moved on to the next exciting thing.

In truth, I don't know how to relax. I've never been to a beach resort. Or even taken a proper vacation.

The cookies catch my eye again, and I peel off the sticky note. I've turned down every offer from Bellamy to try Willa's cookies.

But now, left alone with a whole box...

As though he somehow reads my thoughts from afar, my phone buzzes, and I turn it over to see another text from Bellamy.

BELLAMY

Last text. You get to have my last batch of cookies from Willa. Enjoy. You'll thank me later.

BELLAMY

And if you're thinking about not eating them, I could tell how much you wanted to try them that day in the kitchen. One cookie isn't going to kill your regimented eating.

BELLAMY

Maybe you could work cookies into the contract when you hire her. For me.

With a sigh, I type out a quick response, hoping to catch Bellamy before he gets on the plane. Or maybe hoping I don't.

I don't want to admit what I said to Willa a few minutes ago. But Bellamy needs to know.

ARCHER

The only problem with trying to hire Willa is that I might have told her that she needs to pay a rental fee for use of the kitchen.

BELLAMY

You didn't.

ARCHER

It's a valid requirement and a legitimate business expense for her.

BELLAMY

If you could see me now, my head is in my hands and I'm groaning. My seatmate probably thinks it's because I'm afraid of flying.

BELLAMY

Can you apologize? Tell her you changed your mind?

ARCHER

I'm not sorry. And I haven't changed my mind.

This isn't *entirely* true. But I want it to be true. And I need Bellamy to believe it to be true so he'll stop pushing this.

What *is* true is that the commercial kitchen should be rented. Her business model should have renting a kitchen built in as an expense.

Assuming Willa *has* a business model.

BELLAMY

Then I wish you good luck. Going into airplane mode now. I'll talk to you before the meetings next week. Enjoy the cookies. They'll probably be your last now.

My eyes drop to the box of cookies. When I lift the lid, the now-familiar scent of almond and vanilla fills my nose. Somehow, the smell of Willa's cookies makes my guilt more potent. I try to shove it down, but it won't quite dissipate.

Though the cookies Willa was decorating in the kitchen the other morning had elaborate detail, Bellamy requests simple iced cookies. But I bet he insists on paying whatever the more elaborate ones cost.

These are a light pink, the color of the tank top Willa wore tonight. Though I didn't have much time to dwell on it, given the circumstances, she was wearing pajamas again. Bare feet, short sleep shorts, and a tank top.

Only when she knocked me to the ground and we spent a few long moments lying pressed together was I aware of how much bare skin was on display.

If I'm being completely honest with myself, I think my reaction to Willa in that moment might have fueled my actions. Telling her she needed to rent the kitchen space was a defense mechanism—one I very much regret.

Cookies, I remind myself. *Right now, let's just think about cookies*.

Without allowing myself to overthink, I lift a cookie to my mouth and take a bite.

They're decadently sweet, but somehow not overpowering. The perfect balance between soft and firm, with the icing giving the slightest crunch before melting on my tongue.

One bite and I understand why Bellamy is addicted.

Two bites and I'm wondering if Willa's lips taste just as sweet.

The thought yanks me out of my cookie-induced stupor. I force myself to push away the box.

But I can't bring myself to throw it away.

It's only as I'm falling asleep—still trying to shut off my guilty conscience and banish thoughts of Willa—that I realize when I got back tonight, my apartment door was unlocked.

Chapter Nine
Willa

I'M STILL FUMING mad the next morning, my rage building over time instead of subsiding. It's less like the embers of a cooling fire and more like the very center of an inferno.

"After everything I did to help him," I grumble to Sophie, who hums in agreement as she mixes a bag of compost into the raised bed in front of her. We weeded that one first, and now it's nothing but rich, black dirt.

She took one look at my face this morning when I pounded on her door, said "I know exactly what you need," and then brought me up here to the roof to help prep for spring planting. Sophie insisted that helping her turn over the flower beds would be cathartic. And I guess it kind of is?

But mostly, it's revealing the depths of my rage as I yank up another weed by the root. Every time I toss another one in the compost bag, I imagine I'm throwing it in Archer's face.

Very cathartic indeed.

I pause, setting down my gloves to stretch. My forearms and my back are aching, muscles screaming in the best way possible. Tomorrow, my body might regret this. But today, I'm all in.

"You're doing great. I could use this kind of help on the regular." She brushes a dark curl back from her face with her forearm since her hands are filthy. I don't tell her there's already a streak of dirt across her cheek.

It suits her. Soil is to her what sugar and flour are to me—the hallmarks of our most natural states. She's beautiful up here, dirt under her nails and sun on her cheeks. I bet she'd say the same about me in the kitchen with flour in my hair.

Which reminds me of Archer's announcement last night that he'll be charging me to use The Serendipity's kitchen.

I have tiny moments when I'll forget, feeling good and strong as I do this manual labor, the chilly morning air combined with the warm sun invigorating me. Then I remember, and the anger blazes hot across my skin.

Though that could be the sun. We're having a surprisingly warm day, and it's almost enough to lift my mood.

"Tell me again about the possum." Sophie giggles. "It really came inside the building?"

I've told her twice already, each time remembering a few more details and embellishing others. It makes me happy to think of Archer shrieking as the possum clambered up his body, using his expensive suit like a ladder.

One thing I don't mention in any of these retellings is the intense moment when we found ourselves face to face on the floor. Or the attraction I still feel, even now, underneath my anger.

I wouldn't have wanted to admit feeling anything for him in the first place, and I certainly don't want to admit it *now*.

But then I think of how my breath caught when his eyes locked on mine. The heat of his body so close to mine. The angles of his face softening and his breath catching.

A pang of longing followed quickly by bitterness overwhelms me. I can't remember the last time I felt that kind of electric charge and chemistry with a man.

I yank out a weed with a little too much force and almost fall backwards.

Why *him?* Of all people, why did this happen with Archer Gaines?

He's the bane of my current existence, not a man sparking to life a fiery attraction that has been dormant since Trey.

The thought sends me back into a rage spiral as I recount the possum story for Sophie again, this time emphasizing how ridiculous Archer sounded, with his high-pitched screams.

"I managed to drive it out the front door using a stool I found behind the front desk."

"Like a lion tamer," Sophie says, a note of pride in her voice. "Willa the possum tamer."

I do a fancy bow. "At your service. And right after *that*," I finish, a sharp bitter edge creeping into my voice, "is when Archer told me he'll be charging me a monthly fee for the use of the kitchen."

Effectively putting not just one but *all* the nails in the coffin of Serendipitous Sweets. Archer didn't say how much he'll charge, but it doesn't matter. Even with Bellamy's recurring weekly orders, any extra monthly expenses will push me too far into the red, beyond my current precarious situation and into one that's hopeless.

Sophie's quiet for a moment, then says, "Do you think maybe he likes you?"

I think of the moment when his gaze fell to my lips. Of the way he jumped to help me in the kitchen and let me tie a frilly pink apron around his waist. Of how he sometimes calls me Willa the Person.

Then I tie a cinderblock to those thoughts and toss them into a mental Mariana Trench.

"This isn't third grade when a guy pulls your pigtails because he really has a crush on you. We're adults. And he's just a jerk."

Even as I say it, I don't really know if I believe it. There is something more to Archer. I've seen glimpses of it, and of course, there's what Bellamy said.

But then again, Archer is ruining my business, so I don't need to wonder if there's more to the man. Or care. On the surface, he's a jerk, so we'll stick with that.

"I don't know," Sophie says. "Do we ever mature beyond that? Or do we all just find different, more adult ways to do the same things?"

The question makes me irrationally angry. "Archer does *not* like me. If he did, he wouldn't be putting me out of business."

All traces of humor leave Sophie's face. "I'm sorry, Willa. Truly."

"It's fine. I mean, no—it's not. But I'm failing at all the business stuff anyway. He's just expediting the process."

I like that Sophie is the kind of friend who doesn't try to make me feel better with lies or half-truths.

"It sucks. Men suck."

"Hear, hear."

"It probably means a similar fate for me soon," she says glumly. "If he's making you pay to use the kitchen, he's not going to fund this garden."

When she first moved into the Serendipity, Sophie discovered the garden, overgrown and unkempt. Mostly filled with weeds and a few leftover shrubs and things someone else had planted...and neglected. Everything else, she began to overhaul. First, with her own money, saved when she could, and then with a monthly stipend Galentine added once she saw what Sophie had done.

Galentine had been delighted to see the garden restored to its former glory. And Sophie was more than happy to take on an unofficial role as rooftop gardener since, to my surprise, the job of landscape architect takes place mostly behind a desk. There are raised beds with perennials and flowering bushes. Concrete planters Sophie will fill with annuals in the coming weeks. Trellises and arches stretch overhead with creeping vines. Later in the spring, wisteria will bloom, its lilac flowers hanging like clusters of grapes.

I wince, feeling selfish because I've only been thinking about my situation. The garden isn't something she'll be able to keep up without the stipend. Her financial situation isn't dire like mine, but with some student loans, she's not rolling around in extra money. Definitely not the kind it would take to maintain a garden of this size.

She's right about Archer, of course. His M.O. seems to be business first, people last. If at all.

I wish I could tell her she won't need to worry about Archer ruining what she's created here. But I have zero reassurances. I mean, if he could announce he's going to charge me rent after I helped him with the trash and the possum— and after the moment we shared, which I'm trying to forget we shared—I can't see him continuing to fund Sophie's stipend.

"This is a funny looking weed." I reach for a vine with wide, flat leaves growing up the trunk of a Japanese maple.

Sophie grabs my arm before I can yank it out of the ground. "Leave that one."

"What *is* it?"

"I'm not sure, actually. I haven't been able to identify it. The mystery is kind of giving me life right now."

"You're a weirdo, Soph."

She gives me a light shove. "Takes one to know one."

As we move to the next bed, I say, "Trey's moving home."

Sophie, made of the stuff of epic best friends, gasps. As she should.

"And he's engaged."

Her gasp morphs into a throttled growl of outrage that

makes me smile, despite the words I've said. It's the first time I've had to say them. The first time since dinner with my parents I've thought about them. About *him*. Trey, my newly-engaged-to-someone-else ex, moving back to Serendipity Springs.

It's ... not so bad. I'm not sure if I'm just strangely numb, if I've expended all my emotional energy on the undeserving Archer Gaines, or if I really am *that* over Trey, but it feels nice to feel nothing.

"No," Sophie hisses.

"Yes."

"Tell me everything."

Sophie loves to gather and store information like it's ammunition. For what battle, I'm not sure. But when it comes, I want her on my side.

"My mom didn't tell me much. I guess they met while he was in France, and now they've moved back here."

"A French girl?" Sophie says with a sneer, likely not because of the French but just because it's Trey we're talking about.

"No idea. Maybe she's from Kentucky and he met her on a dating app."

"Why Kentucky?"

"Why not Kentucky?" I shrug and pull a weed with a huge root system. The sound of it being ripped from the dirt is *so* satisfying.

Sophie's button nose, lightly freckled probably from mornings just like this, wrinkles. "Why does Kentucky feel like one of those states that exists but isn't a place anyone's actually from?"

"I don't know, but you're right. Except Trey's hypothetical fiancée, I guess."

"I wonder if she owns horses or has a thick Southern

accent. Maybe she's a debutante who likes to wear fascinators."

"Those all seem like perfect Kentucky clichés. So, probably yes. All of those. Except ... what's a fascinator?"

"Those little hats everyone wears in England. I'm not sure if that's what people wear to the Kentucky Derby. I've never watched it."

"Me neither. It's a lot of anticipation for something that takes two minutes."

Sophie uses what looks like a miniature rake to level the dirt in the bed we just cleared out, and I slump onto a bench, taking a long swig of water.

"So, you're feeling okay about the Trey thing? Do we need to talk it out? Hug it out? Maybe go out for ice cream and eat our feelings? You've had a lot of blows in one week."

There's no heartbreak where Trey is concerned, now that I've had a few days to settle in with the knowledge. Just an uncomfortable, sad, and still somewhat painful feeling. Like a lingering bruise fading from angry purple to a sickly yellow. It's still visible and hurts if you press down hard, but otherwise, it's easy to forget.

Sophie never met Trey. In fact, she and I became friends the first year PT—Post Trey—when it was less of a bruise and more of an open wound I had to tend, carefully wrapping it up every morning in thick layers of self-talk as gauze.

Once I told her the whole story, she agreed that Trey was never the right guy for me.

I think in some ways, I mourned the loss of time and effort, the loss of the idea that I'd found my great love as much as I mourned the relationship itself. The idea of being a young mom, of having my life mapped out.

All gone in an instant—*poof!*

"I'm feeling okay. Not sad, just awkward. I don't want him

thinking I'm still here and single, like our breakup left me in pieces while he's clearly moved on."

An honest answer. I haven't had time yet to imagine my life here with the possibility I could run into my ex and his new fiancée—and, I guess, down the road, his *wife*—at the grocery store. Or even the awareness every time I see Mom that she knows all about Trey's life and how he's doing from *his* mom. The idea exhausts me.

"I mean, I'm over him."

"Of course," Sophie says. "If you weren't, I'd toss you in the compost pile."

I laugh at this, leaning forward until my elbows sink a little into the soft soil I'm turning. The scent of fresh earth, loamy and rich, is a comfort. I much prefer the smell of sugar and vanilla, but I can see the appeal here. I feel better about everything, even if my circumstances have not actually changed. Talking to Sophie and doing something with my hands gives me a fully satisfied feeling.

A *mostly* satisfied feeling.

"But it's a reminder, you know? He's a reminder. Of what I wish I had. What I could have had, I guess. If I were ... different."

Not for the first time, I think about the baby shower cookies for Bronson and the funk they put me in.

Sophie puts down her rake and stomps over to me. Snatching my water bottle, she takes my hands in hers. The dirt on both our palms creates the tiniest friction as she squeezes.

"You are not the reason that relationship didn't work," she says fiercely, her brown eyes blazing. "Do you understand?"

"Please don't make me repeat after you," I say weakly.

She smiles, but it's a smile with an edge. "I won't unless I feel like you need it. But I need you to know that the reason things didn't work with Trey was that he was a jerk. He revealed his character when he put you in an impossible situation. His proposal wasn't a proposal. It was a test. And if someone really loves you, they don't *test* you."

I nod because I agree. I know all this. I've had to remind myself of it so many times. My therapist says the same thing.

I've talked through it with her for the last year, once I finally forced myself to go. And though I still am not fixed—I know that's the wrong word, but sometimes it feels like the best one—it's helped me see things more clearly.

Trey's proposal was dangling the biggest carrot just out of reach of a scared, hungry rabbit. He thought he would be motivation enough to force me past my "issue," as he liked to call it.

My "issue" is that I have severe anxiety attacks when I try to leave Serendipity Springs.

I'd heard of agoraphobia, but I thought of it as being unable to leave home. Like Sigourney Weaver in *Copycat*, another 90s movie, like *The Fugitive*, that my dad loves.

Or *loved*. It hits a little too close to home now, and he hasn't watched it since *before*.

My sophomore year of college, I started having trouble sleeping whenever it was almost time to go back to school. I would spend the ride back to Boston with Trey battling car sickness and irrational worries. Sometimes the feelings eased up once I settled and started classes, but I was never fully okay until I went home to Serendipity Springs.

My junior year, I lost ten pounds I didn't need to lose, and my grades started slipping. I couldn't pinpoint what caused the sudden shift or why leaving home was now an issue.

All this anxiety culminated in a full-blown panic attack my senior year when I tried to drive back to school with Trey after Christmas. My parents, convinced it must be something physical like cancer or a thyroid problem, took me to the hospital and insisted on running every test known to man. We met our deductible that year in January.

Conclusion: a diagnosis of agoraphobia. I finished up my final classes completely online from home, and the university mailed my diploma to Serendipity Springs.

Turns out, agoraphobia doesn't have to be limited to not leaving your house. At its root, it's an anxiety disorder that often manifests when it comes to being in public spaces or crowded spaces—or, apparently, even leaving a larger, broader area like your hometown.

It doesn't make sense to me. Not even after therapy sessions—one of my least favorite things—and doing internet research. I even joined an anonymous online forum to connect with other people who deal with varying presentations of agoraphobia.

Some don't leave their homes, some can't go to grocery stores, malls, or other crowded spaces. A few are unable to ride in vehicles.

A handful are like me: unable to leave the city or town where they currently reside. But it's not common.

Yay, I'm special!

I have no idea why this started. There wasn't an event or trigger I've been able to pinpoint. My therapist says there isn't always a singular moment because anxiety doesn't always follow rules or drive in a straight line.

If my diagnosis was tough for me to wrap my head around, it was impossible for Trey. I still remember the concern on his face when I asked him to pull the car over on the highway as we left Serendipity Springs. My heart was racing, my vision blurry, and I couldn't get enough air. His concern and worry quickly turned to confusion when, through halting breaths, I begged him to drive me back home.

And when we were unpacking my things from Trey's car, his confusion took on a tiny undercurrent of anger.

I get it. Really, I do. This sounds made up. I'd never heard of something like this until it happened to me. I could understand why it was difficult for Trey to understand why we went from being attached at the hip to suddenly being in a long-distance relationship our senior year.

We'd never had real tension before that. He wanted to understand. He tried. He was kind.

But I could always sense his frustration rippling underneath the surface. I'm not sure he ever fully believed me.

Which is why, when he got the job offer for Paris right after graduation, he took it without consulting me, then asked me to marry him and come with him. He really thought that putting me in an impossible position would somehow be the thing I needed to break through my anxiety.

Joke's on you, pal. Anxiety disorders don't respond well to pressure.

Now, with Sophie's kind gaze and her warm hands squeezing mine, I feel what I stopped feeling with Trey. Safe. He stopped being a safe haven, someone I could trust.

There was no way I could marry him and go to Paris. No way I would *want to* when he'd put me in that position. All it did was prove he never really understood. Not if he thought I could just positive-think myself out of the crippling anxiety I faced any time I tried to leave Serendipity Springs.

Trey isn't a horrible person. I have to believe he thought he was helping. He thought this would set me free, giving me something I wanted so much that I'd be able to do something I hadn't done in almost a year—to be physically, mentally, and emotionally able to leave Serendipity Springs.

"I'm sorry you're going through so many things at once," Sophie says, drawing me back to this rooftop moment.

A breeze lifts my hair, stirring it on my shoulders, and I smile. "I'll be okay. I will."

"Duh. You're Willa freaking Smith, a single tiny vowel away from being Will Smith. You can do *anything*."

"Honestly, I feel okay about it. It's going to be awkward when I see him again."

"You think you will?"

"Serendipity Springs is too small for us not to run into each other. Or the stupid town magic."

"Don't badmouth the town magic. If anything, it's good magic. Or luck. Or whatever. Speaking of, any more closet teleportation?"

I don't know why I didn't tell Sophie it happened again. She's my best friend. And she didn't freak out or think I was nuts the first time.

But for some reason, last night when I appeared at her door post possum incident to grab my spare key, I just said I got locked out, not that I transported again.

I feel bad about lying, but I also don't want to talk about it. Preferably, I don't want to acknowledge the situation. Maybe if I pretend it never happened, it won't happen again.

Which feels a little like being a kid and thinking that if your head is under the covers, the monster under the bed can't eat you.

"No more transporting. And I'd like to keep it that way, so let's never speak of it again. Doesn't magic need people to believe in it to work?"

"You're thinking of Tinkerbell. She told Peter Pan if people stopped believing in fairies, they'd all cease to exist."

I lift my water in a silent toast. "Let's do that. We don't believe in or speak of the magic—in my closet or otherwise— and then it doesn't exist."

Or I can forget that I'm lying to my bestie about it.

"I kind of like the idea of magic," Sophie says. "Happy magic, like Galentine always talked about. She said the building helped her find love."

"And how many times did Galentine get married?"

"Four? Seven? I don't remember. That just means the magic did a *really* good job."

"Or it's fickle and unreliable."

"Maybe you transporting into Archer's closet is the building's version of a giving you a meet cute?"

I groan. But I'm also blushing because I'm suddenly thinking about that moment again in the hallway, tucked into Archer's warm chest.

"Can we be done with the magic talk? I'm hungry enough to eat a whole pizza and don't want you spoiling my appetite."

"Fine. Also, pizza will be my treat as a way to thank you for rage-helping with the garden."

I cheer.

"Once we finish this last section," she adds.

I groan.

"You're a cruel, cruel garden taskmaster. But I guess I'll keep you as a friend."

Even if I'm not being a fully honest one to you right now.

Chapter Ten
Willa

DESPITE THE TWO times I've now experienced unwanted closet transportation, I still don't *truly* believe in magic. Or luck—good *or* bad. Not fates or fated mates (though I love both in novels) or even Murphy's Law.

And yet.

And yet.

And yet somehow, despite wanting to avoid Archer like a resurgence of the Bubonic plague, he is everywhere I am over the next few days.

Yes, I know we live in the same building. But there are residents of The Serendipity I've never laid eyes on. And if Sophie and I didn't make plans, literal weeks could go by without seeing each other.

Despite this, Archer is like a whole game of whack-a-mole, and I'm without a little mallet to knock him back into his mole holes.

I see him on the front stairs twice, so I switch to the back stairwell.

Apparently, he has the same idea. Or he just likes stairs. Because he's there too.

After the third time we pass each other in the back, I resign myself to using the elevator.

Only to find Archer there too.

Thankfully, it was a short ride filled with tense silence filling the space like a toxic fog.

Archer is running—shirtless again, ugh—when I'm leaving the building.

He's in the library on the first floor when I stop in to look for a book.

Surveying the pool with those slate gray eyes when I venture into the courtyard on a particularly sunny afternoon.

Oh, and he appears in my apartment by way of a letter taped to my door—a letter announcing a twenty-five percent increase in rent as well as extra fees for the storage units downstairs and the laundry facility.

Because Archer Gaines is the *worst*.

So why is it that right now, when I find Archer on the first floor getting a very loud earful from Frank, I actually feel bad for the man?

Frank rages, echoed by the macaw perched on his shoulder, while Archer listens impassively.

"Where do you get the nerve?" Frank says, shaking the letter from Archer at him.

"The nerve!" the macaw repeats.

Oh—did I forget to mention that the aforementioned letter also announced a strict no pets policy going into effect within ninety days?

Yeah. *All* pets, including birds who talk.

Archer doesn't defend himself—or his indefensible actions—and shows no visible reaction, like he's impervious to other people's opinions being hurled at him in a public space, which is a thing of *my* nightmares.

I agree with Frank (and the bird), but I find myself wanting to step in. To tell Frank to calm down and not to yell (or have his bird yell) in the middle of the lobby. I'm not sure what else I could really say, considering that Archer is ruining our building. There aren't really words to defend him.

But I have a sneaking suspicion that Archer Gaines is like an iceberg. He might appear icy and cold on the surface, but there's a whole lot more underneath.

Okay, so the hidden stuff underneath would *also* be icy and cold if Archer were an iceberg. Maybe I should have picked another analogy.

The point is, I feel bad for him even if I shouldn't. I think this has to bother him more than he lets on. And I want to help even if I am totally not on his side.

Sophie would tell me this is my toxic trait—being *too* helpful—rearing its head. She refers to it as wounded puppy syndrome. In this analogy, I'm not the puppy, but the person who stops for every hurt puppy they see. To which I always argue, who *wouldn't* stop to help a wounded puppy?

Also, Sophie never minds this trait when I'm helping *her*.

I don't stop for Archer.

I don't help.

I continue to the mailboxes by the front staircase, trying not to eavesdrop as Frank, who's always been mild-mannered, and his bird, who is more of a loudmouth, rip into Archer.

Not my circus and Archer is not my fancy-suit-wearing monkey, I tell myself.

Heck, the rent hike announcement had Sophie doing a glum midnight visit to my apartment, where she skipped the cookies and went straight to eating icing directly with a spoon as we googled two-bedroom apartments nearby.

So I get it.

"Do you still think Archer is pulling my pigtails because he has a crush?" I asked her.

She only glared. "My theory was way off base. He's a very bad, no good, horrible man. I think I hate him."

Though we did a little toast to our mutual dislike of Archer Gaines, I find myself wincing now as someone else joins Frank. Someone with a deeper voice and a much more colorful vocabulary describing what kind of man he thinks Archer is.

Well, that's certainly a new combination of words I never thought I'd hear and never want to hear again.

Still silence from Archer, and my heart feels like it's constricting inside my chest.

This is all Bellamy's fault. He's the one who keeps texting me. They started innocently enough, talking about cookies. The man is slightly obsessed, and I'm here for it. But then his texts shift to ask about Archer.

How is he?

Have you seen him?

I'm not sure he has anyone to talk to, so if you see him, could you check in on him? He'd hate it if he knew I said this.

I think he's concerned about how Archer's doing on his own.

Then, this very morning, Bellamy called to place an order for cookies this weekend.

"I guess this means you'll be coming back soon?" I asked.

"I wish it were sooner. I'm putting out fires, and new ones keep cropping up."

"So, is this a delayed order, then? Because I still don't ship."

"This one is for Archer, but I need you to say they're for me."

My skin prickled uncomfortably, both at the idea of Archer eating my cookies and at having to talk to him again. "I'd ... rather not lie?"

I expected Bellamy to demand to know why or to argue with me, but instead, he sighed. "Given what he's been doing, I get it."

"Okay, good."

"But…"

"I don't want a *but*, Bellamy."

He chuckled. "I'm going to give you one anyway. Archer could use a little kindness."

"He certainly hasn't shown me—or any of the other residents—any kindness. If you're trying to convince me that he's got a hard outside with an ooey-gooey center, I don't believe you."

"I wouldn't describe any parts of him as ooey-gooey. But I would say there's more to him than what he shows. He's had a rough go of it."

"He's a billionaire. How rough, exactly, could his life be?"

Even as the words came out of my mouth, I regretted them. I know—though not from experience—that having money can only shield you from so much. It doesn't equal happiness or freedom from terrible things.

I'm grateful Bellamy didn't call me on my harsh statement or my assumptions. "He's worth a chance. I promise you."

"We're not talking chances. We're just talking cookies." And I don't want to even give him those.

I hated how disappointed Bellamy sounded when he said, "I understand. But I'd ask that you still do this. For me."

"For you … but it's really for him?" I asked.

"Smart girl."

"Why? Give me a reason, Bellamy."

He was quiet for so long, I had to check to make sure the call hadn't dropped. "His story isn't mine to tell. Just think about it."

Ugh. Why did Bellamy have to humanize him? Archer fit perfectly into the evil robot villain box in my head. An evil robot villain with fantastic abs, that is.

I keep seeing flashes of humanity. Like, for example, just

now, when pretending not to watch Frank and the bird both squawk at Archer, I noticed something.

That little tin of mints Archer is always pulling out of his pocket is in his hand. And as I walked by, he was popping them into his mouth one after another like a chain smoker. Or, I guess, a chain mint-chewer.

Maybe it's nothing. Maybe Bellamy's words are getting to me. But I have a sneaking suspicion Archer is not okay. That he is barely managing his anxiety with an iron fist and a thin thread.

It's something I recognize a little too well.

The yelling finally stops, and Archer rounds the corner to the mailboxes, looking remarkably unscathed from his human and avian tongue-lashing. But his mints are still in hand. Our eyes meet for the briefest second before we both pretend they didn't.

I retrieve my mail—mostly bills and junk—slowly, watching Archer struggle with the combination. Navigating the little mailbox dials is a rite of passage at The Serendipity. They're original to the building, which means they're old and finicky. It usually takes the help of a longtime resident to break in newbies.

I could offer to help. Despite everything Archer has done, I *want* to.

I've just opened my mouth to do so when Roberta catches my eye from her mailbox. Roberta lives on the first floor, and I only know her because she's always eager to make passing conversation.

And by conversation, I mean gossip.

Today, though, she just gives me a silent shake of the head, as if to say, *Don't you dare offer to help the man ruining all of our lives.*

I close my mouth, but I don't feel good about it. Especially not when Roberta and I both walk away, leaving Archer still fiddling with the dial, another mint crunching between his teeth.

Chapter Eleven
Willa

BECAUSE I'M LIVING out the adage of *a watched pot never boils* in the form of an *unwanted man always appears*, I run into Trey at the grocery store after I leave Archer at the mailboxes.

My ex is at the other end of the cereal aisle, though it takes a good ten seconds of staring at the back of his head for me to recognize him. It's the hair. Trey always kept his light brown locks neatly trimmed while we were dating. He had a standing once-monthly hair appointment all through college, while I've always been more of a *take scissors to my hair when the mood hits* kind of person.

Which is why mine is currently just brushing my shoulders. I chopped seven inches off last month when two people canceled their cookie orders in the same week. I'm still getting used to the length, but I think it suits me.

Trey's hair is pulled back in a baby ponytail that's clearly a man bun in the making. I think maybe I'm wrong—because since when was Trey into man buns?—until I see his unmistakable profile as he grabs a box of cereal. An ultra healthy organic brand, I can't help but notice.

Is this what happens when you spend a few years in France

—you trade short hair for a wannabe man bun and a love of Cap'n Crunch for organic foods that promote healthy digestion and have all the taste of a flattened cardboard box?

I immediately go into stealth mode, ducking down behind the grocery cart and pulling the closest box of cereal in front of my face. *Please don't let him turn around*, I plead silently with the universe. I'm not sure why since it clearly hates me. Thankfully, Trey turns left toward the crackers and snack aisle, totally unaware of me surreptitiously peeking at him.

As soon as he's gone, I backtrack, zipping back down the aisle the way I came and turning toward the seafood area. One thing France can't have changed is Trey's shellfish allergy. I'll just hang out and talk to the lobsters in the tank while I wait a reasonable amount of time for Trey to vacate the premises.

"Hey, guys," I tell the lobsters as I duck down to their level. "Don't worry. I'm not going to buy and boil you. I just need to hide out for a bit."

They wave their rubber-banded claws in either their best version of a thumbs-up or a slow-mo plea for their freedom.

The only thing worse than running into Trey at all would be running into him *here*. Grocery shopping is one of my all-time favorite activities. It's also my go-to when I'm stressed, even now, when money is a huge stress point. Adding things to my cart can lift my lowest mood.

And this particular Spring Foods location is my personal happy place. Even though there are other stores closer to my parents' house, I started shopping here in college, long before I lived at The Serendipity. Since it's downtown, it's a little more of a neighborhood store. There's just a vibe.

Trey knows this. More than once, he accompanied me to this exact store when we were home on break. I have a whole host of memories with him here, like making out in the greeting card aisle. And the frozen foods section. And—well, never mind. Probably more places than I want to think about now.

The first few times I came here after the breakup were tough, but I finally managed to exorcise the memories of Trey so I didn't have to give up my favorite store.

It's totally unfair that he's here now. Moving back to town *and* shopping in my store? No way.

He and I barely talked after I rejected his proposal, but I assumed I got custody of this store in the split. He can have every other Spring Foods and all the Hannafords. Even a Walmart grocery store if he wants to go that route.

Wherever Trey wants to shop, that's fine. But this is *my* Spring Foods, and he knows it.

Or he *should*. Even after four years apart, Trey should remember that this is *my* signature store and choose another out of respect. But maybe he's moved on to the point that he doesn't remember. Or care.

I honestly don't know which is worse: him not remembering, or him remembering and not caring.

It's a moot point when what I'm *really* worried about right now is Trey spotting me. Because I am in no way mentally or emotionally or vocabulary-ally prepared to speak to him right now. I will absolutely end up having an *I carried a watermelon* word vomit moment if he tries to talk to me.

I thought I had time before running into him. Like, maybe a few months. Or a year. Plenty of time to go over potential scenarios in my head and come up with wonderful and witty things to say. The kinds of things that don't make me sound like a total loser who's still living in the same town, still single, and about to bankrupt my small business, while he's back from France with a new fiancée.

And an attempt at a man bun, I remind myself, which gives me some small semblance of satisfaction. I mean, good for guys who can pull off a man bun. Some do exist. Usually the lumberjack type, pairing it with a full beard, soulful eyes, and flannel.

But that's a very short list, and I can guarantee Trey will never be on it. I'm not being petty. Just honest. He's got more of a soft, happy face without the kind of bone structure that can offset a man bun.

"Just think of the bullet I dodged," I tell the lobsters. But they've lost interest in my drama and have slowly drifted toward the other end of the tank.

Where, unfortunately for me and my verbal processing to captive crustaceans, an actual customer now stands. Since I'm still crouching, the first thing I see through the tank is a dark suit. Who wears a suit grocery shopping?

With almost as much cold dread as I felt seeing Trey, my brain immediately thinks of one person who would *absolutely* wear a suit to the grocery store. He'd probably also wear it to get a new driver's license or to a sporting event, were he to ever attend such a thing.

Archer Gaines. Because of course he would also be shopping at my favorite store right now. It's how my life works.

But I'm not positive it's him until Archer ducks down, his face appearing on the other side of the tank. Our gazes lock with lobsters between us. His irritated expression is comically distorted through the water, making his normally sharp jaw look wider and rounder, giving Mr. Potato Head vibes. It also creates the illusion of Eugene Levy eyebrows.

I stand up. Across from me, Archer straightens to his full height, frowning deeply.

"You're ubiquitous," I tell him, shaking my head.

His frown deepens. "I'm what?"

"It means everywhere at once."

I don't know why, but I remember almost all my high school vocabulary words, and *ubiquitous* was one. Perfect for Archer since I can't escape him. Even when I really, really want to. Like right now, when I'm already trying to avoid someone else I really don't want to see.

Get in line, buddy.

Though, in this case, I'm surprised to feel like Archer is the lesser of two evils. I can't even muster up anger when I think about him ruining my business and essentially kicking me out of my apartment.

"What brings you to Spring Foods on this fine day?" I ask. "Spring Foods doesn't really seem like your scene."

I glance pointedly at the giant chicken mural above our heads. Since we're in the seafood section, it's a chicken with a mermaid tail, which I guess makes it a merchicken?

When I was in high school, Spring Foods decided to start a loyalty program for customers. And whatever genius was in charge of this campaign named the loyalty members Spring Chickens. Serendipity Springs heartily embraced this, which led to the company really going all in on the Spring Chickens thing. There are chickens everywhere. Bumper stickers that say *I'm a Spring Chicken!* And a whole line of t-shirts. The first official day of spring every year, the stores all have someone dress up like a chicken and take pictures with kids, kind of like Santa or the Easter Bunny.

Needless to say, Archer Gaines is no Spring Chicken.

Archer's gaze follows mine to the merchicken, and his grumpy expression intensifies. "Grocery stores in general aren't *my scene*," he mutters. "But I couldn't get delivery to work."

"What do you mean you couldn't get it to work?" I know for a fact that several different stores will deliver groceries to The Serendipity. If I have to worry about running into both Trey *and* Archer here, I might be forced to switch to delivery myself.

"It just ... wouldn't work." Archer glares down at the phone in his hand, and I don't miss the way his grip tightens around it. "Like everything else right now," he mutters. "*Nothing* works."

Bellamy's words choose this moment to come back to me. *He deserves a chance.*

The stubborn part of me still doesn't want to give him one. But I'm softening as I watch the tension radiating off him.

Archer strikes me as intensely private and closed off. But I can't miss the obvious signs of stress. The mints are nowhere to be seen, but it's in the flush of his cheeks and the white-knuckled grip on his phone. There's almost a visible shimmer of tension radiating off his body, like heat on a summer blacktop.

This is more than stress. It's the tight coil of anxiety I wish I weren't intimately familiar with.

I don't want to feel sympathy or empathy or any other -*pathy* toward Archer. And yet the man seems to be constantly drawing my unwanted feelings to the surface.

Like the attraction I felt tying on his apron or when we were lying on the floor during the possum incident. That was some *intense* chemistry—until I remembered who I was chemistry-ing with. Definitely didn't want to feel that.

Or any echo of it now, staring at Archer across a lobster tank and underneath a merchicken mural.

I don't want to be attracted to Archer, and I *also* don't want to have compassion for him.

"Were you talking to the lobsters?" he asks.

"I, um … no? Okay, fine. Yes." I glance back into the tank, where the lobsters are now ignoring us. "A little. They're good listeners."

"Do you always talk to your dinner before eating it?" he asks.

I blink at him. His stern, handsome face only shows the slightest hint of amusement in the tiniest curl on one side of his lips. "Another joke from you. I think you met your quota for the month. Anyway, I don't eat lobster. Or anything I have to look in the eyes."

"You're a vegetarian?"

"Not technically. Not fully. Just"—I give the lobsters another look—"if I have to face my food."

Which is partly because watching so many cute cow videos on Instagram makes it hard to eat hamburgers, but also because I'm on a tight budget.

"Are *you* buying lobsters?" I ask, hoping the answer is no. I'm getting a little attached. These are my *emotional support when you run into your ex and also your sworn enemy you're also attracted to* lobsters.

"I don't even like seafood," Archer says. "But I can't find anything in this store. I'm just walking in circles."

One glance at his cart shows me it is completely empty, save a lonely head of cabbage. "You found the cabbage. That's a start."

"That's not lettuce?"

I'm starting to wonder if Archer has ever set foot in a grocery store before today. "No, it's not lettuce."

He stares at the cabbage like it's a complicated math formula. "But I can still eat it in a salad."

"Not unless you're making a slaw. Do you want some help?"

Archer's frown becomes frownier. "I can figure it out."

"I'm sure you can," I say, though the cabbage he thought was lettuce tells a different story. "But I'm here and—"

"Willa?"

Turns out, not even lobsters can shield me from Trey. Because here he is, standing at the end of the lobster tank, placing me in the most awkward non-love triangle possible between my ex and a man I barely know but whose closet I've magically transported to twice.

I would give my right arm to step into my closet right now and be magically transported to anywhere but here.

On the plus side, there is no rush of strong, painful feelings as I square my shoulders and face my ex for the first time in four years. There's no longing for what we had, no sense of regret. Not even nostalgia, if I'm being honest. Overall, I feel a surprising but pleasing lack of deep feelings as I come face-to-face with my ex-almost-fiancé.

But the moment *is* painfully and potently awkward. It practically shimmers in the air as Trey and I size each other up.

With his hair pulled back, Trey's face looks rounder. Or maybe that's just the result of a lot of French food? I remember once feeling like I could get lost in his eyes, which now look to me like a very forgettable basic brown. I'm having a hard time remembering why I fell for him—and especially why I stayed with him for so long.

I know we had good times, but even as I try to locate a bright, happy memory, they all seem a little *meh*.

"Hey, Trey." I barely restrain myself from adding *long time no see*, but unfortunately *do* blurt out, "Ha—that rhymes."

I briefly consider climbing into the lobster tank, but instead I plaster a smile on my face that feels half deranged while trying to decide what to do with my arms.

Why is it that anytime I'm in an uncomfortable situation, my arms suddenly become the only thing I'm aware of? I cross them over my chest, which looks too defensive and confrontational, but when I drop them, it feels like they're dead weight attached to my body. Like Frankenstein arms, sewn on from some other person.

Ew. Apparently, it's not just my arms that get weird but my brain.

Trey offers me a smile that's a little too genuine, then says, "I can see you haven't changed."

Though I don't think he means this to be offensive, I'm offended all the same. But I choose to be the better person and hold my tongue rather than make a snarky comment about his attempt at a man bun.

"So, I hear you're back in town," I say.

"I am." He pauses, his expression shifting. "Did you also hear that I'm engaged?"

Again, there's nothing painful about hearing his words, but the awkward-o-meter is now reaching maximum levels. I mean, did he *have* to bring it up? He's basically creating a new, horrible core memory in my favorite grocery store.

"Congrats," I say, hating that the word sounds insincere.

The last thing I want is for Trey to think I'm not over him. I don't want him to imagine me pining over him for the last four years. Which would be acutely embarrassing. And untrue.

"That's really great. Is she French?"

He laughs, and I'm not sure why this is a funny question. Then he stops abruptly, staring in a way that makes me even more uncomfortable.

It's shock mixed with a little bit of what looks like guilt.

"I thought your mom would have told you," Trey says.

"Told me what?"

But before he can drop the anvil of whatever horrible truth my mother failed in her maternal duty to tell me, a throat clears.

I turn, and Archer has left his cart and is now standing at my elbow. Though I still think it's ridiculous he's wearing a suit in a grocery store, he does wear it well. And I mean *well*.

Archer clears his throat again, his gaze never leaving mine. His face is always hard to read—a problem when your jaw seems chiseled from stone and permanently set in a frown— but I try anyway. And fail. Whatever he's trying to silently convey, I'm not getting the message.

Wait, is he ... trying to rescue me from this clearly uncomfortable situation?

Nothing in my interactions with Archer has given me the impression he likes to *help* people. Me, in particular.

"How long will this take?" he demands.

I suspect Archer didn't intend for this question to come out so harshly, in a cracked whip of words. But the man is a snapping turtle in a suit.

I find myself grinning. Why is his grouchiness suddenly so amusing to me?

Oh, right—because he's wedging it right between my ex and me like a solid wall of protective grump.

There's a good chance Archer isn't trying to save me at all but is actually in a hurry to get done shopping and has decided he does want my help. That seems more likely given our interactions, but either way, I'll take it.

Now, Trey is the one clearing his throat, bringing me back to myself.

"Right. Archer, this is Trey Fletcher. Trey, Archer Gaines."

I don't offer up any titles or explanations. At this point, they don't seem necessary and could only make things more awkward.

"There you are! I thought I lost you." Another voice, almost—no, *more*—unwelcome than Trey's cuts in.

The woman walking toward us is all brown doe eyes and a bubblegum smile—until she sees me. Then the smile slips right off her face as her gaze shifts to Trey. I can't miss the ring on her finger. The thing could be used to direct planes to the right runway.

"Hey, Mel," I say. "It's been a while."

Long enough for you to get engaged to my ex.

Mel and I are old friends in the sense of old news. As in, our friendship is totally a thing of the past.

And I'm glad because if it hadn't been, it would be now.

I'm not one of those women who feels like they can keep some kind of claim on an ex. I feel no ownership over Trey. Not after four years.

I wish him happiness. Long life. Love, I guess.

But love with a woman who had been one of my closest friends for *years*—a woman who met Trey through *me* when we were dating?

She places her hand over Trey's on the cart handle, like they're about to walk through the store, pushing it together as a show of couple unity. It makes me want to barf.

It just feels so intentionally dramatic. Like, let's not just stab you in the back, but do it with ten pitchforks, a couple of swords, and then run you over with a steamroller for good measure. Especially considering the way Mel disappeared at a particularly critical time for me—just after I said no to Trey's proposal and he left for France.

Only now I'm wondering if *this* is the reason why my friendship with Mel ended. Did she ghost me because she was angling to be my replacement with Trey?

Not cool, Mel. Or Trey. Not cool either *of you.*

Archer moves slightly, leaning in so his arm rests against mine. It's an oddly comforting gesture coming from him. I glance up, and his gray-blue eyes lock on mine.

"Sorry to cut this reunion short," Archer says, not looking sorry and not looking at them at all, "but we need to get going."

Does he realize how ... couple-y that sounds?

"We should have dinner!" Mel *definitely* got the couple vibe, and her features brighten as I drag my gaze away from Archer. "Just the four of us!"

Trey looks like she's just suggested he go skinny-dipping in a piranha tank. I'm sure my face expresses similar horror.

"Mel," Trey says, a note of pleading in his tone. Like

maybe they've talked about this before, and he's already told her it's a bad idea.

I'm trying to find a vague way of saying no, not even if this were the zombie apocalypse and they were the only ones with a fortified shelter and a stockpile of food, when Archer says, "We're busy."

With two words—two and a half, if we're being technical about the contraction—Archer just declined the terrible offer while doubling down on the couple thing.

The idea has my cheeks going hot. Also, now I feel terrible for not helping him with something so simple as a mailbox combination when he's stepping in to save me from a dreadful ex encounter.

"Oh. Okay. That's fine." Mel's face falls, but I can't bring myself to feel bad for her.

I distinctly remember texting Mel in the dark days after Trey left for Paris. She sent back things like crying face emojis. Then stopped responding at all.

Yeah … that ship has sailed. Sorry not sorry, Mel. Shrugging emoji.

Trey offers up a tight-lipped smile and starts to steer the cart away with a half-hearted goodbye.

If I were a stronger, mouthier woman who spoke come-backs out loud instead of replaying the moment with the perfect reaction hours later, I'd call after Trey and tell him to pick a different store because this one is *mine*.

But I just lift a hand and give a limp wave of relief to see them go.

Archer shows zero interest in goodbyes or pleasantries of any kind, and I respect that. His attention is still focused solely on me, and I wonder briefly what it would be like to have this kind of intensity directed my way in a different context.

I shiver. Archer frowns.

Then he shocks me for a second time by taking off his suit jacket and draping it over my shoulders.

"You're cold," he says.

I'm really not, but I am instantly warmer as I push my arms through the too-big sleeves.

"Thank you."

Archer only nods, then glances down at his phone, where I can see a grocery list.

Right—I said I'd help him with groceries. I lost the plot there for a moment.

I mentally prepare for him to ask intrusive questions like, *Who were those people* and *You dated* that *guy?* but thankfully, Archer doesn't.

He just stands there, like a big, handsome tree trunk of a grump in his button-down shirt and tie.

"Sorry about my, uh, friends," I say.

"They didn't seem like friends."

He's right—more than he can possibly know—and I admire his perceptiveness. It also kind of terrifies me.

What else does this man see?

"Well, thank you for stepping in."

Archer's steely eyes study me, and I tug his jacket tighter around my body. "You didn't need saving. But someone *did* need to put that uncomfortable conversation out of its misery."

I can't help but laugh at this, and as the corner of Archer's mouth lifts a fraction, Bellamy's words start looping through my mind again.

Maybe my best cookie client is right about his boss. At least partially. Archer is still putting me out of business and basically evicting me due to rent increases, so he's not *all* good.

So why am I thawing toward the man?

It's more than a thaw, as I realize how close we're still

standing and how warm his jacket is and how handsome he is when his face softens a little.

Oh, who am I kidding. I am starting to melt for a man I halfway hate. What does this say about me?

The lobsters wave their antennas at me, almost like they're offering up encouragement. If one of them pops out of the tank and starts singing "Kiss the Girl," it won't shock me. Not after the last ten days of coincidences and unexplained phenomena.

Also, I'd be lying if the idea of kissing Archer hasn't tiptoed through my mind as I stand here in his jacket, cocooned in his masculine scent. Especially not after he just helped me through the kind of awkward moment people usually only experience in their nightmares.

"I have a proposition for you," Archer says.

"Okay. Shoot."

"You offered to help me with groceries."

"I did."

The long pause is almost enough to make me grab him by the tie and yank the words out of him.

"I need ... more help."

He says the word help like it's the dirtiest of all four-letter words, and I find myself biting back a smile. I don't want to laugh *at* him. But he's making it hard just by being himself.

"I need to hire someone who can help manage things at The Serendipity."

Well, *that* was unexpected.

He pauses, like he's waiting for me to fill in the blanks. And in a strange kind of irony, it seems like he's offering me a job, but I'm still not fully comprehending.

Archer wants to hire *me* to help manage The Serendipity?

"Bellamy suggested I ask you," he adds.

Ah, Bellamy. This makes much more sense. I can't see this

being Archer's idea. Though with the confusing cocktail of signals Archer has been serving up, you never know.

"Is this just until Bellamy gets back?"

Archer shakes his head. "Bellamy mostly handles things related to my business in New York. He won't be helping much with the day-to-day operations here, and that's what I need. Someone who knows the area and the building and is good with details and ... people."

It's a job, the lobsters seem to be telling me. *Stop questioning it and say yes!*

Honestly, the idea of a job practically has me salivating. I won't have to think about moving—or worse, moving home.

Working with Archer, however, I'm less sure of. For multiple reasons. His prickly personality, for one, and the fact that he is the reason I *need* a job.

Then there are the moments, fueled by some kind of temporary insanity, in which I feel a sharp tug of attraction to Archer. I definitely don't want to put myself in a position to encourage any of *that* nonsense.

"How do you know *I'm* good at those things?" I ask.

"Your cookies," he says simply.

"My cookies?"

"Baking is precise. So is your attention to detail in decorating."

"Oh. Thanks." My cheeks feel suddenly too warm.

"And just about anyone is better at dealing with people than me."

I can't help it. I snort. Then cover my mouth.

Archer looks shocked for a moment, then there's that tiny tilt in his lips again. Not a half smile, but a quarter smile.

"Would this be full-time? Part-time? Benefits?"

"Whatever you need it to be."

"Short-term or long-term?"

"Again, it could be either. I know you have your business to run."

Ha! That's where he's wrong.

Although working for Archer would buy me some time to make Serendipitous Sweets profitable. Maybe I could even negotiate working in the commercial kitchen as part of the package.

"One of your tasks could be to find a longer-term replacement for you so you can focus on your business. Or if you'd like to stay on, we can consider this on a trial basis."

"What would my duties be?"

To his credit, Archer answers all my questions without any hint that he's frustrated or impatient. "At first, putting out a number of fires. I can't seem to get anyone to call me back, and I need a service to clean the building, an exterminator for the opossums, a plumber for the backed-up sink on the third floor. As well as some things that would fall more under the role of a personal assistant. Taking messages, completing simple administrative tasks."

"Okay," I find myself saying. "Yes. But I have a condition."

"Only one?"

I can't tell if he's teasing or not, so I just barrel on as though he's not. "I'd like to have use of the commercial kitchen be a part of the employment package."

His jaw flexes once. Irritation? Begrudging respect?

A toothache?

"You can have that regardless of whether you accept the job. Any other conditions?"

I desperately want to add a laundry list of them since he's being so accommodating, but his response momentarily shocks me into silence.

"Fine. What's your phone number?" he says.

Though I know he's not asking for personal reasons, I still

have a nervous, fluttery feeling as I recite my number. Immediately, my phone buzzes with a text.

"Now you have mine as well," Archer says. "Also, I sent my grocery list. You can start with that. Just bring the groceries up to my apartment when you get back."

And without giving me even a moment to respond, Archer turns on his heel, leaving me with his jacket, a grocery list, and an ogling pair of lobsters. Oh, and a new job I might really regret—namely, because of my new boss.

Chapter Twelve

Archer

I HAVE MET and surpassed my quota for mistakes this month, so hiring Willa cannot be anything but a success. This is what I tell myself after the first hour of her first day.

This must work. It will. I will adjust and it will be just—

"Hey, boss?"

I cringe at the term, which Willa has been using exclusively from the moment she waltzed into my apartment this morning. I technically am her boss and the boss to—by last count—a few thousand employees. But no one *calls* me boss. It makes me feel like we're two twentysomethings running a sandwich shop in a beach town on summer break.

Not that I have any idea what *that* would be like. But Willa calling me boss in that cheeky tone gives me some faint idea.

I walk across the apartment to my office and hover in the doorway. "Archer is fine," I tell her, not for the first time.

Her smile tells me she knows it's fine and is choosing to call me boss because she knows I'd prefer that she *not*.

Willa is sitting in my chair with her feet up on my desk. Technically, I suppose it's Galentine's chair and Galentine's desk. But seeing Willa there stirs up a sense of possessiveness. But oddly, in a way that makes me like thinking of those things as mine and seeing her using my things. In the same way I liked seeing her in my jacket yesterday at the grocery store. I was sad when she brought it back but telling her to keep it might have seemed weird.

"For the exterminator, do you want services set up on a schedule?" she asks.

"As opposed to having him come whenever he wants to?"

She laughs, but I wasn't joking. I don't know how exterminators work. Do they usually set up an annual or semi-annual schedule? I have no idea how often buildings need to be sprayed to keep out pests.

Willa misses the seriousness of my question at first. Then, she seems to realize I'm legitimately asking and quickly straightens out her expression. "As opposed to us having to call him whenever the building is overrun with possums. Or roaches."

She makes a face, one that seems to indicate that she finds roaches worse than opossums. I would disagree. Not that I want either in the building or anywhere near it.

"What do you think?" I ask.

"I vote schedule," she says. "Most people schedule quarterly services."

"Schedule it is."

"I'll set it up." Willa scribbles a note on her pink clipboard. Seeing my hard stare, she waves a hand. "Don't worry. I'll make sure there are digital records. This just makes it easier for my brain. Using pen and paper helps me process. I'm tactile. I need to touch things."

Her cheeks burn a sudden, bright pink. I hadn't read anything into her words. But now I am.

Especially as the pink spreads over her cheeks and down

her neck. I find my gaze tracking the rise of color, wondering how far the blush extends on her skin.

"Like, not *all* things. I don't go around touching everything or everyone. I didn't mean anything weird or ..."

She trails off here, and I find myself mesmerized and suspect I'm also a little red-faced.

Willa at no point indicated that she wanted to touch *me*. Yet that's where my mind went. Where my mind still is. Those slender, delicate fingers on my jaw or curving around the back of my neck and dragging up into my hair.

When was the last time I had thoughts like this?

I don't know the answer, and it disturbs me that it's this woman, Willa, I'm having them about. Though I meant what I said about her precision and attention to detail, outside of her impossibly perfect cookies, Willa is chaos personified.

Blond hair falling down around her shoulders in messy waves. Words falling freely from her mouth, seemingly without care. Sometimes, Willa herself is falling down, as she did during the opossum incident and again yesterday when she brought up my groceries and went sprawling on the way in.

This morning, she asked to go out on the balcony before getting to work, and I swear, if I hadn't stepped outside and cleared my throat, she looked ready to hop up and climb along the railing like it was her own personal tightrope.

Almost half the time I've seen her, she's been wearing pajamas. Often, there is some evidence of baking on her person, whether food coloring staining her fingertips or powdered sugar on her jaw. And she always smells of sweet almond and vanilla.

To which I'm quickly becoming addicted. Willa consistently disarms me, seemingly without intent.

I'm not sure what my face is communicating right now,

but it must be *something* because Willa's blue eyes go wide and she practically shouts, "I'll keep my hands to myself!"

Then she lifts the silly pink clipboard so it's blocking her face. And I'm glad because it hides my smile. It's gone when she peeks at me again.

"Am I fired?" she whispers.

"Why would I fire you?" She opens her mouth but before she can speak, I add, "I mean, there are several options. For trespassing in my apartment that one time or for allowing an opossum into the building?"

Willa narrows her eyes, their focus falling to my mouth, where I am again smiling. This time, I don't tuck it away. Her mouth quirks too, though she's still glaring as her eyes meet mine.

"The possum incident was not my fault, and I got it back out of the building, thank you very much. And I wasn't trespassing. Intentionally," she adds quickly. "For what I hope will be the last time, I did not break into your apartment."

I've thought about my first meeting with Willa more times than I'd care to admit, mostly because it still doesn't add up. She isn't a liar. Almost everything she's feeling shows clearly on her face.

But if she wasn't lying, what's the explanation for how she came to be in my closet? The thought is a splinter, lodged and irksome. For now, I ignore it.

"The possum getting into the building was as much your fault as mine." Willa removes her feet from the desk, planting them on the floor like she's preparing for a fight.

"You knocked the bag out of my hands, which propped open the door when you tackled me."

"But you incited the possum to choose violence."

"*O*possum. And I did nothing of the sort. Regardless of aforementioned circumstances, no. You're not fired."

Because, despite being a complete distraction in ways I

didn't expect, Willa has accomplished in an hour the things that I could not do in a few days. Honestly, it's frustrating. How can she be so effective where I failed?

I have an MBA from Northwestern. And for as many terrible things as he's done over the years, personally and professionally, my dad gave me a working education in what it takes to run powerful, multinational enterprises.

But I couldn't get an exterminator to return a phone call.

I pull out my mints and pop one into my mouth. I have to ration them now, as I've run through so many this week. I'm waiting for a new shipment to arrive. Hopefully tomorrow.

"What flavor are those?" Willa asks. "I didn't recognize the brand."

"Barkley's Ginger Mints." I hesitate, then step closer and hold out the tin. "Would you like to try one?"

"Absolutely." Willa drops her clipboard and snatches the mints from my hand, popping one in her mouth before handing the tin back.

Her eyes are wide and curious, but almost immediately, her expression turns sour, and she spits the mint into her hand. "Ew! Archer, these taste like spicy dirt! How can you eat these?"

While I do like the taste, she isn't wrong in her description. "I suppose I happen to like spicy dirt."

Leaning around the side of the desk, Willa drops her mint in the trash and shudders. "Oh, before I forget, can we talk about groceries? I'd like to help set up delivery for you. Can I see your phone?" She holds out her hand.

"I—yes."

Why does it feel like such a big ask? Why does putting my unlocked phone into Willa's hand feel like such a vulnerable act?

Maybe because the second I step back, her grin turns wicked. She immediately takes a selfie. "Adding this to my

154

contact info. Now ... which store would you like to use? There's Spring Foods, which is where we were yesterday, Whole Foods, and Hannafords. I'm going to assume Walmart is out. What's that face? Do you *love* Walmart? This will disrupt everything I know about the world if you're a Walmart shopper."

"Spring Foods is fine." I pause. "Who was that man there ... Trey?"

I don't mean to ask the question, but I find that the moment it's out of my mouth, I'm dying to know. An ex, obviously. From the pinched but resigned look on Willa's face, one that indicates their obviously awkward history. But not heartbreak. Which adds the tiniest bit of lightness to my mood.

Willa sets down my phone with a sigh and leans back in the chair. "He was my college boyfriend."

"And when was college for you?"

"I graduated four years ago." She pauses. "We broke up right after."

Four years ago. Which would make Willa around twenty-six? Twenty-seven? I'm surprised. I thought she was much younger. She's so ... youthful. Being around her makes me feel ancient, but I like knowing there's only seven or eight years between us.

Not that it matters. It shouldn't matter. It *doesn't* matter.

I shift. "And he lives here in Serendipity Springs."

"He just moved back. From Paris." There's a tension in her voice, matched by tightness in her shoulders. As I watch, she twists her fingers, then seems to realize she's doing it and stops. "He proposed to me right after graduation."

This surprises me. Not the idea of someone proposing to Willa—that idea makes me want to smash something. I'm surprised their relationship progressed all the way to a proposal, only to fall apart somehow.

How did he let this woman get away?

I wait, sensing Willa wants to say more. Or maybe it's just that I'm *hoping* she wants to say more.

"Now, what about this office?" Willa asks.

"What about it?"

"It's a mess." She sets down the clipboard, measuring the closest stack of folders with her hands, as though they hold their own system of measurement. Maybe in Willa's world, they do. "And from what I've picked up, I suspect you are a man who abhors mess."

"*Abhor?*"

"It means *to hate*. As in, I abhor your ginger mints."

"You and your vocabulary."

She beams at me, her smile so genuine and disarming that it makes me take a small step backward. "You inspire me to use my big words. Am I wrong?"

"About vocabulary?"

"About abhorring mess and disorganization. I'm assuming this is how Galentine left things? She never let me in here, but this looks very much like her handiwork."

"I already did a first round of cleaning," I tell her. "This is what's left."

"Then, thank you. Would you like me to organize all this? Do you have a particular system? A way you like things?"

"I just want to be able to find what I'm looking for without having to dig my way through mountains of papers that may or may not be of any significance."

"And I just want a pony for Christmas. But this—I think I can do."

"You want a pony for Christmas?"

Willa laughs. "No. It's an expression." She tilts her head. "Maybe it's just one my family uses?"

"I've never heard it. But then, my family wasn't really the type to have phrases."

I immediately regret bringing up my family. Especially

when Willa sets her elbows on one of the stacks of folders and drops her chin in her hands. She looks far too inquisitive. And far too ... something else. The word that comes to mind is *tempting*.

"What is your family like? Are they still in New York?" She must see the way my whole body tightens at the mention of my family because she grimaces. "I'm sorry. Rude. Not everyone wants to talk about their family. And I'm supposed to be working, not talking your ear off and asking intrusive personal questions."

She may be apologizing, but she still looks eager for an answer.

It's only fair, considering the way I was just prying into her personal life. I slide my clenched hands into my pockets, then lean against the doorway, feigning a casualness I certainly don't feel when talking about my family.

"I guess you didn't google me?"

There's the head tilt again. "Should I have?"

"I'm glad you didn't."

I pause, measuring the best way to start the conversation. I don't usually have this conversation. Have I *ever* had this conversation? Anyone I've ever dated already knew me and knew my father. Maybe that's one reason none of my relationships ever worked.

That, and my inability to form a connection that wasn't surface deep.

"Archer," Willa says, her voice as soft as her blue eyes. "You don't have to talk to me about this. I shouldn't have pried."

"It's okay," I tell her, and it is.

Though I don't speak of my childhood or my upbringing often, I've had to give answers for the occasional interview I couldn't avoid. I have pat answers prepared.

"I never knew my mother. She left right after I was born

and died not long after. My father raised me. Or rather, my father hired a series of nannies to raise me. He was busy building his empire and finding new women to marry." I manage to keep the bitterness from my voice. Barely. "So, no, my family was never close."

Willa looks as though she's tempted to say she's sorry. I'm glad she doesn't.

"You used past tense," she says quietly. "Does that mean you're closer now?"

"My father is going to jail." The words come easier now that I've started. Or maybe it's simply easy talking to Willa.

Her face goes slack. She tries to corral it into a more casual expression but then gives up and stares with wide eyes. "Jail? Did he murder someone?"

She whispers this last part, and I cough to hide my laugh. There's nothing funny about murder. But if she knew my father, a mousy little coward of a man, she might understand why it's funny. It's like asking if a tiny dog scared away a pit bull.

"He's been charged with a whole slew of white-collar crimes. Interesting that your mind went straight to murder."

Willa bites her lip to hide the smallest of smiles. "Too many true crime documentaries, I guess. Sorry."

"Don't apologize on my behalf. He should go to jail. He's guilty."

I don't mention that if it weren't for the fact that we split off our businesses years before, I would have been implicated in my father's crimes. Or that he actively tried to implicate me.

More like ... he tried to make me take the fall.

I wasn't shocked when I heard about his arrest, but I also didn't know about his actions. If I had, I wouldn't have stood by silently, even if it put me in the awkward position of having to turn in my own father.

Which isn't so different from the position I'm in now that he's appealing. His lawyers keep calling, and I keep blocking them. Whatever they want from me, I don't want to give them.

"How do you ... I mean, how is—" Willa stops and drags a hand through her hair. One piece falls over her eye, and she blows it back before speaking again. "That's a lot to process. Are you okay?"

This is a question I'm rarely asked. And when I am, my answer is quick. *I'm fine.* I always am. Even when I'm not.

But here, in an office so cluttered I normally can't think much less speak, with a woman I don't know quite well enough to trust, I find myself wanting to give an honest response. Wanting to mull over her question rather than let it slide by.

Am I okay?

The short answer is yes. My assets are protected. My business is mostly fine, other than the stain brought by association with my father. Though I've done everything possible to cooperate with the investigation, the press wants more of a story. It creates a strain with investors, the board, and has even degraded trust with lower-level employees. There's doubt in the looks I receive now.

Now, the best thing is for me to be away from the city. Hence my relocation to Serendipity Springs, taking on this venture as a distraction. A challenge. Which ... I am admittedly not good at. The residents hate me, and though I shouldn't care, I do. Reminding myself the changes are part of a long-term goal isn't much of a comfort. I'm also not sure how I'll actually make any changes when I couldn't get an exterminator to return my phone calls.

Willa is on track to accomplish that, and more.

Maybe Galentine's stories about the building weren't so

far off, and The Serendipity has deemed me unworthy, foiling my communication.

In any case, yes. I am still okay. *Just* okay.

"Yes," I say finally. "My father and I divided our businesses years ago, so there was less direct impact on me. I'm okay."

Willa purses her lips, and a crease appears between her brows. "You didn't answer my question."

I shrug. "I did answer. I'm okay."

"No, Archer," she says. "You answered as though I asked if your *business* is okay. Or your money. What I asked is, how are *you*? You, the man whose father is in jail. Are you okay, as a person?"

Willa is right. I didn't even realize that my answers were exactly as she just pointed out—related to business and logistics, not myself.

But this question—the one she asked, the one I completely missed—is not one I feel like I can answer.

In fact, even trying to think about it, my hands begin sweating in my pockets, and the back of my neck starts to itch. I rub a finger along the edge of my mint tin.

Are you okay?

The kind of simple question Bellamy doesn't even ask. Or, maybe he does, but in other ways. Because he knows I wouldn't answer directly, just as I find myself edging out the door.

"I'm fine personally as well," I say, the bitter tang of a lie making it hard to swallow.

I think she reads the lie in my face because her gaze drops. "Okay," she says. "Well, I'm glad."

"I've got to make some calls," I tell her, though what I *really* need is some space. From her. "Are you all set?"

Willa lifts her clipboard and salutes me with it. "I'm good here, boss. I'll have you up and running in no time. Possums: gone. Plumbing: plumbed. Office: organized. Trust me."

I do. But I'm not sure why that fact makes me feel both exhilarated and deeply unsettled.

Chapter Thirteen
Willa

I glare at my therapist.

She stares beatifically back, with her pristine white hair and blue eyes.

I recross my legs, adjusting in my seat. Judith does the same.

I give an exasperated sigh, and she does the thing where she smiles without smiling. It's faint and might not register to a stranger, but I've been coming here long enough to recognize the twinkle in her eyes and the slight twitch in the corner of her lips.

Go to therapy, they said.

It will be great, they said.

They're all a bunch of dirty, dirty liars.

Fine—no one said it would be great, per se. They did say it might help me, and so far, I see no sign that it has done squat. I'm not sure I've made any progress at all in the year I've been seeing Judith. The other thing that hasn't changed is my dread every week on therapy day.

Maybe to some, the experience of laying bare the most

vulnerable parts of themselves to a stranger with a degree feels good. Healthy. Rewarding. Cathartic.

For *me*, it's like someone handed over a skimpy two-piece bathing suit and told me I'd be walking a mile-long runway under the most unflattering lights in subzero temperatures—in front of a football stadium of people who all have binoculars to examine my every flaw.

Actually, I might prefer that.

On therapy days, my hands start to sweat and tremble a few hours before my appointment. My stomach ties itself into a tight knot, and my thoughts turn into Formula 1 racecars.

The sessions all start the same: Judith and I engaged in a standoff to see who will break first and speak. She seems to enjoy it, while in me, it makes anger bubble and build. She says she wants to give me space to *start the conversation* (her words), and every week, I prefer to see exactly how long we can sit in uncomfortable silence. The record so far is nine minutes and forty-seven seconds.

What no one ever told me is that therapy is war. And while Judith is the one I feel like I'm waging war against, I know it's actually me battling against myself.

It's uncomfortable. Painful. And though I'm sure Judith hears all kinds of stories, I can't help feeling humiliated by mine.

The only reason I still come every week is because I prepaid for a package her practice offered through a Facebook ad. That should have been a red flag to me. Something as serious as mental health shouldn't come in prepaid discount packages advertised on social media.

But also ... I want to, at some point in my life, be able to leave Serendipity Springs again.

Judith clears her throat and adjusts her glasses on the bridge of her tiny, perfect nose. She has the adorable, pert features of a

Disney cartoon. One of the nice side characters who helps the main character on their journey. She also has all the doggedness of a bloodhound following the scent of all my secrets.

I sigh again and turn to study the curtains, which are a thin, multicolored fabric that clashes with the more traditional maroon rug and the handful of bright bean bag chairs scattered around. I asked Judith once about the decor of the room. It's a sunny addition on the back of a small house she repurposed into a therapy practice.

"I like to mix things up," she answered. "It may not match, but having different styles is inviting. There are more options for people to relate to, which might make different kinds of people feel at home."

There's nothing in this room I relate to. Not even the gorgeous midcentury modern chairs Judith and I are currently sitting in for our face-off. Sophie would love them. And while I appreciate them, they're too stiff for comfort, the wooden legs too aggressively pointy.

But I'm not sure any decor would make me feel more comfortable in this situation.

"So," Judith begins, as she always does. "How have things been since our last session?"

"You wouldn't believe me if I told you," I mutter, wondering what she'd say if I started off by telling her my closet transported me across a building and up two floors.

"Pardon?"

Judith leans forward with interest, resting pointy elbows on spindly knees. I've tried to pinpoint her age, but so far, I have failed to narrow it down to a specific decade. She has few visible wrinkles, but her short hair is solid white. She chooses a nondescript wardrobe of black or navy pants paired with a solid-colored blouse. No jewelry, save for a simple diamond with a platinum band. She's thoughtful and kind but with a sassy edge that makes her *real*.

I think if I met her in any other context, I'd really like her.

But in this room, Judith is trying to make me talk about things I don't want to talk about. Which means I *can't* like her.

"A lot happened," I say. "I'm not sure an hour will be enough time to cover it."

Forty-nine minutes now, but who's counting?

"I'd love for you to try."

Well, she asked for it.

Leaving out the part about how my closet has some kind of fickle magic transportation powers, I back my struggle bus up and unload on Judith.

Meeting the grumpy new building owner, surviving a possum attack, the death of my business thanks to the same new building owner, running into my newly engaged ex and my former friend who's now his fiancée. I end with my new job, which I'm shocked to find I like.

One of the other things that bugs me about therapy is that though I'm expected to share *everything*, Judith is a vault. It's rare to get any reaction from her aside from the occasional encouraging smile.

But today I get two: a soft *humph* when I recount the grocery store encounter with Trey and Mel, and a curious *hmm* at the mention of my new job working for Archer.

"So, you know, just a typical week," I say.

"I'm not sure *typical* is the word I'd use." Judith raises a sculpted white brow.

"What word would you use?"

"What's another word *you* might use?" she counters. "Aside from typical."

Ugh. Judith asks so many questions. Which is, I guess, her job. But still.

"I might say ...stupid. Dramatic. Ridiculous." I pause, thinking about this week. "But not boring."

She smiles. "Definitely not boring. You almost seem"—Judith tilts her head, examining me—"energized talking about it."

Though my first response is to say something snarky about showing her energized, I find myself considering her words. Maybe I *am* energized.

By *frustration*. I'm energized by frustration, mostly aimed toward one grumpy man who has toppled over the comfortable chaos of my life. Although the frustration has morphed now into a whole new set of complicated emotions.

Interest with a side of empathy. Hard to be angry with the man for his cold demeanor now that I know his background. Attraction, which shows no sign of slowing.

And yes—still frustration.

He might have given me the kitchen space without cost, but with the rent increasing, it's a moot point. So, yeah, I'm still mad at him.

And I think about kissing him more than I should.

Such a strong mix of opposing reactions can't be healthy, right? I almost ask Judith but then remember I don't like talking to her.

"How are you feeling about the new job?"

"It's a job. I need the money."

"Your new boss came up quite a bit." Judith stares with what I like to call her laser eyes. They tell me she knows I'm not giving her the full story.

I stare back, which tells her I don't *want* to give her the full story.

For a moment, the room is quiet, aside from my fingers drumming on the arm of the chair. "I think I'm good at it. The job." Might as well go back to her first question, which is easier to answer.

Archer seems very appreciative, which he expresses by way of frowning a little less. He even gave me a clipped *thank you* at the end of my second day. I also notice he's binge-eating fewer of his disgusting mints. I'm not sure I should get all the credit, but I'm happy to take it.

"You seemed to have mixed but strong feelings about your boss when you talked about him."

That's one way to put it.

I wish I didn't. I'd prefer to have mixed-but-meh feelings about him. But even Judith's question has my heart picking up its pace.

Slow down there, little buddy. No need to get excited about that guy. I'm too young for you to get overworked.

"You're frowning," Judith says.

"My new boss has that effect."

"But a moment before, you were smiling."

"Has anyone ever told you it's rude to stare?"

"I'm simply observing. Switching gears, how are you doing with your steps?" Judith asks.

My steps. I'd rather talk about Archer for the remaining time.

"I still haven't really made much progress on that front."

"Have you tried?" Her question is gentle but prodding. It sinks into me like a blade, leaving a sharp tug where it lodges in my chest. "Remember, we're not trying for perfection, only progress."

It sounds so simple when she says it, but the reality is a lot more difficult for me. So is progress.

"Two weeks ago, I drove past the city sign," I admit, a hot flush of shame creeping up my neck. Because this sounds too small to celebrate. Even if it's the first time I've left the technical city limits in years.

But Judith beams. "Willa—that really is something to celebrate. It's progress."

"I made it a mile before I had to turn around." Even now, remembering has my palms starting to sweat. One minute, I was grinning and whooping and feeling like just *maybe* I could do this. Maybe I was done with the weird mental and physiological block keeping me stuck here.

And then I had to pull over so I could dry heave on the shoulder of the road.

Judith leans forward again, her expression somehow both sharp and soft as she says, "Don't downplay your accomplishments. Honor them. Repeat them. Then build on them."

I nod numbly, understanding and accepting what she says on an intellectual, logical level. On an emotional level, however, I'm frustrated with myself that what counts as something to celebrate is so very small.

Serendipity Springs is a great place to live. I didn't grow up with grand plans to move to a bigger city or travel the world. But now that I'm trapped, I think about all the places I'd go if I could. Beaches. Islands. Mountains.

Not Paris. But maybe London or Venice?

I'd fly on a plane and ride in a boat. Try snowboarding or scuba diving (not in the same location, obviously) or zip lining.

I'm not sure I'd like all of these activities or if I'd want to try them under normal circumstances. But being stuck has me dreaming big. Even if I'm not necessarily being brave or doing the hard work I should be doing.

"And how was seeing Trey?" Judith's question about my ex is actually a welcome change of topic.

"I thought it would be worse. My mom dropped the engagement bomb, so I was mentally prepared for that."

Mom did not, however, mention Trey was engaged to *Mel*, and I'm still debating how to bring this up. Or if I should. Right now, I'm too hurt.

Ever since my diagnosis, my parents have struggled to speak hard truths—or any truths, really—to me. Which makes me feel worse about everything and more out of sorts. As an only child, I had the kind of upbringing where my parents treated me like a mini adult. But now, I'm an adult being treated more like a baby.

"It was awkward, but I didn't feel heartbroken, which I'll take as a win."

"Good," Judith says, her mouth a firm line. Though she's never actually said as much out loud, I get the sense she doesn't like Trey.

I can't blame her. I'm not sure how much I like him either.

And to think—you came this close *to marrying him*.

I would have, too, had he not proposed in the way he did, making our future contingent on one he'd planned without me. Or planned *for* me, even knowing the struggles I was just starting to parse through.

Honestly, this has sabotaged every dating relationship I've tried to have since. If I could be *so* wrong about Trey and *so* ready to marry him, how can I trust my own judgment?

Then there's the pesky matter of thinking about dating and having to tell a guy, *Oh, by the way, I can't leave Serendipity Springs. Hope you like it here and sorry for the inconvenience!*

My only gauge for knowing how a guy might respond to this is Trey. Who sent a message loud and clear: You're broken, and I can fix you by giving you an impossible ultimatum!

So, it's no surprise I'm not eager to lead off with this information.

I remember the potent feeling of nausea I felt staring down at Trey's earnest face, as he was on one knee with a velvet box in his hand. I didn't even see the ring.

All I could see was his lack of understanding.

It felt like being given some kind of loyalty test by a person you thought you'd already proven yourself to. A kick in the gut instead of a kiss.

But in a way, he was the one who set up a test and then failed it himself.

Bullet dodged! Thanks, agoraphobia, for saving me from a marriage mistake!

For some reason, this makes me think of Archer, saving me in the grocery store. Or not saving me, really, but stepping in. And telling me that Trey and Mel didn't seem like friends. The thought warms my heart a little bit, and I almost forget I'm still in a therapy session.

Until Judith jumps in with another question.

"Did this leave you feeling a new sense of closure? And maybe make you more open to a relationship?"

Heat shoots up my neck and across my cheeks. "A relationship with my *boss?* Isn't that unethical? I'm a little surprised you're suggesting that."

"I didn't suggest it." Judith smiles. "In fact, I wasn't thinking about your boss—Archer, was it?—when I mentioned a relationship. But clearly, you were."

She's got me there.

"As far as ethics," she continues, "dating a coworker or even a boss can be tricky. But your situation sounds a little less formal. Didn't you say it was temporary?"

"I—yes."

Though I've enjoyed the change of pace and the dopamine rush from completing tasks, managing a building or being an assistant isn't my dream. Then again, it's making me wonder if a cookie business is actually my dream. I love the cookie part. But it's been a relief to not worry about Serendipitous Sweets. Maybe that's not what I want either.

The best part about my new job, if I'm being fully honest,

is seeing Archer. My skin prickles every time he strides into the office, with his blazing eyes and firm mouth, ordering me to do something. Even when that *something* is calling the plumber.

The deep timbre of his voice is like a tuning fork. It makes my heart hum.

My favorite thing, though, is the way he'll hesitate in the doorway a few times a day like he wants to say something. Like he's starved for some kind of human contact. He never brings himself to speak, so I happily jump to fill the silence by either babbling inanely or asking him questions.

Oh, no...

My conversations with Archer are my conversations with Judith, only in reverse. I groan, dropping my head into my hands. Awesome. I am therapist-ing Archer.

Except he wants to be there. He keeps coming back, dispensing orders and then softening a little, hovering just inside the office with a look that's almost hopeful. That is *not* like Judith and me.

I feel *slightly* better.

"I think ultimately, it would depend on the power dynamics between you. In a healthy relationship, both parties are on equal ground," Judith says. "You wouldn't want him to be your boss outside of work."

A sly smile overtakes her face, and I realize I was wrong. She's not a supportive side character in a cartoon movie. She's a straight-up villain.

"Unless you want him to boss you around ... elsewhere."

I gulp. Then I glare, but it's hard to do so when my face feels like it's melting right off my bones. "I don't think it's ... we're not ..."

"Do you feel like you can freely express yourself with Archer? Could you be partners?"

She's back in business mode, thankfully. No smiles. No

innuendos—was that an innuendo? Are therapists allowed to make those?

Whatever it was, I'm still recovering. But I force myself to think about her question.

I think of bossing him around in the kitchen while he wore a pink, frilly apron. Despite his commanding and somewhat intimidating presence, I've never had a problem speaking freely. Even the night we met.

But it doesn't matter because I'm not seriously considering this, am I?

I can think of at least five or ten good reasons not to. Perhaps the biggest one, which has become more clear as I've heard bits and pieces of Archer's conversations with Bellamy and others, is that his real life is in New York. He's said nothing about going back, but he'd have to, wouldn't he?

A billionaire would be bored in Serendipity Springs.

And even if the idea of living in a bigger city like New York excites me, I can't. Literally. It would be Paris and Trey all over again.

It would be different, some small voice insists. *Archer isn't Trey.*

But the parallel between the two situations has been made, leaving me with a sour feeling in my gut.

The alarm on my phone beeps, and I jump to my feet, relieved I've survived another week of war. And safely avoided answering her questions about Archer. He is a pothole—no, a sinkhole—up ahead on the road I'm driving. And the best option is for me to steer right around him and keep going.

So why is my foot twitching to hit the gas and drive straight into him?

"If you can, take that drive again," Judith says. "Only as far as you already went. Unless you want to go beyond. But Willa?"

"Hm?" I turn at the doorway, where I've got one foot out of the room already.

"Go easy on yourself."

I give her a tight smile, not sure this is something I can do.

Chapter Fourteen
Willa

THE PROBLEM with being good at my new job is that I forget all about my other one.

Which means on Friday, I find myself pulling an all-nighter, baking and decorating cookies the moment they're cool enough. This is not how I like to do things—last minute, rushed. It's also not my favorite to be awake past midnight. I don't turn into a pumpkin or a Gremlin, but it's close.

My feet keep going numb, and I'm not doing the best job with my flooding because I keep making my icing too thin. I've remade it two times but keep ending up with the same consistency, somehow. Rather than simply filling in the outlined sections, it's *literally* flooding over the edges of the cookies.

At least Sophie will have no shortage of samples. I could also probably sell them to Bellamy—he doesn't care about how pretty they are.

"They're never going to dry." I say this out loud, because one o'clock in the morning is apparently the time of night when my thoughts need to be vocalized.

Or I'm just trying anything at all to stay awake. Coffee is

no longer helping. There's a certain point at which caffeine reaches max levels and bottoms out. I might as well be drinking water. Each time I take a sip, it's like the warm liquid is giving me a pitying pat on the back, saying *There, there, child* instead of the caffeine zinging into my bloodstream like the jolt of electricity I need.

To be clear, I'm still drinking it, nursing the same pot of coffee I made at eight o'clock. Right after a text from my client came in saying how excited she was to see the cookies.

Actually, what she *said* was that she was excited and then she asked for a sneak peek. I was forced to lie and tell her the cookies were already packaged.

Which would have been true—had I not forgotten to make them in the first place. What makes it all worse is that this is someone I know from high school. Angie and I have always been more acquaintances than friends, barely keeping in touch via social media. I was surprised when she reached out via the contact form. The message was filled with exclamation points and emojis and a few mentions of supposedly shared high school events I had no memory of.

I'm not sure if she actually remembered us as friends more than I did or if she was angling for a discount, but I gave her twenty percent off. And agreed to stay for a little while when I dropped the cookies off before the party.

The latter concession hurt more than the discount, which definitely hurt. I'm such a pushover.

The only saving grace to this order is that it's relatively simple. It's a mermaid themed birthday party, one of my most popular birthday packages. I could practically scallop mermaid tails in my sleep.

Honestly? That's almost what I'm doing. If this were last month's order of incredibly detailed flowers for a garden club that required true-to-life colors and details, I wouldn't have been able to manage. Right now, my eyes are blurred with sleep and my hands have the slightest tremble of exhaustion.

I'm mid-yawn when the swinging kitchen door flies open. My yawn becomes a shriek as Archer strides into the kitchen with the force and intent of someone coming to object at a wedding.

I don't realize I've squeezed a fist around the piping bag until Archer says my name sharply, his laser eyes dragging my gaze down to the counter in front of me, where there's now a whole pile of icing like a big turquoise turd.

Groaning, I drop the bag and spin to the sink, washing my hands before the food coloring stains my fingers.

"You can't just burst into rooms like that!" I practically yell. "Now I have to make a third batch of royal icing."

"I'm ... sorry?" His words are hesitant, like apologies are a new-fangled invention to him.

I dry my hands on a dish towel and turn to face him. He's still in a suit—because of course he is—but he's lost the jacket and tie and is just wearing a light blue button-down tucked into black slacks. I wonder if this is Archer Gaines's version of business casual. Or pajamas. The thought almost makes me burst into hysterical laughter.

"Do you sleep in a suit, boss?"

His brow furrows as he glances down at himself. "What? I —no."

Before my thoughts can devolve into imagining Archer in low-slung pajama pants and no shirt—too late!—I ask, "What has you barging into the kitchen in the middle of the night?"

"Couldn't sleep. What has you decorating cookies in the middle of the night?"

I slide a spatula under the pile of icing, lift it, and unceremoniously dump it in the trash. "I forgot an order," I mutter. "I'm sure it's hard to imagine since that big Ivy League-educated brain of yours probably never forgets things, but we can't all be so lucky."

As I pull out an unopened bag of confectioner's sugar and the meringue powder, Archer leans a hip against the counter, staring down at the cookies I've finished.

The good news is I'm a little over halfway done. The bad news is that I still have a dozen cookies to ice. And then I have to hope they dry so I can package them. If I had a dehydrator, I could use that, but it's not exactly in the budget. I can use the oven at a super low temperature if I need to, which I suspect I will. I hate doing that because I don't want the consistency of the cookies to change. I'm also always afraid I'll fall asleep and burn them.

"I keep lists," Archer says, and I glance over at him, noting for the first time how tired he looks.

"What?"

"I forget things all the time. I have to keep lists. Then, I share them with Bellamy so he can remind me in case the list isn't enough." He lifts a shoulder in a half shrug. "My 'big, Ivy League-educated brain' isn't much help."

"So, you're *not* a suit-wearing robot. Good to know." His face pinches a little at my words, and I wonder if I hit a nerve somehow. I don't have time to delve into it. "Well, it's been fun catching up, but I've got to make more icing."

"Do you need help?"

The only person I've ever legitimately let help me prepare an order—and only in desperation—was Sophie. She turned out to be less useful in baking than I am in gardening. I had to remake an entire batch of cookies after she somehow mistakenly used salt instead of sugar.

"But how?" I remember shouting at her. We were lucky a cookie broke and Sophie took a bite. They didn't look like they were made with salt instead of sugar. I can't imagine what would have happened if I had iced and then delivered them. "How?!"

"I don't know!" Sophie shouted back. "I do flowers, not flour!"

That still didn't explain it. I mean, sure—table salt and sugar are both small white crystals. But I had them in labeled glass containers with lids. It feels like an impossible mistake to make.

So, I'm not exactly eager to let anyone else help. Besides, baking cookies is something most people—besides Sophie, obviously—can do, as long as they follow a recipe. The problem is that I'm at the decorating stage. Learning how to pipe, flood, and then decorate with royal icing isn't something a person can just learn and do.

Judith's words from our session earlier in the week return: *Could you be partners?*

"You can help keep me awake." Yawning again drives the point home.

"Okay," Archer says. "How?"

I point to a stool Sophie often inhabits if she's down here when I'm working. "Sit," I order. "Talk to me."

I like bossing him around. It's the best kind of turning of the tables, even if I'm sure it doesn't elicit the same kind of reaction in him as it does in me.

But he does obey, fussing with the stool a little—probably trying to get it up to what I suspect are impossibly high stool standards—before he sits.

"Here—wear this." I snag the same pink frilly apron off the counter. Tonight, I was too stressed to even put one on. It's too late for me now.

"Is this really necessary?" Archer asks.

I smile. "No. But do it anyway."

"Do I get to call you boss now?"

"Do you want to call me boss?" I ask. This is the weirdest

flirting I've ever done, but it also has more impact on me than anything I can remember.

Archer's blue-gray eyes stay fixed on mine, only disappearing as he drops the apron over his head. "I think I prefer calling you Willa the Person."

So do I.

"What else can I do?" He's already managed to tie the apron strings in back, probably faster than I would have. It's hard to remember how to tie a bow when you're standing close to a man who fills out a suit like Archer does.

He looks surprisingly eager for instructions, given that it's after one in the morning and we're in a commercial kitchen. I decide to push him a little, emboldened by middle-of-the-night magic.

"Put your right arm in," I tell him.

He looks down at the apron. "Put my right arm in what?"

"In," I snap, holding my arm straight out in front of me to demonstrate.

Archer mirrors my movement, slowly holding out his arm as he raises a brow. "Okay, and?"

I am barely keeping in what I know will be an avalanche of laughter once it releases. "Put your right arm out."

Before he can ask what out means, I throw my arm straight behind me.

After a moment of hesitation, Archer does the same.

"Now, put your right arm in, and shake it all about."

Archer doesn't copy me as I flail my arm around. Instead, he drops his hand to his lap and squints at me.

"Are you ... okay?" he asks.

It's the sincerity in his voice that tips me over the edge, and down I go, tumbling into hysterical, honking laughter that has me bent over at the waist. I clutch my cramping stomach, gasping for breath.

"Willa?" he says, and now tears are running down my cheeks, which ache from the size of the smile on my face.

I straighten so suddenly that little sparkles dance across my vision for a moment. Swiping my fingertips at the wetness underneath my eyes, I grin at Archer.

"Thank you," I tell him.

He shifts, his gaze bouncing around the room, everywhere but at me. "You're welcome?"

It's only when my laughter subsides that I realize how distinctly uncomfortable he looks. It's an incongruous display of self-conscious discomfort from a man whose entire personality otherwise screams with excessive confidence.

"What are you thanking me for? And what *was* that?"

I freeze, realization slapping me like a rogue wave. "Do you ..." I swallow, the question suddenly sounding so stupid. Archer's gaze returns to mine, briefly, then flits away. He looks like he's wishing for a hole to open up in the floor and drop him into one of the circles of Dante's Inferno. "Do you know what 'The Hokey Pokey' is?"

I wince as I ask. Because it seems like such a stupid question. Who *doesn't* know "The Hokey Pokey"? But I'm also wincing because if he doesn't, it makes me feel like some kind of monster for making a joke he doesn't understand.

"No." Archer shakes his head, still not looking at me, and I squeeze my eyes closed, pinching the bridge of my nose.

"I'm sorry," I say. "It's really dumb. Just a kid's dance that people do at birthday parties."

A thought strikes me and almost makes me shudder with a strange kind of sadness. With the snippets Archer has told me about his childhood, would he have attended birthday parties? Has he been inside a skating rink and laced up the ugly brown roller skates with split laces and orange wheels?

Of course he hasn't.

And it's only because I want to climb inside of his embarrassment alongside him that I do what I do next.

I start to sing in the warbly, off-key voice I've been not-so blessed with. "You put your right hand in, you put your right hand out. You put your right hand in, and you shake it all about."

My Hokey Pokey moves are almost as bad as my voice, because singing and dancing at the same time is well beyond my skill set. But I continue. This is my penance for pointing out what should be a shared cultural experience that Archer has been left out of, thanks to his upbringing.

"You do The Hokey Pokey and you turn yourself around— that's what it's all a-bout!" I shimmy in a circle as I sing, hips swaying not to the rhythm, but I do manage to pull off the lifting of one knee to clap under it as I sing the last part.

When I'm finished, Archer is completely motionless on his stool. I'm not sure he's breathing.

I feel both stupid and weirdly energized. Because even though I looked like a fool, I think I was successful in my quest to ease Archer's discomfort. Now, he doesn't look embarrassed, just a little shell-shocked.

"I'm not a singer. Or a dancer," I say. "Obviously."

He says nothing.

A flush rises in my cheeks. "Right. Well, that was ... something."

I turn my back and start in on the royal icing, which I really should have made already. If I ever want to sleep, that is.

At this point, I'm not sure I'll ever sleep again. Instead, I'll be haunted by the memory of this moment, humiliation getting me in a chokehold. I'd give up my expensive mixer to make Archer shift into boss mode and order me to do something. Even if that something was repeating my performance. Which I hope to never do again.

"The Hokey Pokey" is now dead to me.

"I guess they don't do it at billionaire birthday parties," I mutter.

I measure out the powdered sugar and meringue powder, then add the vanilla and almond extracts, the familiar smell a comfort when I'm feeling so distinctly uncomfortable.

"I never went to a birthday party," Archer says. "At least, not one intended for children."

I keep my focus on the mixer because I'm not sure I can look at Archer in the face without crying. Or doing something even stupider like crossing the room to throw my arms around him in a hug he probably doesn't want. Even if it's what he might *need*.

"Even my own weren't for me," he continues. "They were an excuse for my dad to expand his social circles and display his wealth. I was the only child in attendance."

I may not know Archer well, but I am absolutely certain he wouldn't want even a trace of anything resembling pity. This makes it hard for me to respond. The urge to hug him now reaches a level so intense that my entire body feels like it's collapsing in on itself.

This is the only explanation for why I turn on the stand mixer before adding water or putting on the protective plastic cover, which I rarely use because it annoys me trying to wrestle it on top of the mixer. A cloud of vanilla and almond scented powdered sugar envelops me, and I immediately turn off the mixer and step back and sneeze violently six times in a row.

A lot of people talk or joke about peaking in high school. I think I just did the opposite—I bottomed out at twenty-six years old at one thirty-seven a.m. in The Serendipity's kitchen.

I move to the sink and toss cold water on my face, wiping

away the powdered sugar and discreetly scrubbing at my nose. Just in case the sneezing knocked anything loose. My mother hates the word booger more than any curse word in existence, so I grew up forced to use the word motto, a term Mom and her childhood best friend made up. The only way I can sink lower is if Archer sees me with a motto hanging out of my nose.

Sufficiently assured my face is as fine as it's going to get given the current set of circumstances, I turn and catch Archer smiling.

No—it's not a smile. It is a full-on *grin*.

The sight throws me. Not just because this version of Archer is almost as attractive as the frowning boss one. But because he looks almost *boyish*.

This, I think, *is how young Archer would have smiled at a birthday party where kids did The Hokey Pokey.*

"You should come with me tomorrow," I blurt.

His smile disappears, but I think it's more because I'm looking directly at him and not because of my words. "Come with you where?"

"To the party. I have to drop these off tomorrow. I can't promise there will be The Hokey Pokey, but..." I don't know how to end this sentence. "There might be juice boxes?"

Archer swallows, a movement I normally wouldn't notice, except right now I feel like I'm hyper aware of every single detail about him. It must be the lack of sleep. I rub my eyes.

"You want me to come to a child's birthday party tomorrow." He's repeating, not asking a question. "With you."

I'll choose not to be offended by the last part. One thing I've learned after spending time with Archer is that there is rarely subtext with him. He is blunt and simple, which at times makes him harder to understand. He usually doesn't mean the kinds of loaded things other people would when they say something like *with you*. But he'll also say unguarded, too honest things most people would hold back.

With a teasing smile, I say, "Think about it. You can cross it off your bucket list and never again have to say you haven't been to a real backyard birthday party." I dramatically roll my eyes. "I mean, embarrassing."

My risky choice pays off. Archer's eyes are on me again. "Fine. But there had better be juice boxes." He pauses. "What is a juice box?"

I laugh. "You'll see. And if they don't have them, I'll take you out after to get one."

"Deal."

I swear, he looked like he wanted to say, *It's a date*. Or maybe I wanted him to say that? Do I want to go on a date with Archer Gaines?

Does he want to go on one with me?

"Now I need you to do something for me," I tell him.

"What do you want, Willa the Person?" he asks, and I'm tempted to ask for something ridiculous like a yacht or a rare diamond. Just to see his response.

Instead, I say, "Just talk to me. Tell me more about these non-child birthday parties or what you were like in college— oh my gosh, did you ever order pizza after midnight like a normal person? Or tell me about your dating history—since now you know some of mine. I'd be fascinated to know about the kinds of women you've dated."

I didn't mean to ask the last one. Even if it makes my cheeks flush.

"Strike that last question from the record please. Sorry."

"I'm not sorry," Archer counters. "I'll tell you my dating history if you tell me yours."

"Um. Okay."

Archer shifts, moving his stool a little closer to me and

then settling again. "Fair warning: my dating resume is short and uneventful."

Why does this make me so happy? It really, really does.

His eyes catch mine. "So far," he adds, his intense blue-gray eyes issuing what seems like a challenge.

And this makes me even happier.

Chapter Fifteen
Archer

ATTENDING a child's birthday party was never on my bucket list. Probably because I hadn't heard the term *bucket list*. I had to google it after leaving Willa in the kitchen at almost four o'clock this morning.

Honestly, now that I know what a bucket list is, I think the whole idea is kind of morbid. I mean ... a list of things to do before kicking the proverbial bucket?

No thank you. I'd prefer something like a *living* list. Maybe it's just semantics, but to me, it seems significant.

Semantics aside, I don't keep this kind of list, but if I did, what Willa and I find when we walk through the gate of a white picket fence would *not* be on it.

"Oh, boy," Willa says, coming to a full stop inside the backyard. It's a chaotic sea of screaming children, balloons, and an inflatable castle. Music blasts through speakers I don't see, and two dogs chase each other. Two shirtless boys are perched in a tree, throwing what appear to be water balloons.

It is the exact antithesis of the kind of parties my father threw in my name but for his own purposes. I was usually the only non-adult in attendance, with a nanny hovering nearby in the early years and Bellamy standing as sentry in the later ones, his smile sharper than his suit as he fended off various people who, I know now, were probably trying to get something from my father by being nice to me.

I realize suddenly that this is one of the first times I've even entertained the idea of attending any kind of social gathering without Bellamy by my side. Normally, I would have thought about this beforehand, but it didn't cross my mind.

Maybe because I didn't consider a children's birthday party to be a social event—or maybe I was just happy for Willa to invite me somewhere. Though I'm already excited to leave, I don't have the usual ugly twist of anxiety in my gut. Just straight-up dislike, and I can manage that on my own. Or with Willa.

Anyway, if Bellamy were here rather than spending a few unplanned extra days in New York, he'd be slipping off his shoes, leaving them in the messy pile outside of the bouncy castle to jump with the kids.

"Welcome to your first official kids' backyard birthday party." Willa nudges my arm with her shoulder. We're each holding a box of her cookies, which she somehow managed to finish after I left last night. Or, technically, this morning. I'm grateful to have something to do with my hands. "Aren't you *so* glad you came?" she asks.

"Ye-e-es."

She grins. "Are you *sure?*"

At that moment, a little girl with pigtails and an ice cream cone streaks by, leaving a smear of chocolate on my trouser leg. I opted not to wear a suit today, foregoing the jacket and tie for a simple button-down shirt and slacks—which will now need dry-cleaning.

"Positive," I say through gritted teeth.

In truth, I'm happy to be just about anywhere—yes, this horrendous party included—if it means spending time with Willa. I can't get enough of her. All week I've found various excuses to duck into my office. She clearly doesn't need any micromanaging as she's knocked out a whole list of things I couldn't manage to do, but I ask anyway. And then stay for whatever personal questions she throws at me before I go.

It's safe to say Willa already knows more about me than any of my previous girlfriends.

Not that she's a girlfriend. She's just ... Willa. For now. I've been trying to work up the courage to ask her on an actual date, but I'm not sure about the protocol, considering she is currently my one employee—and her office is inside my apartment. It seems like an ethical violation on every level.

Would Willa even want to date me? Has she been flirting, or just being nice? Would it make her uncomfortable if I asked her on a date? Could she be honest if I did?

I don't know the answer to any of these questions yet, which means I'm happy to be here with her. Not a date. But we're out of my apartment, out of the building. It's a good middle ground to see how things feel between us when we're somewhere besides our usual territory.

"Let me just deliver these cookies and we can go," she says. "I didn't plan to stay long."

I think I've seen enough of the party already. But not of Willa.

"I don't mind."

She nudges me again. "Come on, boss."

I've grown used to the nickname and find that I particularly like it, especially when we're in a situation like this one where I'm *not* the boss.

I follow Willa along a sidewalk to the covered patio behind the house. A long table covered in a sparkly silver tablecloth holds an assortment of food and buckets of ice where cans of beer and colorful children's drinks coexist.

I lean close to Willa and nod toward the closest ice bucket. And if I place my lips a little closer to her ear than I have any business doing, so be it. Sue me. I've got good lawyers and know how to plead the fifth. "Juice boxes?"

She laughs and, if I'm not mistaken, leans into me a little bit. "Juice boxes. Though I might prefer a beer."

"Do you want one?"

"Not right now. Maybe ..." Willa bites her lip, then glances up at me shyly. "Maybe after? Somewhere not here?"

"With me?" I think I know this is what she means, but I need to be sure.

"With you."

"Sounds perfect."

She grins at this. "Okay. Now I really want to drop these off and get out of here."

Me too.

But this is easier said than done. So far, none of the adults have acknowledged our presence. And the long table, decorated to match the mermaid cookies Willa made, is completely full.

I'm about to ask what to do with the boxes when a woman with dark hair and a very bald baby shrieks at the sight of Willa. Somewhere inside the house, I'm sure all the glassware just shattered.

The still-shrieking woman hands off the baby to a man next to her, which forces him to juggle a baby and a beer. He does so expertly, as though this is a skill he's been preparing his whole life for. Maybe it is, because as the baby's pudgy fists grab for the beer, he manages to keep it out of reach and take a long swig without missing whatever his buddy is saying.

The woman proceeds to smother Willa in a hug. "You're here!"

"Watch the cookies!" Willa says with a laugh I can tell is slightly forced. "Good to see you, Angie."

"Wow," Angie says, stepping back, and at first I think she means the cookies, but quickly realize she's looking at Willa. "Don't you look great!"

It should be a compliment, but the way it comes out is pure, undiluted jealousy.

Willa is wearing a pink dress, and her loose waves are down, barely brushing her shoulders. She *does* look great. But I also liked her last night in the kitchen, sleepy and casually dressed, with powdered sugar on her cheeks. And I don't like how uncomfortable she seems now.

I notice a few other people on the patio looking at us and whispering. The familiar prickle of discomfort climbs up my spine until I realize they're not looking at me but Willa. Then I get angry because it's clear they're talking about her. She can't have missed it either, but she pretends she's just fine.

"Thanks." She gives a nervous laugh and holds out the box as she glances around. "I thought we were early."

Angie waves a hand, and several rings flash on her fingers. "Oh, this is just the pregame." She laughs. "Most people will be coming in an hour."

The backyard is already teeming with people, and we had a hard time finding parking within a block of the house. Maybe children's birthday parties aren't so different from the kind my father threw "for" me after all. I'm surprised at how unaffected I feel. Usually, the sight of this many people would have me searching for an exit.

I don't know if it's Willa's presence, which turns out to have a surprisingly calming effect on me not unlike Bellamy's, or if it's because this is *her* thing. Next to Willa in her pink dress, I'm practically invisible.

Of course, the moment I think this, Angie's gaze snaps to me. Her blatant perusal makes me want to take Willa by the hand and bolt for the nearest exit. But we're still holding the boxes of cookies.

"Oh, hello," she says. "I'm Angie Solomon. Have we met?"

"No."

"Angie, this is Archer. He's here with me."

A succinct but vague answer. I like it.

"People are really excited to see you," Angie says, clapping her hands. I noticed her fingernails are painted to match the decor. "You have no idea."

Willa shifts, suddenly looking unsure. "People? People like who?"

Angie rolls her eyes. The motion is so exaggerated that I'm honestly surprised her eyelashes, which appear to be glued on and slightly crooked, stay in place. "People from high school, silly. A lot of us still keep in touch, but you don't ever hang out with us!"

Willa's *unsure* ratchets up to a *definitely sure* she doesn't want to be here. "Actually, I..."

Someone calls Angie's name, and she spins away in a cloud of too-sweet perfume, leaving us standing on the patio under a turquoise and silver balloon arch, still holding boxes of cookies. Willa turns, her blue eyes wide and panicked.

Just like when we were in the grocery store, I find myself overcome with an urge to protect her that's nearly impossible to ignore.

"What is it?" I ask.

"There's someone specific Angie might have invited. Someone I definitely don't want to see again."

My grip on the box tightens, and I force myself to relax so I don't crush the cookies. "Who? What did they do? Were you bullied?"

"Nothing like that. Simmer down. But we do need to go."

"Where should we put the cookies?" I ask.

"Great question." Willa's head whips back and forth, looking for any available space.

"I'll trade you." The man with the beer and the baby steps up and somehow manages to hand Willa the child and take both boxes of cookies without spilling his beer. I'm impressed, and he's pretty pleased with himself before he disappears with the cookies inside the house.

Leaving me and Willa ... and a baby.

"Hello, you," Willa says.

There's an unexpected tug inside my chest as I watch Willa soften. She readjusts the baby against her chest until they're almost nose to nose. I'm glad she knows how to hold him—or her?—because I certainly wouldn't if someone thrust a baby at me.

"I don't even know your name," Willa says, and the child laughs, revealing a toothless grin. "Or how old you are. Three months? Four?"

The baby gurgles up at her, delighted, then flails tiny fists until he or she has snagged Willa's hair.

She winces, leaning forward as the baby tugs. "Ouch! Oh my, that's quite a grip. A little help, boss?"

"I, uh ..." I don't know the first thing about babies. I can't recall the last time I was this close to one. Maybe never.

The baby yanks hard, and Willa cries out. Immediately, I step closer, gently prying tiny fingers one by one from Willa's hair.

"Hair pulling isn't polite," I say in my softest, most reasonable tone. "You can have my fingers, though."

It's really a concession, considering the baby already has my fingers in a tight grip, which leaves me practically draped over Willa. I don't mind. The baby clasping my fingers *or* being this close to Willa.

"Baby likes you," Willa says.

"Does s...he?"

If I sound dubious, it's because I am. The wide eyes focused on me appear to be about two seconds from tears. In fact, when the baby blinks, a wet sheen forms and its lip trembles. Panic clutches at my chest. "Hey, now. None of that," I say in just above a whisper. "Crying isn't allowed at birthday parties."

Or, it shouldn't be. I distinctly remember crying at one of my own after overhearing a conversation between two older ladies who were discussing my mother's absence.

"So sad," one of the women had said, sipping from the drink in her hand. I remember the blood-red mark of her lips left on the rim of the glass. "His mother must really have hated him to completely abandon them both."

After years of the words slinking like shadows through my mind, I realized the *him* might have referred to my father, not me. That's more likely.

Because as I stare down at this baby, I know this for certain: I could *never* do the same.

Even when he or she crams one fist—still holding my finger, straight into its mouth.

"I hope you washed your hands today," Willa says.

"At least twice."

She grins up at me, but as our eyes meet, the smile slowly fades into a softer, more serious expression. Tender.

"You seem to have a way with babies," she says, her voice a little shaky.

I shake my head, not letting my gaze leave hers for a moment. "This is the first."

"You're kidding."

"Nope. Not many babies in my world. But I rather like this one. Though if he or she had teeth, I might feel differently." The baby is gnawing at its own hand, and I'm grateful my finger is protected in its fist, though I'm not safe from drool.

"Willa! Oh, thank heavens," Angie appears, having flung the sliding door right off its track. "I thought Jeff lost Baba."

"Baba?" Willa says.

"The baby you're holding, silly. Bring her inside."

Willa and I exchange a look as we move toward the house, stepping awkwardly since the baby is still in her arms but not releasing my hands.

"I hope that's a nickname," Willa whispers, leaning close to the baby and nuzzling her cheek. "Because you're going to have a long, hard road ahead of you if not."

Inside, Angie manages to disentangle us both from the baby—whose name really better not be Baba—and then disappears back outside.

The kitchen looks newly renovated and still smells of fresh paint. We're totally alone. But now that I realize how loud it was in the backyard, the quiet is refreshing.

"She was supposed to pay me, but ..." Willa hesitates, glancing toward the sliding door, which Angie must have gotten back on its track. Willa looks just as eager to go back outside as I feel. "Let's just go."

I hate the idea of Willa not getting paid. But when she grabs my hand, I'm the one forgetting. Because I like the feel of her palm sliding into mine. Her skin is warm and soft, and though this smacks of desperation to get out of here for fear of running into whomever she doesn't want to see from her past, for me, it's something else entirely.

To the point where I almost feel a little guilty enjoying it so much when Willa is clearly panicked about whomever she doesn't want to see.

We're almost to the front door when it swings open. The couple entering is looking at each other, not us, but I immediately recognize them from the grocery store.

Clearly, Willa's ex and his fiancée are the ones she was hoping to avoid.

Willa yanks me to the left. We stumble through a door, and she quickly slams it behind us. We're in a dim and very cramped half-bathroom. I know this because my hip is jammed right up against the pedestal sink. Willa is still holding my hand—crushing it in hers, really—and she takes her other and slaps it over my mouth.

"Shh," she whispers.

I wasn't going to say anything, but I don't argue or pull away. We're pressed together, almost as close as we were the night we were trying to escape the opossum. And just like that night, the air between us feels weighty and electric, like something is building, a storm gaining strength.

Voices pass outside the door, and without thinking, I reach behind me and flip the lock. Just in time, too, as the door handle rattles. Then there's a knock.

"Hello?" a woman's voice calls.

"Occupied!" Willa calls in a high falsetto that makes me snort.

Her eyes go right to mine, and she grins as the voices move away. There's a loud, happy scream that sounds like Angie before there's a thud like the sliding glass door shutting and then quiet.

A beat passes. Then two. Willa relaxes and starts to drop her hand away from my mouth.

I'm not sure what possesses me because I've never been ... *possessed*. I grab Willa's wrist, keeping her hand in place against my lips.

I don't know what I'm doing. But that doesn't stop me from doing it.

My breath is suddenly trapped behind my ribs. If I have any breath at all. And I'm not sure I do.

Willa's eyes are *so* blue. I don't think I've seen a sky that compares. Even as her pupils expand, ink bleeding over a page until there's only the smallest ring of navy at the edge.

"What are you doing?" she whispers.

"I don't know."

With every syllable my lips brush against her hand, a sweet sigh of a touch. Have I ever been so delicate with anyone? Have I ever wanted to be?

"I want..." I start but can't verbalize what I want.

Or maybe *want* is too small a word for the huge, strange things I'm feeling. Or maybe this room is too small to contain it.

I'm grateful for the tiny space, though, the uncomfortable ridge of the sink pressing into my hip, anchoring me firmly in the tactile reality of the moment. It sharpens my senses into blades as I hear the short gusts of Willa's breaths, feel the rise and fall of her torso against mine, see the wonder and surprise in her face, an expression sliding heavily into desire. A mirror of my own face, I'm sure.

The moment is so poignant, it's almost painful.

Before it slips away, as moments always do, I kiss Willa's palm. Soft, slow, a lingering press.

Her gasp is quick and soft. Lids dropping low, her gaze tracks the movement of my lips as I lower her hand, guiding it to my waist. Her fingers clutch at my shirt, tugging me as though we're not close enough. She'd have to climb into my skin to be closer, but I understand the desperation because it's humming underneath my skin, a buzz in my blood growing harder to ignore.

I'm cupping her cheek without knowing how my hand got there. She nuzzles into me, eyes fluttering closed, her lashes resting on the apples of her cheeks. I want to count each eyelash, to study her delicate features until I could conjure up a completely flawless memory of her.

I think I—

"Yes," Willa whispers, surging forward a little until the

door is against my back. Her eyes are open again, on my mouth again, still ink ringed in blue.

"What?" The question comes out strangled, almost a groan.

"You didn't ask, but I'm telling you yes—you can kiss me."

I don't wait for another invitation.

Kissing Willa feels like the bravest thing I've ever done. The bravest ... and also the most dangerous. I've counted no costs, run no risk analysis. Zero projections for long-term success.

The only thought in my head as my mouth moves hungrily against hers is *Why did I wait so long?*

Not as in, so long since we've been in this bathroom, but why—and how—did I wait so long in my adult life, how did I *live* without this kiss?

Without *Willa?*

The thought is a pulse, driving my hand from her cheek to the back of her neck. She makes a little sound when my fingers reach into her hair. Not a whimper, not a moan. A new sound, uncategorized by labels and definitions. An elusive, rare new species I'll name and keep completely to myself.

Her lips are soft against mine, her mouth sweet but not *easy.* She kisses me like we're arguing again. A back-and-forth that builds the energy between us as her hand yanks my shirt right out of my pants until her fingertips rest on the skin just below my ribs. They don't move or explore, but claim only this space as though, for now, she's satisfied with these few inches of me.

"Willa," I groan, sliding my other hand up her spine, the fabric of her pink dress silky against my palm.

"What are we doing?" she asks, punctuating the question with a fierce kiss on the corner of my mouth as her teeth skim my bottom lip. "You don't even *like* me."

I freeze. Muscles locking and breath caught and held.

Willa tenses against me, pulling back to stare up at me. My hands drop to her shoulders, squeezing once. Then again.

"You think ... I don't *like* you?"

"Do you?" There's so much vulnerability in her question, so much raw emotion, fear twining with the glow of hope.

I gently massage her shoulders, strong but so small underneath my palms. "Willa, yes. You are ..."

I search for words. I wish I had the exact ones to explain the way I'm so impressed by her. Enamored. Her bravery in wanting to help me after I've been so snappish with her. The skill of her creativity and her ability to make sugar into actual art. Her humor and kindness.

"You are so Willa—as in *Willa*. Not Willow."

It takes a moment for this phrase, an echo of our conversation the night we met, to click. She grins, fast and bright.

Her cheeks are flushed, and I'm not sure if it's from the kissing or the trapped heat in the room or my words. A flash of my own vulnerability pulses through me—does she like me? And *why?*

I've been horrible to her on several occasions. From the night we met—I shove away the uncomfortable reminder that she still hasn't told me the truth about how she got into my closet—to deciding she needed to pay rent for using the kitchen. Sure—I took it back. But the damage was done from doing it in the first place.

Guilt slices through me. I'll fix the rent issue later. And pay her for the cookies today if Angie doesn't.

There's a bang outside the door, making us both jump— the sliding glass door again. Voices in the kitchen. Laughter and then a male voice saying, "The bathroom's in the front hall."

"Uh-oh." Willa takes a step back, but she's smiling as she pulls her hand out from where it's been burrowed inside my shirt. "Sorry I wrinkled your shirt. Can I iron it for you later?"

"Absolutely not."

She narrows her eyes as footsteps approach. "Why? Is that not in the list of tasks for me? Or are you going to fire me now that we're .... whatever this is?"

I lean forward, pressing a soft, lingering kiss against her lips that makes me want to start all over again. "It's not that," I whisper, kissing her cheek, then her jaw, ignoring whoever is now jiggling the door handle. "It's that I don't trust you with a hot iron."

Chapter Sixteen
Willa

"YOU'RE TAKING me to the rooftop garden?" Archer asks.

I stop on the stairs, my hand falling limp in his as I turn back to face him. I'm a step above as I've been basically dragging him, so now we're eye to eye. "You've already been up here?"

Archer lifts a hand, slowly drawing his fingertips down my cheek. "Hey." His rumbly voice is a shade softer. "Don't be disappointed. Galentine gave me a brief tour when I moved in. Yours will be better."

I wanted him to experience it with me for the first time, but when his lips find mine, disappointment falls away. My eyes drift closed. "Mm-kay."

When he chuckles, his mouth moves deliciously against mine, and I find myself chasing the sound.

"Don't be so easy to convince," he murmurs.

"Don't be so convincing, boss."

He wraps an arm around my waist, tugging me closer. "You're the one in control here, Willa. Not me." Archer's voice sounds strained as he deepens the kiss, like he really is barely holding onto a very thin shred of control.

Stairway kissing is highly underrated. I like having Archer on my level. But I also like his height when we're on even ground. His height makes me feel small and sheltered. Protected.

But then ... that's just how I feel around Archer.

It's been a few days since our first kiss. A few days of walking on sunshine or rainbows or cloud nine. (What makes cloud nine the special one, by the way?) Archer and I have slipped so easily into this new...thing without pausing to examine the fine print of what the parameters are.

Because nothing is more of a buzzkill when you're on a kissing high than having a conversation about things like boundaries and exclusivity and whether you want to get married and start having babies.

I do *not* plan on discussing the last one anytime soon—I'm smart enough to know that's exactly how to lose a guy in *less than* ten days. But I'd be lying to myself if I claimed that seeing Archer with Angie's baby didn't have me thinking about it. My ovaries started revving their idling engines the moment he made eye contact with Baba—*worst baby name ever*—and started talking sweetly to her. I was a *goner*.

And that was *before* I pulled him into the bathroom and he kissed me.

Now, I'm just plain ruined.

Which is fine by me! Because being ruined by Archer Gaines is the best outcome I could hope for.

I'd be lying if I said it doesn't keep me up when I leave his apartment at night. I can surmise that we're exclusive because Archer is with me almost all day, every day since I'm working out of his office. And though we're still getting to know each other through quick conversations between actual work and frantic kisses in work breaks, I know *this* about him—he is too serious about everything else to be *un*serious about relationships.

This gives me some security when my panic at the lack of defined boundaries rears its head.

We'll talk about the future, including when or if he'll return to New York and why I wouldn't be able to see him or go with him—a thought that has me going icy-cold down to my toenails.

We'll figure it out. All of it. But for now, I feel utterly safe. If not a little impatient.

Archer's trying to say something, but I'm not ready to break the kiss. Not yet. After another moment of his mouth moving slowly and purposefully against mine, he gently cups my jaw and pulls us apart. We're both breathing heavily, and his dark hair is mussed.

Did I do that? I want to do it more.

"I like this look on you," I tell him, smoothing back the unruly strands. "You're a little messy. Like me."

"I like your mess," Archer says.

From anyone else, I'm not sure I'd take this as the compliment I know it is coming from him. He's also not a man who says things he doesn't mean. And normally, he isn't a man who appreciates disorder. So if he says he likes my mess, he means it. And that means something.

"Hang on," I say. "I have a question."

"Yes?"

I keep my face as serious as I can. "Did you kiss Galentine on the roof?"

Archer laughs, the sound deep and rich, echoing down the stairwell in full surround-sound effect. I'm grinning by the time his gaze returns to mine. "Why? Are you planning to kiss me on the roof?"

"Maybe. Answer the question, boss."

I cannot in any world imagine Archer and Galentine kissing. I asked mostly as a joke. But now I'd really like him to answer.

"Would you be jealous?"

"Yes," I say simply. "But also it's important factual information to know before we go up there."

"I did not kiss Galentine. On the roof or elsewhere. I must disclose that I gave her a handkerchief—"

"You carry handkerchiefs?"

Without missing a beat, Archer pulls one from the inside pocket of his suit jacket, like some kind of magician. It's monogrammed with his initials, though I realize I don't know his middle name. "—and she told me she prefers her men blond."

Now I'm the one laughing because I can totally picture it. "That is so very Galentine."

"Here." Archer presses the handkerchief into my palm. "It seems only right that you have one too."

"What's your middle name?" I ask, tracing my finger over the scrolling letters. The G for his last name is larger in the center with the initials spelling out *AGO*.

"Oliver. What's yours?"

"I don't have a middle name. But I wish I did because my full name is one letter away from Will Smith. Which means if the *a* gets left off, people expect Will Smith. Then they're disappointed."

Archer kisses the corner of my mouth. "I, on the other hand, would be highly disappointed if I got Will Smith instead of you."

"Perhaps the best compliment I've ever received."

"That is a low bar. I'll make it a point to raise that bar very soon and very often."

Whenever Archer says things like this, things that imply a future, my stomach dips and then soars, like a kite with the strong breeze of hope carrying it along.

"So ... the garden?" he says.

"Hm?"

"Were you going to take me up to the roof?"

"Right. Yes. Come on." Biting my lip, I turn quickly before I can get lost in him again. Bolting up the last stairs, I tuck the handkerchief in my pocket and pull out the roof key. It's the same one that unlocks the front door, and I'm sure Archer has one. But I'm not waiting for him.

Or letting him distract me again—because I have a plan.

Just as I hoped, the fairy lights Sophie hung are lit, criss-crossing over the rooftop garden. It really looks...magical.

No—I need a different word. Because magic makes me think about the closet that facilitated my meeting with Archer. Our meet cute, as Sophie called it. It's one more thing on a long list of items Archer and I have not discussed, and I don't plan to.

I still can't explain it, and somehow, I don't think Archer will believe the truth. So I'm going to continue avoiding my closet and pretend the unexplained transportation didn't happen. Or that there's some logical explanation I simply don't know.

I'd rather bury the memory of it all and keep the prize: Archer.

"This is the rooftop garden," I tell him, spreading my arms wide and doing a little spin. Trying to sell it.

Because while I do plan to kiss Archer up here, my ulterior motive tonight is to get him to sign off on continued funding for Sophie. I'm assuming he doesn't know about it yet, so I'm both dropping a bomb and then asking him to hang onto it.

A cute little garden bomb. With flowering roses and fairy lights.

My palms start to sweat a little. Because this is only stage one of my plan. For the last few days, even before the kiss, I've been trying to think of ways to broach the subject of Archer's proposed changes to The Serendipity. Like the rent increase that is going to force me out. Or the new pet policy that puts people like Sara and Frank in tough positions. That's stage two.

I mean, stage one won't even matter if Sophie has to move out because of the rent increase. But it feels like a good baby step, a place to start, a way to dip my toe in rather than taking the full arctic plunge.

Archer said he had already decided to not charge me for the kitchen when I agreed to work for him. That was the first hint of a heart somewhere underneath his hard exterior. Now, I've seen more evidence of his heart. No, it's not ooey-gooey, as I joked with Bellamy. But he was right—there is more to Archer.

I sense a battle in Archer between the part of him that wants to be a practical businessman, focused only on the bottom line, and the more human part of him. Part of the evidence came from Google. I learned that even if Archer had a head start from what his father had built, after they split up the Gaines empire, Archer quickly surpassed and then eclipsed his father's holdings and net worth.

Part of me wonders if maybe his father committed the financial crimes he did in an attempt not to be bested by his son. I don't know their dynamic, but from what I *do* know, this doesn't sound so far off. But the most interesting article was a tiny one that didn't make any of the major news outlets. Or ... they chose to ignore it because it didn't fit their narrative.

After his father's arrest and the collapse of his father's companies, Archer tried to take care of the employees impacted. Creating what amounted to severance packages he was in no way responsible for, helping executives find new positions, even creating or opening new positions in his own company.

Archer is an astute businessman. But he also is a man with

a very big heart not many people get to see. Maybe one he actively tries to keep under wraps.

I just need him to turn that same big heart toward The Serendipity.

"Well," I say, taking Archer's hand and linking our fingers. "What do you think?"

I lead him under the arch of wisteria. It's not in full bloom, but after a few warm days, the lilac blooms are just starting to show. It really is romantic up here. And it's for this reason, not in any way because I'm nervous to talk to Archer about continuing Sophie's monthly stipend or lowering the rent, that I link my arms behind Archer's neck and tug his mouth down to mine.

His big hands slide down my spine, making me shiver, and stop at my waist. He's warm, and the night air is a little crisp, so I lean in closer.

"Do you bring all your boyfriends up here?" Archer asks, trailing his lips across my jaw.

"Now who's jealous?" I tease.

"Me." The word comes out almost as a growl against a spot just under my jaw.

"You don't need to be. I've never come up here with anyone."

"Good." The word hangs in the air, heavy with meaning, even before he pulls back and catches my gaze, sending a silent message with his intensity.

Maybe I'm reading into things, but I feel like he's telling me I'll never come up here with another guy again.

"Enjoying the ambiance, I see?"

We both turn to see Sophie leaning against one of the cement planters, smirking. She has been nothing but smug since I told her Archer kissed me. I'd be annoyed by it, but ... I don't actually care. I'll happily admit I was wrong about Archer liking me all day long.

But she hasn't been around Archer and me together. I'm actually not sure if they've met. Taking Archer's hand again, we walk over, meeting her by the beds she and I worked on just last week.

"Sophie, have you met Archer?"

I'm surprised when he says, "We've met."

"When did this happen?" I ask, glancing between them.

"You've been a little busy," Sophie says, smiling. "Just like when I walked up here."

Some friends might be mad or feel like they've been ditched with how much time I've spent with Archer these last few days. Sophie isn't one of them. Other than being insufferably smug, she's been so happy for me. Even if we haven't hung out as much. She's been busy too, apparently, which is good timing for me.

"We actually met this week and talked about the stipend for the garden," Archer says, and my mouth drops open.

"You *what?*" I don't know which one of them to glare at first. So I glare at both of their grinning faces and then I yank them into a group hug where I'm the one squished in the middle.

"Are you happy or angry?" Archer asks, and I can hear the smile in his voice. But I can't see it because my face ended up squished into his chest.

No complaints there.

"Happy," I say with a sniff, not sure where this threat of tears is coming from.

"Okay, okay," Sophie says, giving my shoulder a squeeze and disentangling us. "Not a big deal."

I shoot her a look because it's a very big deal. And I really, really hope it's an indication that stage two will be successful when I work up the courage to ask Archer about it.

"Oh, hey." I point behind Sophie to the flower bed with the non-weed I tried to pull when we were working and I was griping about Archer ruining my business. "Your UFO is blooming."

"Her UFO?" Archer asks.

"Unidentified floral object," Sophie says, stepping closer and bending down to examine the flower. Its petals are white with a deep pink center, resembling a mix of an orchid and a lily. "I haven't been able to figure out what this plant is. But I guess it's one that blooms at night. Interesting."

I smile at Archer and give him a little eye roll. "Yes. Plant mysteries are *very* interesting."

"Oh, shut it, Willa. Why don't you guys go back to making out?"

"Right here? Okay." I start to reach up on my toes for Archer, who's looking very amenable to the idea.

"No!" Sophie says. "You'll scare the flowers. But you have my blessing to christen the rest of the building with your kissing."

"Mm—sounds like a plan." I give Archer a flirty grin, and his hand finds mine, squeezing tight. "'Night, Soph!"

She doesn't respond, caught up in staring at the flowers on the vine, which I'm glad I didn't remove last week. Maybe now she'll be able to solve her mystery.

But I'm no longer thinking about flowers when we step inside the building and Archer spins me, gently pressing my back into the wall as his lips brush my ear. "How long do you think it would take to christen the whole building?"

"Guess we'll have to find out."

Chapter Seventeen
Willa

"WELL, ISN'T THIS COZY?"

At the sound of Bellamy's voice, Archer and I jerk apart. We are teenagers making out in a basement, caught mid-kiss by a snooping parent. Only in this case, we're two grown adults who should be working but instead have been making out in his kitchen.

Story of my life this last week since the birthday party. Not the *getting caught* part so much as the *kissing* part. Like, a record-breaking amount of kissing, if there's anyone who tracks this kind of thing. Someone call Guinness!

No complaints here. I never knew kissing could be so great either.

Guess I was never kissing the right person.

With Archer being eight years older, I wondered at first if things between us might move at a faster pace or be more ... I don't know, serious? Like dating him would be the equivalent of taking a stuffy PhD lecture rather than an intro class taught by the fun professor who comes to campus wearing jeans and wants to know how your weekend was.

I mean, Archer is a fairly intense, serious dude, in addition to being older. I assumed maybe after a day or two, he might initiate some kind of sit-down DTR with a lawyer present.

But things between us have felt light and fresh. Fun. Archer is *playful* with me. Who knew the man had a playful setting?

As illustrated by my current position seated on the kitchen counter while Bellamy is smiling smugly at us. As though this is exactly how he thought he'd find us when he finally returned from his extended stay in the city.

I quickly hop down and tug at the hem of my dress, which was riding up just a little above my knees. I already miss the cool marble against my skin and the insistent press of Archer's fingertips on my thighs.

The counter would definitely offer some relief to my flaming hot face right now.

"Welcome back, Alfred!" I give Bellamy an impromptu hug.

Bellamy, as it turns out, is a hugger. He squeezes me tightly, laughing. "Good to see you again, little baker. I hope you have some cookies waiting for me."

When he releases me, I turn and find the box on the countertop. "Archer ate the first order, but I made you another."

"Excellent." Bellamy wastes no time, flipping open the box and taking a bite. "Mmm. I missed these."

"You didn't say you missed me," Archer says.

"No," Bellamy says with a smile and a mouthful of cookie. "I certainly didn't."

I turn back to Archer, then hesitate. Other than Sophie on the rooftop last night, we haven't yet tried on our relationship in front of other people in our lives. *Assumed* relationship. I mean, it's as shippy as any relationship I've had. Definitely leagues beyond anything I've had since Trey. We're definitely *dating*: a few romantic dinners, strolling through downtown hand in hand, oh—and he tried to make me go running with him, which gave me a good laugh. But it's been very isolated, a little bubble of happiness.

I'm not sure how Archer wants to play this in front of Bellamy.

Whatever. He already saw us making out. No reason to avoid touching Archer in front of him now.

I fold myself into him, pressing against his side. His arm curves around my shoulders, and I sink into his chest with a sigh. I don't know how expensive his suits are or what they're made of, but the fabric is so soft. I'd like to smuggle out one of his jackets and have someone sew it into a pillow for me.

Archer presses a quick kiss against my forehead, then glares at Bellamy. "Don't you say a word."

Bellamy's smile is huge. "What*ever* would I say? Can I at least offer a congratulations?"

"Yes. And thank you," Archer says.

"Also: I saw this coming."

"That," Archer says, pointing a finger at Bellamy. "That's the kind of thing I meant."

"Oops." Bellamy gives a casual shrug, still grinning like a scoundrel. "I guess it's true what they say: While the cat's away..."

"Bell." Archer's plea is almost a groan, and Bellamy holds up both hands.

"Fine. We'll pretend this is all very casual. No different than the first night we all met in this very room," Bellamy says.

A sharp prickle of discomfort snakes its way up my spine at the thought. Because I don't want to think or talk about that night. I've been conveniently forgetting about my magical closet, and it's been acting on its best, normal closet behavior. I'd like to keep it that way.

Despite how things have been with Archer, telling him

I've been magically transported not once, but two times into his apartment is a test I'm not ready to take yet.

Later. We can talk about my magical closet later. Or maybe never.

"Well, I should get back to work after my ... break." I pull away, backing toward the office. Truth be told, I'm not getting *back* to work. I never started.

Because the moment I walked in the door, Archer was on me, lifting me up onto the counter with his mouth on mine. A ripple of happiness moves through me, and I bite back a smile.

"Maybe the three of us could catch up over dinner," Bellamy says. "Any plans?"

"Actually ..." I glance at Archer, who shifts and clears his throat.

"We're having dinner at Willa's parents' house," he says.

Bellamy's eyes widen, and so does his smile. "Meeting the parents already? Wow. I missed a lot."

"No, no, no—not like that," I say, though it really is at least a *little* like that. I can't read Archer's expression, but I'm hoping this doesn't feel like too much. "My dad called yesterday, and Archer happened to answer my phone, and one thing led to another, and ... yeah. You should come!" I say to Bellamy quickly.

This is a bad idea, mostly because I think my dad would have *way* too much fun with Bellamy. I suspect the two of them would give Archer and me both a ridiculously hard time —and fully relish every moment of doing so.

"Oh, no," Bellamy says, starting in on his third—fourth?— cookie. "I couldn't. But I can't wait to hear how it goes."

I disappear into the office, giving Archer a last look before closing the door and leaving them to discuss whatever important business things have been stressing Archer out this week.

Underneath all the sweet, happy, kissy times, I've detected

an undercurrent of something heavier with him. Tension triggered whenever Bellamy calls, or whenever Archer gets a call he refuses to answer. New York area codes. No names saved in his phone. Extra frowny frown as he stares at the screen before sending it to voicemail.

I'm not sure if this is normal or if it's related to the things with his father or what. Once, the name of a lawyer's office flashed across the screen, so my guess is at least some of it relates to that. I know the appeal trial is impending, but he hasn't mentioned it. Or if he plans to go.

His father is one area he's carefully skirted around in our conversations.

In between the slow lazy minutes or hours we were making out like teenagers, Archer and I talk. Silly things like ice cream flavors (I love any chocolate; Archer rarely eats ice cream because he's a monster and when he does, it's raspberry sorbet which I argue doesn't actually count because it's sorbet) and pet preferences (I love all animals but don't feel responsible enough to feed them; Archer likes few animals but would take a cat because of their cleanliness and independence). More serious things like his struggle with reading social or interpersonal cues, my barely surviving business, and going a little deeper into our past relationship failures.

Turns out, we share the common theme of having not emotionally connected with people we've dated. And I swear, when our eyes met during that discussion, we shared a sense of knowing *this* was different.

Because it is.

Archer is a juxtaposition of unexpected parts somehow fitting together seamlessly. He's measured and possesses more careful control than I have in my entire genetic makeup. And yet he kisses me with an unbridled fervor that holds nothing back.

I can still sense the restraint in him, still sense how careful he is with me. Not because he thinks I'm breakable, but more like I'm some precious commodity. He cherishes me, but I also feel like he wants to *consume* me.

The restraint also extends to himself. I know there are things he's holding back. Not *hiding*, per se, but more like he's cautiously extending a little more of himself every day. Testing the boundaries.

It makes me sad, because this feels like the actions of a man who, when he's made himself vulnerable in the past, was punished for it. Or, at the least, unappreciated.

Archer's natural resting state may still be serious and at least a little grumpy, but I've also heard his booming laughter and witnessed boyish—even roguish—smiles. I keep squinting at him when he's not looking—on the phone or frowning down at paperwork or something on his laptop—trying to see the jagged edges of where all the pieces of this simple yet complicated man fit together.

And I think I could keep doing so forever.

———

"Why are you nervous?" I ask, glancing away from the road for a moment at the tense man seated next to me.

"Who says I'm nervous?"

"Your hands look like they're about to shatter the wine bottle."

At this, Archer clears his throat and loosens his grip—just the slightest bit—on the wine he's bringing my parents. We're on the way to their house for dinner, and Archer looks like a pressure cooker about to blow its lid and take out half a kitchen.

"Hey, that reminds me—you haven't been eating your ginger mints. I haven't seen you pull them out in days.

Chewing those disgusting things seemed like your destressing go-to."

Archer's quiet for a moment. "You didn't like them. I didn't want to taste like—what did you call them, spicy dirt?—when we were kissing."

I wish I weren't driving so I could give him a hug. A tiny, but very thoughtful gesture. "That's really sweet."

"I also haven't felt as stressed lately." When I glance over, he's smiling. "For some reason."

Even sweeter. Though not entirely true. Unless ... unless the tension he's tried to keep a lid on this week would have been worse without me. I don't like that thought.

"Seriously, though. You've got nothing to worry about. My parents are easy. And I'm sure you've met the parents of someone you're dating before."

"A few times."

I'm speared with an irrational jealousy over these past girlfriends whose parents—*multiple* parents—he's met.

It's *tear out someone's hair* level jealousy.

"Were you nervous then?" I force myself to sound like a normal human and not a homicidal maniac stifling the desire to stab all of Archer's exes.

"No."

"Okay," I say slowly. "What makes this different? Or why are you nervous now?"

"Because before, I knew their parents wanted to meet me because they thought I could give them something. Money, clout, social standing."

"Well, that's plain horrible."

"Yes." He pauses, and I can hear the hesitation in his voice.

"But?"

"At least in that context, I know what to expect. I have

something to offer. With your parents ..." He shrugs. "I don't know how to impress them."

I reach over and squeeze his hand, turning to face him as I stop at a red light. "It's not about impressing them."

When his gray-blue eyes meet mine, they're stormier than usual, with a vulnerability that makes me ache. "I want them to approve. I want them to *like* me. I don't know how to make them do that."

"You don't need to *make* them like you. You don't need to make *anyone* like you. It's not something you can force. Just be yourself, and I promise, they'll see you and like you. My parents already like you because I've told them so much."

Maybe *too* much. I think they're honestly equal parts excited and scared. They're thrilled because I sound happy, and it's been so long since I've talked to them about any guy. If Mom and Dad are a little hesitant, it's because of how *much* I had to say and how quickly things have been moving.

"You don't think this is all progressing a little fast?" Mom had asked, her voice hesitant.

Honestly, no. I can't put it into words yet, but with Archer, I want to jam my foot on the gas. I'm ready to end the test drive and take this puppy out on the Autobahn, full speed.

Sure, there are a few things to work out. Like ... the fact that I haven't told him about my agoraphobia. Or the way I'm hoping against hope he never brings up the night we met and how I got into his apartment.

I also don't know if his long-term plans involve me. Or going back to New York, which would obviously pose a problem for me.

Then there's the little matter of his sweeping changes to The Serendipity and how Archer has basically served me an eviction notice.

So, yeah—we've still got some things to discuss.

See, Mom? We're not moving that *fast.*

"What if you've given them expectations that are too high?" Archer asks. "What if they're disappointed?"

He looks so miserable, I want to cup his face in my hands and kiss him until he's too distracted to worry. Too bad I'm driving. Or maybe it's a good thing, as otherwise, we'd be very late.

"They'll love you, boss."

"But how do you *know?*"

"I just know." My voice is fierce. "I know they'll love you because I—"

The word cuts off, lodged in my throat as I realize what I almost said.

Love. I almost said love.

I'm sure it almost slipped out because I just said *love* when talking about my parents liking him. Love, as in I love cold pizza for breakfast and the very first sip of coffee in the morning.

Even if I had said *I love you*, it wouldn't have been *that* kind of love. The big one.

I mean, I *like* Archer. I don't *love* him. It's way too early for that. Isn't it?

"They'll like you because *I* like you," I say quickly, trying to distract myself from a little too much self-reflection. "And because you are a wonderful man. All they want for me is someone kind and good. You are both those things."

And I'm right, of course. They *do* love Archer.

I had a momentary hot flash of panic when we first walked inside the house. I saw Archer standing in his very expensive suit against the backdrop of my parents' very normal, very middle-class home. Framed family pictures that all need dusting, some of the photos slightly out of focus. A house plant clearly no one has remembered to water based on the leaves it's shed all over the floor.

Has the rug in this front hallway always been so worn and faded?

Before I could start hyperventilating, Archer stepped forward, right into the center of the definitely-needs-to-be-replaced rug and smiled at my parents. The big, wide smile I never would have imagined him capable of when I first met him but looks so dang good on his handsome face.

Issue the man a ticket for public disturbance good.

"I'm Archer Gaines, and I'm going to pretend I'm not nervous to meet you even though I want to run right back out the front door."

With that adorably honest statement, he handed my dad the bottle of wine, let my mom give him a hug, and basically won my entire heart.

It only got worse from there. Worse, as in, losing all chance at protecting myself against tumbling Jack-and-Jill style down a steep hill for this man.

I tried to stop Dad from dragging Archer to the basement but couldn't. And when I was no longer physically able to keep myself upstairs, I crept down to find Archer wearing Dad's Optivisor, the two of them bent over a piece of track, discussing train stuff.

Archer glanced up at me, his eyes distorted and swimming through the magnifier, and I wondered what was wrong with me that seeing him like that made me want to yank him into the nearest closet to steam up the lenses of the Optivisor.

During dinner, Archer is charming and polite, if not a little quiet. My parents do enough talking for him and me both. I play referee—issuing penalties and yellow cards for any too-nosy questions and kicking Mom under the table whenever she and Dad get a little lovey-dovey. I'm not sure I stop smiling the whole time, even when I'm chewing.

Angel hair pasta wasn't necessarily the best choice for a meeting-the-parents dinner, as all four of us end up with tiny splatters of tomato sauce on our cheeks and chins. Archer's going to need to dry clean his shirt. Or is he the type to just throw away dirty clothes rather than trying to get a stain out? Another fun fact I need to learn.

It's not until we're all sopping up the extra sauce with garlic bread that my dad commits a personal foul. "So, Archer. What's it like to be a billionaire?"

I choke.

Not legitimately—though needing someone to give me the Heimlich might have saved Archer from having to answer the question. But enough bread goes down the wrong way that I need a long gulp of water. Too bad I don't have time for such trivial things now.

"Dad!" I scold through hacking coughs, my eyes watering. "You can't just say things like that!"

I glare at him, but he just smiles his gap-toothed smile, which makes it hard to stay angry with him. "What? It's not rude if it's a google-able fact."

Archer passes me my water, squeezing my arm and giving me the kind of pure male look that says, *Step aside, little lady. I can handle this.*

"I wouldn't know what it's like *not* to be a billionaire," Archer says simply. "And though money certainly makes a lot of things easy that might otherwise be hard, I wouldn't say I had an ideal childhood, by any means."

I reach over and squeeze his hand under the table. He squeezes right back.

"I'm sure you might have other questions if you actually did search for my name or my family name." Archer leans back in his chair, still keeping our fingers linked. "I'm happy to answer any questions you might have."

"Within reason." I shoot my parents warning glances, which they ignore.

"Or *un*reasonable," Archer says firmly.

My parents keep it reasonable. Mostly. They ask about his relationship with his father, before and after his arrest. I can see both Mom and Dad getting fired up and protective when they pick up on how lacking in any paternal instincts Archer's dad is. Archer skates over the subject of the mother he never knew and doesn't mention the fact that he'll have to testify at his father's trial. I think my mom might have pulled out a pitchfork and marched straight to New York if he had.

They ask about The Serendipity, and Archer uses this as an excuse to talk *me* up and how I solved simple problems that stumped him. Only when Dad asks if there are any big plans for the building is there any hesitation on Archer's part.

Immediately, my radar goes off. I haven't moved to stage two yet, suggesting that Archer pull back on—or set fire to—the rent hike and pet policy. His guilty expression has me wondering if Archer has some bigger picture I haven't even thought about yet. I guess it won't matter if I'm no longer a resident, though I have developed sentimental feelings about The Serendipity.

Will Archer actually stick with his plan to raise the rent if he knows it means I'll have to find a new place to live?

I'd like to think no, but then I also don't want him to make exceptions just for me. It's easier to think about him doing it for the good of the whole building. Not, like, a personal favor for his girlfriend.

But also—maybe living in a building owned by your boyfriend while also working for him is a complication we'd do better without.

I'm both relieved and suddenly fearful when the phone rings, interrupting Mom's latest question about Archer's education.

"Dad," I warn, but he's already up and out of his seat, lunging for the phone.

"What's wrong?" Archer asks.

"Nothing, really. I just hoped you might not have to witness this."

But the call is short, with Dad only asking two questions before the salesperson on the other end of the line reads the vibe and disconnects the call.

Grumbling, Dad returns to the table. "I like to have a little fun with the telemarketers," he explains.

"He looks forward to this all day," Mom says proudly, the way you'd talk about someone winning a distinguished work award.

"You know how they are—always calling at dinner," Dad says.

Archer looks fascinated and slightly confused. "I don't know, actually."

Apparently, telemarketers fall under the umbrella of things like juice boxes that Archer's never experienced. So when the next call comes, right after Mom and Dad explained how this works while I tried to remember why I thought bringing Archer to dinner was a good idea, both Dad *and* Archer jump up.

"No," I whisper, as Mom cackles.

Dad and Archer debate who's going to answer. The phone in our kitchen is so old, it doesn't have a speakerphone option. It's so ancient they should really charge tickets or make it an elementary school field trip destination to see an artifact from another time. Dad finally steps back, pointing to Archer and then the phone.

"Have at it," Dad says.

Archer runs his hands down the thighs of his trousers and clears his throat twice. At this rate, he's going to miss the call completely.

"Hello," he says, and I wonder how it's possible that this man looks hot even with a mustard-yellow relic of a phone held to his face. It brings out the square in his jaw.

"Don't say the word *yes*!" Dad hisses. "They sometimes record it and then use it as consent for other things!"

But the warning must freak Archer out because he immediately starts saying the very word. "Ye-men. Sorry. No. I used to live in … Yemen."

I'm laughing so hard that it makes no sound, silent tears leaking from my cheeks. Mom has a hand over her heart, and Dad's nodding emphatically.

"Sorry. That was irrelevant information. Please continue. I am very interested in hearing about your funding needs and how I might be able to contribute."

Dad claps a hand over Archer's back and stands only an inch away from him, leaning in so he can hear what the guy is saying on the other end of the line.

Mom sighs. "I think you've found a good one," she says. "Definitely better than Trey."

"No contest," I agree, and I can't help but hope, as I watch Archer carry on a stilted conversation with a telemarketer, that he'll respond differently than Trey did when I finally confess that I'm currently trapped in Serendipity Springs indefinitely.

Chapter Eighteen

Archer

WILLA WANTS to talk to me about something.

How do I know this? Because ever since she strolled out of the office ten minutes ago and announced she was done working for the day, Willa's been wandering around my apartment *not* talking.

I'm almost positive I know exactly what she wants to talk about. But for now, I'm pretending to be immersed in my laptop screen while secretly watching her. This could easily become my favorite pastime. It's definitely the best distraction from the fact that I have to leave in three days for my father's trial.

And Willa isn't the only one with something she wants to talk about. I can't shake the idea of asking Willa to come with me. Every time I consider it, my stomach clenches with nerves and my palms sweat, but the idea of being in the courtroom without her makes me feel worse.

She'd come if I asked. I know she would. But I haven't been able to work up the nerve to mention it. Yet.

Willa's humming now, circling my kitchen island with her fingertips skimming the surface. Every so often she pauses, pressing her palms flat against the marble, like she's testing its strength. Or ... measuring? With her fingers spread wide, she stops humming and stares down at her hands, lips moving as she counts.

"Need a ruler?" I ask. "Measuring tape?"

"I'm good."

And then she's on the move again. I drop my gaze to my laptop, where a spreadsheet swims in front of me. I've had it open for at least an hour, but it's just lines and numbers at this point. Don't know, don't care.

The past few days since Bellamy returned, my interest in business has waned, eclipsed by my newly found interest in train sets. Actually, it would be more precise to say that my interest in my business has evaporated, burned up under the heat of a brighter sun.

Look at me—emulating a bad poet instead of a good businessman.

But Willa has become like my sun. Lighting up corners in my life I didn't know were shadowed. Reviving things I thought were long dead or didn't know existed. Like: a true desire for a family of my own.

It only took standing next to Willa holding a baby who was gnawing on my hand to stir up paternal instincts I never knew I had. Having an upbringing like mine soured me on the idea of being a parent. I barely dated anyone long enough for the subject of kids to come up, and if it ever did, I shut the conversation down.

I've known Willa for very little time and hadn't even kissed her when she was holding the baby. Yet ... now I'm thinking about fatherhood. Considering it. Discovering there's a part of me that *longs* to build a family. Not that I'd know the first thing about how to do so. Seeing Willa with her parents only cemented it, giving me hope that there are decent, healthy families out there. Maybe I could have one.

Of course, I'm not saying this out loud to Willa. I suspect

she feels the same way, mostly because Willa's face broadcasts the things she feels no matter how she tries to hide them.

Which is another reason I know she's biding her time about something she's nervous to say. I briefly consider putting her out of her misery and bringing it up but watching her work up the nerve to tell me is far too much fun.

Willa crosses the room, now singing softly. It's a vaguely familiar tune, sweet and soft. A Christmas carol, I realize—the one with all the *fa la la*s. I find myself grinning.

Today Willa's wearing a pink dress I've seen her in before—actually, it was on the day of the birthday party almost two weeks ago. The day we first kissed. I remember trying admirably not to stare at her legs. I don't bother trying now.

I like that Willa wears things more than once. This is a great dress on her—it would be a shame if she didn't wear it often. And it may seem simple, but to me, it's refreshing. One of the women I dated casually bragged once about donating her outfits after wearing them once. "A tax write-off," she'd said with a laugh.

It made me uncomfortable then but not nearly as uncomfortable as it makes me *now*. Getting out of New York has certainly given me perspective. On myself, on my life and its direction, on what a *normal* life looks like. Normal, as in not existing inside the elite bubble of extreme wealth and privilege.

Leaving has been the best decision I've ever made. For *many* reasons. And I'm not eager to return.

Also for many reasons, but mostly because of the one circling my apartment.

With my head still angled toward my laptop, I surreptitiously watch as Willa pauses in front of a floor lamp. It's new—did Bellamy bring this in? Or was it Willa? There's also now a little side table next to the lamp I don't recognize, holding an artfully arranged stack of books and a gold picture frame.

With a photo of …

I squint, then snort. It's a photograph of Archibald the dog.

"Seems like you've done a little shopping this week," I say.

Willa clicks the lamp off and on a few times, finally leaving it on and straightening the books, which are already straight. "Bellamy and I agreed your apartment needed a little more … life."

"And you thought you'd bring in more life with a framed picture of a dog who attempted to maul me?"

"He was trying to maul the *possum*. Not you. Archibald likes *you*." She turns, hands folded behind her back like she's holding a secret there, mouth upturned in a smirk. "*Really* likes you."

Growling, I snap my laptop closed so quickly that it makes Willa jump a little. But she knows me well enough now to see through my facade of anger. Though I wouldn't say I'm *thrilled* about the declaration of doggy love Archibald gave my thigh a few days ago in the lobby.

"Too soon to tease you about it?" she asks.

"It'll *always* be too soon."

"Sara promised to get him fixed this month. Or next."

"We can only hope. What else did you add to my apartment?" I ask.

Willa laughs. "You really didn't notice? Bellamy said you wouldn't, but I didn't believe him. I think I'll let you discover things on your own. Like a little treasure hunt."

"I'm not sure if I like you and Bellamy in collusion."

"Better get used to it," Willa says, wandering over to the windows. "He also gave me your credit card. He said that would be okay too."

"It is. You made the apartment look better. New curtains?"

"Yes. Your windows were too naked." Willa turns, her face a little hesitant. "You don't mind?"

"The curtains? No, you're right about my nude windows."

"The curtains *or* me using your credit card. I'm not trying to use you for your money," she adds quickly.

"Trust me, I'm well aware of what being used for my money looks like, and I know that's not what you're doing. You probably only bought things that were on sale." I can tell by her surprised expression that I guessed correctly. I pat the cushion next to me. "Now, come. Sit. Talk to me about what you've been trying to work up the courage to say."

Willa smiles, but it's wobbly. "That obvious, huh?"

"Little bit. Come on."

Willa cautiously moves to sit down, keeping half a cushion between us with her knees together and feet flat on the floor. Much too prim and proper. I hook an arm around her waist and tug her over until she's practically in my lap.

"Much better. Now, go ahead and ask. If it helps, please know that the answer is yes—I'll change my mind."

Willa tenses, practically turning to stone. She doesn't look at me. "Change your mind about what?" she whispers.

Does she think I could possibly mean about *her?*

Maybe I was wrong about what she planned to say. I pull her closer and press a gentle kiss on her temple. "There's a possibility I guessed incorrectly. I thought you were going to talk to me about the letter I sent to residents."

"The one with the rent increases and the no-pet edict?"

"I'd hardly call it an edict, but yes."

My father would tell me I'm being sentimental, but I'm starting to see that as not such a bad thing.

"I've already drafted another letter announcing that I won't be raising rent or kicking out puppies or parrots or anything else. Life at The Serendipity will continue as normal."

Willa spins to face me, her blue eyes gleaming brightly. "Really?"

"Don't look so surprised. I'm not a *monster*. Even if my first instinct is to prioritize the bottom line over the human element. In this case, I had a change of heart about the building. I don't need the money I'd make from selling luxury condos. And it would make people happy."

Willa especially, but I've started to feel oddly attached to The Serendipity. Or maybe it's the people who live here. I've heard so many stories while fielding the complaints and rebukes.

Like the Hathaways. The other day, the older couple stopped me on their way up to the rooftop garden. They told me how they met and fell in love here years ago. After their children were grown, they decided to return to The Serendipity to live out the rest of their days.

Then there's Matteo, the chef whose grandparents used to live here. They were famous for throwing dinners in the courtyard for anyone who wanted to come, which inspired his love of cooking. He even invited me to eat at Aria, his restaurant, on the house.

After telling me I really should reconsider my plans, of course.

Nori Sinclair, who looks to be about Willa's age, has lived here since she was four and told me she wanted to stay here forever—but the rent increase might force her to leave.

Sara tearfully begged me not to make pets leave while Archibald assaulted me with his tongue. Again.

And on it goes. I think I've met almost every resident now—mostly against my will and in uncomfortable confrontations—but the conversations have unexpectedly softened me.

Willa gasps. "You were going to turn The Serendipity into condos? Archer!" She pokes me in the chest. "Actually, I could totally see that working. But please don't. I like where I live, and none of the other options are anywhere close to the price or character."

I grab her wrist and bring her hand to my mouth, kissing her fingertips. "You were looking at other places to live?"

"Yes," she admits. "Sophie and I were trying to find a two-bedroom place together."

"Why didn't you tell me?"

"I didn't want you to make the decision just because you felt sorry for me."

I kiss her wrist now, hovering there as I try to feel her pulse against my lips. "The last thing I feel for you is sorry, Willa."

She draws in a deep breath. "But I *am* struggling. Financially."

"I picked up on that."

"But you didn't say anything."

"I didn't want to overstep or assume you'd want my help, though I would freely offer anything you need. Actually"—I release Willa's wrist and lean forward to grab my laptop—"I did do something for you. Look."

Once I've navigated to the window I want, I balance the laptop on her knees, watching her expression as she frowns at the screen. When she realizes what it is, her jaw goes slack.

"A business plan for Serendipitous Sweets? When did you have time to do this?" she asks.

I don't tell her that I was doing this instead of the things I should have been doing. My work week mostly consisted of telling Bellamy to handle decisions while I spent time creating a business plan—when I wasn't scouring Subreddits about model trains.

"It was nothing," I say simply. "You don't have to use it, of course. But I think it will help. It's clear that you love all the baking and hate all the business stuff. I'm also happy to help you with anything you need in that regard."

"But you're busy," she says. "Running your billion-dollar company that does—what does it do again?"

"Mostly real estate. It's boring. This was a lot more fun."

"Archer, this is *amazing*," Willa says. "Thank you!"

I'm unprepared for her to throw her arms around my neck, practically knocking me sideways on the sofa. I chuckle, securing her against me with one hand while moving my laptop out of the way with the other. She kisses her way up my neck, punctuating each kiss with a thank you.

"Watch out," I say, hearing the gravel in my voice as her lips graze my earlobe. "This kind of thanks is going to inspire a lot more pampering. Now, do you feel better after talking to me?"

Willa groans and drops her head to my shoulder. "Well— that's not what I wanted to talk to you about, so no. How did you know I had something to say? Am I that easy to read?"

"You've been pacing around the apartment *not* talking for twenty minutes. Kind of a dead giveaway." I reposition her next to me on the couch and place my fingertips underneath her chin, gently lifting until her gaze meets mine. "You can tell me anything. It's not going to scare me off."

"Are you sure?" Her smile wobbles.

It only ramps up my urge to protect her. To assure her that nothing she could say would change how I feel. But that might mean admitting exactly how *I* feel—and I'm a little worried my big feelings might scare *her* off.

"Yes," I say, infusing my voice with as much deep command as I can. "And then I have something to ask you."

"You go first," she says.

"Nope. You start."

She sighs, glancing down and picking at the hem of her dress. "It's just … I told someone before, and it didn't go well."

Trey. She doesn't say his name, and I'm not sure how I know, but I do.

"I'm not him," I tell her. "You can trust me. Whatever it is, Willa, I'm not going anywhere."

There's a long pause in which she stares so hard at the rug, I half expect it to go up in flames. "That's the thing," she says finally. Miserably. "Neither am I."

I'm so caught up in my thoughts, I miss Bellamy's question the first time he asks. And also the second.

I've been distracted all morning, the back of my mind replaying my conversation with Willa last night.

The front of my mind, meanwhile, is focused on a message I'm waiting on in regard to a rare train I tracked down for her father. It's a vintage Lionel steam locomotive; one George had a poster of on the basement wall. He called it his White Whale. Apparently, his grandfather owned one, and when he died, his wife didn't realize how much it was worth and donated it to Goodwill.

I couldn't stop thinking about it, and when I found a collector selling one in the Boston area, I reached out.

Bellamy clears his throat so loudly, a few birds startle out of the hedges surrounding the pool area.

"I'm sorry," I tell him, putting a hand over my eyes to shade the sun. "Could you repeat the question?"

We're having a meeting before he heads back to New York and, at his insistence, this meeting is taking place by the courtyard pool. Honestly, not a terrible idea. Both of us have our jackets off and shirtsleeves rolled up. It's bright and warm with a light breeze—like the weather decided to perfectly cooperate on the first day of spring. It's actually really lovely out here. If I hadn't already canceled my meeting with the architect to discuss plans to close in this space to add on to the building, I'd probably do so now.

The only downside is that being out here leaves me exposed to the residents, most of whom would still like to throw me into the pool. A few might actually try. I saw Frank and his bird glaring with equal vehemence through one of the windows a few minutes ago.

I really need to draft a new letter walking back my proposed changes before they band together and mutiny.

"I asked what your plan is." Bellamy holds up three fingers. "Three times."

Guess I missed his question *more* than twice.

"My plan," I repeat, speaking just as slowly as he did. "Hm. A cookie might help me think."

Bellamy snatches the box from the table between our lounge chairs and moves it to his other side, out of my reach.

"I thought you were happy to see me eating cookies," I complain.

"No—I was happy to see you break out of the rigidity that made you think cookies were evil. I am less happy to share my cookies with you. You're the one dating the baker. Get your own."

I do have my own stash upstairs. Though Willa has had an uptick of orders recently, she's still found the time to keep Bellamy and now me in a steady supply. Even if she's started returning a portion of the outrageous tips we've been leaving.

It became something of a game when I realized Bellamy was tipping Willa almost forty percent for every box. Not to be outdone, I placed an order and tipped forty-five. He went fifty. I don't want to admit the current amount, but suffice to say, we both tipped so far above what the cookies actually cost that Willa yelled at us both. She said she couldn't possibly keep our money and threatened to stop making cookies for us altogether.

I might continue over-tipping like this, if for no other reason than to see her angry. I love seeing Willa ruffled, and it's far too easy to do. Her blue eyes blaze, and her hair gets wilder, like her anger sparks static electricity that infuses every strand. And true to her word, Willa hasn't been keeping the money. Or, at least, not all of it. I've been finding cash stuffed in strange places throughout the apartment. In my silverware drawer. Underneath the bathroom cabinet. In my pillowcase.

I intend to sneak it all back into her possession. Like the bills I stuffed into her glove compartment when I tagged along with her on a trip to Spring Foods the other day. An envelope filled with twenties is now waiting to be discovered underneath the butter in the commercial kitchen.

"Your plan?" Bellamy reminds me, making a show of savoring his cookie.

The truth is—I don't have a long-term plan with Willa. At least, nothing that's solidified. The future is a hazy, soft-edged, lazy sort of dream where Willa and I build a life together.

But where? My life has always been in New York. I never thought I'd leave the city aside from college. I've started to acclimate here, maybe even enjoy the change, but I'm not sure if that's the location or simply being around Willa.

Would I want to stay in Serendipity Springs forever? Or even long-term?

It's a question I must consider—especially now that I know Willa can't leave.

I had never heard of agoraphobia specific to a city or larger geographic area. But anxiety is something I'm familiar with. And last night I shared with Willa about my own struggles with social anxiety. The only other people who know are Bellamy, who was instrumental in getting me the help I needed years ago, and my father, who dismissed the idea as a

233

form of weakness. I appreciate that, to some degree, Willa and I can understand each other.

But where my anxiety is manageable, it's clear Willa's still greatly impacts her life in ways she wishes it didn't.

"It's like I'm in that sci-fi show about the town with the invisible dome over it." I wasn't familiar, but she continued anyway. "I hadn't given serious thought to moving anywhere else after college, but now that I *can't* leave, I just keep thinking of all the places I can't go. I've got a whole Pinterest board dedicated to travel. If," she said, and I could see her fighting back tears, "I can ever leave again."

Immediately, I wanted to track down her Pinterest board —whatever that is—and start planning to take her to every one of those places. Which right now is impossible.

So is the idea of living in New York. Which means if I choose Willa, for now, at least, I'd be choosing a life here.

I check my phone again—still no update on the train parts.

"I'm not completely sure," I finally admit to Bellamy. I don't mention the agoraphobia, as it's not my place to share. "It's a conversation Willa and I need to have. Is it too soon, do you think?"

Bellamy smiles wide. "I was talking about your plans with the company, but this is far more interesting. Go on."

I backpedal. "As for the company, I'd like to take a step back," I say quickly. "A *bigger* step back. Which would allow me to stay here longer than I planned."

"And how would you spend your time in Serendipity Springs now that Willa helped you find a new building manager?" Bellamy asks.

Yesterday, Willa and I interviewed Steve, a young Black man with a penchant for sweater vests and organization. He's motivated and loves history. Apparently, he applied for the position not because he's ever managed a building, but because he's fascinated by The Serendipity. He seemed a little less fascinated when Willa mentioned the basement storage unit full of unorganized files Galentine apparently left behind but agreed he would take care of organizing and digitizing whatever needed it.

I hired him on the spot, and he'll start working next week from the parlor downstairs, a room that's seldom used. It has a great conference table, a strong Wi-Fi signal, and it overlooks the pool. It's a salaried position but does not include living arrangements.

Meanwhile, Willa pitched me the idea of renting out the basement apartment. I can't see anyone being thrilled about being the only resident paying to live in the basement next to a storage area. But Willa thinks that the outside entrance, leading up to the pocket park next to The Serendipity, makes the apartment unique. We'll see.

"There will still be a lot for me to do, just from afar," I say. "You've practically been running everything on your own for the last five years anyway. And doing a fine job of it."

"A compliment," Bellamy says, plucking another cookie from his box. "I like the effect Willa has on you."

I do too.

"You don't think things are moving too quickly?" I ask. My phone dings, and I'm thrilled to see a message from the train seller, who accepted my offer. "Excellent."

"What's excellent?"

I look up. "Oh—just a train thing for Willa's father. Don't worry about it."

Bellamy leans back in his chair, crossing his legs and grinning up at the bright blue sky. "Oh, I'm far from worried. I feel certain that you're on a path toward something greater, and I love it."

My mind goes to the question I had recently about Bellamy. "Can I ask you something? It's personal."

Without turning his face away from the sun, Bellamy says, "Go right ahead."

"Is there a particular reason you're still single?"

He hums, crossing and recrossing his legs before he answers. "There was someone—a long time ago. I made poor choices and lived to regret it."

I want to press him, but it's clear he's said all he wants to say. At least for now. "I'm sorry."

"Thank you. I've had years to make my peace. And make peace I did. As it turns out, I'm more content alone than I would be if I married someone who wasn't *her*." Now, he turns to look at me, flipping his sunglasses up on top of his white hair. "So, I'd urge you to consider your own contentment and make choices you can live with for a long time."

"Noted," I say lightly, though his words have sunk in deep.

"How are you doing with the trial? It's in three days, and you haven't mentioned it," Bellamy says, and now I'm the one turning my face up to the sun, eyes closed and heat warming my cheeks even as a deep chill moves through me.

"Fine," I tell him, willing the word to be true.

The trial has been lurking in the back of my mind, a shadow looming larger as the date approaches. I don't want to deal with the media circus again. Or with testifying—something I wouldn't be doing had I not been subpoenaed.

But what I really don't want is to see my father.

"Have you told Willa? Or asked her to come with you?"

I swallow, remembering Willa's face as she told me how she's unable to leave Serendipity Springs. "I wouldn't subject her to the circus that my father's trial will be."

"She'd come to support you. Just ask her."

"We'll see," I tell him, and I'm grateful when someone clearing their throat nearby interrupts us. Just thinking about the trial has me feeling a spike in my blood pressure.

The Hathaways stand near our deck chairs. Norman is

wearing an old-fashioned bowler hat with a flower on the brim, the same light lilac as his wife's hair. They're both smiling widely.

I see them around the building a lot. Always together. Always with their arms linked as he leans on his cane.

"We don't mean to disturb you," Jane says, smiling.

"She says while disturbing him." Norman chuckles and shakes his head. "We wanted to come by and introduce ourselves to your friend. And my wife thought the more we talked to you, the harder it would be to kick us out of the building."

Well, that's direct. Bellamy stifles a chuckle behind me. "This is Bellamy. And I don't plan to kick anyone out of the building."

"But that's exactly what you're doing by raising the rent." Jane's smile is soft and her voice sweet, but I get the very distinct impression she's a shark underneath. At least, when she needs to be. "It's just more passive than actually sending out eviction letters so you can feel better about yourself and sleep better at night."

She's not wrong. And neither was I in my assessment of her. The only inaccuracy in her statement is that I'm feeling better about myself or sleeping at night. Though some of it has to do with my father's trial, I've also had several nightmares related to the building and its residents.

Norman leans over to kiss her cheek. "What Jane means to say is we hope you reconsider. We fell in love here."

"Thanks to a little nudge," Jane adds with a wink. "I'm not sure he would have noticed me if we hadn't gotten stuck in the elevator. And believe me, I was trying to get him to notice."

The story, which they also told me the other day, reminds me of Galentine and her whispered pleas to the universe ... or the building.

This building definitely has a type. And I'm not sure what it says about me that I've started to settle in here.

Bellamy says, "We'd love to hear the story, if you have time."

The short *version of the story*, I want to add since I've already heard it once.

I turn to Bellamy and ask, "Don't you need to get back to the city?"

"I've got a little time," Bellamy says.

"And we've got nothing but time." Moving faster than it seems possible for someone with a cane, Norman drags over nearby chairs for his wife and himself for what I know will be anything but short.

———

Bellamy leaves, and with Willa working on an order, my apartment feels emptier than it did the night I moved in. Forget the new curtains and the tiny details Willa's added—the space feels cavernous and bare.

Solitude used to be a comfort to me. Now, it feels ... stifling.

I rub a hand over my chest, deciding that maybe a run will help dispel the tight clutch of emotion pinching my chest.

What did you want to tell me? Willa asked after she finished talking last night.

After she shared her struggle with agoraphobia, there was no way I could ask her to come to New York with me for my father's trial.

I said it was nothing important and that we could talk about it later.

Thankfully, she didn't press me on it. Today, she's been busy and didn't follow up. Which is just as well. The last thing I'd want is for Willa to feel pressured.

Willa's struggle with agoraphobia must feel absolutely crippling—especially after how Trey responded and what he did. I've never wanted to resort to violence more than after she told me what he did. I can only hope I don't see him again anytime soon.

But finding out Willa can't leave Serendipity Springs right before I was going to ask her to come with me to New York feels somehow pointed. Intentionally specific. Darkly ironic.

And now, I'm dreading the trial even more than before.

I don't usually run at night, but I've got restless energy I need to burn off. Heading to my room, I loosen my tie and unbutton my shirt, leaving my clothes scattered behind as I walk. I toe off my dress shoes one at a time, stepping out of them in the doorway, ignoring the tremor in my hands and the increasing tightness in my chest.

It doesn't matter, I tell myself. *You never planned on having Willa with you in the courtroom. Nothing's changed. Bellamy will be there. You'll be fine.*

It's been years since I've felt this build of pressure in my limbs, so I don't realize at first that it's more than simple anxiety or worry.

But as I slide open a drawer to pull out my running shorts, my vision blurs and my chest tightens until I collapse to my knees on the rug at the end of my bed, fighting for every breath in the clutches of a full-blown anxiety attack.

Chapter Nineteen
Willa

It's been weeks since my closet has hurled me through its fickle, invisible, improbably impossible portal.

So, as I'm rooting around in there for my pajama pants after I've finished the cookie order, I'm wholly unprepared to find myself suddenly tripping over shiny dress shoes.

A collection of shoes that probably cost as much as the trade-in value on my Hyundai.

This passage from closet to closet felt a whole lot more violent than either time before, and my stomach is churning. I take a moment to orient myself, steadying one hand against the wall as I draw in a breath and wait for my gut to settle. The closet door is cracked, so I'm not in pitch darkness, which is helpful.

What's *less* helpful is the fact that Archer is home. Or, at least, he was just minutes ago when I left his apartment.

And here I had *just* started to convince myself that I had somehow misremembered the magical closet.

That sounds illogical, I know—but does it sound any more illogical than the truth? But as weeks passed with no activity, I started to think it hadn't really happened. Maybe I just didn't *want* to believe it. And if I didn't believe it, then it couldn't be true.

Kind of like the year my mom said if I didn't believe in Santa, I wouldn't get good gifts. To which I agreed: "Yeah, I didn't believe last year, and I didn't get much."

I didn't understand why Mom and Dad were laughing so hard until years later.

Too bad my childhood Santa theory didn't work in this situation. Because, believe it or not, I'm now in Archer's closet. And I can't see a way around having to explain myself to him.

I stare down at his shiny, expensive shoes. He'll believe me. He will. Probably?

This isn't like the first time it happened, when I was just some strange woman appearing in his closet. I'm Willa—Willa the Person. *His* person.

But if there's one thing I know to be true about Archer, it's that he's rooted in logical thinking. Something the closets in this building, apparently, are not.

And now, in addition to telling him about my agoraphobia, which he handled so perfectly and with so much kindness, I'm going to need to tell him about my magical closet.

Or our magical closets? I'm not sure if his closet is pulling me in or if mine is pushing me out, or if I should just blame the whole stupid building at this point.

How many huge, weird things can a straightlaced, practical man like Archer handle in a single week? I wonder. *Guess I'm about to find out.*

Maybe I'm lucky and he's gone down to get the mail or something. I can let myself out and—

I hear a sniff. No—a sniffle. It's wetter than a sniff. Followed by a shaky breath. Neither of which are sounds I'm used to hearing from Archer.

Because...those are crying sounds. I know them well.

My panic about having to explain magic disappears, sucked into a deeper vortex of panic these sounds elicit, and I swing the door open and step outside.

Immediately, I see Archer. The sick feeling in my gut intensifies. Because he's across the room, lying right on the rug with his back to me, still in his suit pants but only an undershirt. His tie and button-down and shoes are scattered in very un-Archer-like fashion around the room.

I'm on the floor behind him before I can second guess. He doesn't react when I lean over him, curling my body protectively over his.

I drag my fingers through his hair, massaging his scalp.

"Hey," I say softly, brushing my lips over his cheek. It's wet, and my heart throbs with worry. "Hey, I'm here."

I swallow down all the questions I want to ask when he sighs, a deep release of breath that relaxes his whole body. One of his hands lifts enough to clasp my forearm, hugging it to his chest. I can feel his heart racing, and he's breathing much too fast.

"Willa," he says, then sniffs again. His voice is missing the normally deep roughness, the solid command I'm so used to.

What could possibly have happened since I last saw him?

"Hi, boss." I hook a leg over his until I'm a mix of a spoon and a blanket. I struggle to keep the worry out of my voice. What he needs right now is my calm. "You're warm."

He sighs again, then tightens his grip on my arm. "You too."

For a few moments that stretch like an eternity of worry, I stroke his hair and listen to his breathing, all while wondering what brought this strong man to his knees.

It's killing me not to just ask what's wrong. But I'm a little scared of the answer...and even more scared he might not answer at all. After I shared about my agoraphobia, he wouldn't say whatever he planned to tell me. Now I'm worried it was something much bigger than what he'd let on. I suspected it was about his father's trial, since he's going back this week for it. But he hardly mentioned it.

Which maybe means it's buried deep.

"Do you want to talk about it?" I ask after a few minutes.

"It's nothing," he says.

"You don't have to talk to me about it, but it's not nothing, Archer."

"I don't want to talk about it with you."

I ignore the dagger slicing through me at those two little words: *with you*. But this isn't about me, so I swallow my hurt and my pride as I say, "Want me to call Bellamy?"

"*No.*"

We sit quietly for a few more minutes, the tension building to a level that feels impossible to bear. I'm a can inside a trash compactor, unable to fight off the crushing pressure.

"Please? You know that you can trust me, Archer. I don't know how to be here for you if you won't talk to me."

He tenses, then releases a slow breath. "You've already helped," he says.

"Have you ever had a panic attack before?"

"Once."

He doesn't elaborate, and I'd like to borrow a toolkit from a professional thief so I can pick the locks Archer has around himself.

Actually, forget the fancy tools. Give me a sledgehammer and a blowtorch.

"Was there anything in particular that helped you get through it?"

"I like what you're doing with my hair," Archer says, and I double down on my head rub. "But you need to go do cookies, don't you?"

"I do. But this is more important. *You* are more important." I pause, keeping up the rhythmic drag of my fingers through his dark hair. "I don't know if this has to do with the trial this week, but I've been thinking about it. About you. I can't imagine how hard that would be. I wish ... I wish I could go with you. Not that you asked," I add quickly. "But if you wanted me there, I would want to be there."

He's quiet for so long that I sit up a little, looking down at him. Archer rolls onto his back, adjusting me so I'm tucked into the crook of his arm, my head on his shoulder. It's comfortable, but it means I can't see his face.

Which is maybe how he wants it. Talking is easier without eye contact.

But he still says nothing.

I'll admit it; I'm disappointed. It's selfish to want him to want me there when I know I can't go. I also hate that he's not talking to me about what's wrong. Especially after I pretty much opened a vein earlier in sharing what I did. It's like being on a seesaw with a hippopotamus on the other side—a complete imbalance of emotional weight and vulnerability.

Give him time, I tell myself, even if it's the opposite of my instinct, which wants me to pry and beg and force my way inside.

Archer's lips brush over my forehead. I tighten my jaw, willing it not to wobble or shake.

Archer is the one dealing with something huge right now—whatever it is. Not me. I won't make this about me.

"Thank you," he says finally. "I'll go to New York and deal with it. Then I'll be back. It will be fine. Okay?"

He's minimizing. I can hear him talking himself into believing his words, the same way I've done with so many things.

In the past almost five years, I've never felt so frustrated about my inability to leave Serendipity Springs. It makes me wish I'd started therapy earlier or not fought Judith at every turn. Not told her no when she suggested I try cognitive behavioral therapy, whatever that is.

Maybe, if I'd done more or tried harder, I would have been able to go with Archer now. I could have insisted and tagged along, hiding in his luggage if needed. Just to show my support. But I can't, and the thought burns.

I know Judith would tell me I'm being too critical. But Judith also would applaud the sudden burning need I have to do whatever work I can to see if it would help.

Because I don't want to be left in this position again—where I feel like my choices and my agency are being taken from me.

Four and a half years ago, I was crushed when Trey asked me to go to France with him—even though the moment he asked, I knew I wouldn't want to go, even if I could.

Now, Archer is acting like he doesn't need me in New York, and all I want is to be with him there.

After a few more minutes of silence, I extricate myself from Archer and he walks me to the door.

"I'll see you in the morning? I need to get things ready for Steve to start next week," I say.

Archer's gaze moves past me. "I think ... I might just go to the city a day early."

"You're leaving tomorrow?"

"I think that's best."

Why does it feel like we're having a fight even though we're not fighting?

I ignore the feeling and press up on my toes to kiss him. "Hurry back."

His gaze heats as he chases my mouth, deepening the kiss for not nearly long enough. "As soon as I can."

Okay, maybe things aren't so dire. Maybe it's all in my

head. Maybe I'm being overly dramatic, and Archer just needs more time to open up to me.

But as Archer turns the deadbolt, he pauses and frowns, staring at it. I watch the growing crease between his brows as he runs a finger over the lock.

And it's at this moment I remember how I got here. My stomach lands somewhere in the vicinity of the laundry room in the basement.

Archer glances at me. "How did you get into my apartment? Did Bellamy give you his key?"

"I—no." My thoughts are running like a scared mob, trampling over one another.

Make an excuse!

Tell the truth!

RUN!

"I was planning to give you a key tonight but forgot," Archer says. "I wrapped it up in a box and put it in a drawer—did you find it?"

Such a sweet gesture. I only wish he'd remembered to do it. Because then I could lie and tell him I used my key. Lying would be so much easier.

I shake my head. "No," I whisper.

His features tense as I watch, like a door slowly closing. "Then how did you get into my apartment, Willa?"

"Before you say anything, let me explain. Please."

Archer doesn't say anything. But as he crosses his arms and takes the smallest step back, his body says a lot.

"I guess I shouldn't say I'm going to *explain* because, honestly, I can't explain it. But this is the truth—sometimes, when I walk into my closet, I end up in your closet. And I know how that sounds. I promise, I know. There are rumors the building is magical, and I have no idea if that's true and I honestly don't even really believe in magic. If it hadn't happened to me—three times now, actually—I wouldn't believe it at all."

I pause and take a breath, keeping my gaze focused on Archer's undershirt, which is as clean and pressed as his starchy button-downs.

"Say something," I plead. "Ask me questions! I'll answer what I can, even if I don't know how. Or why."

I finally dare to look up at him and wish I hadn't. His face is as closed and impassive as the day I met him, when we had a similar discussion in the same room.

"Three times?" Archer asks, finally. "I know about the first time you claimed this happened and now tonight. You were in my apartment a third time?"

"Y-yes. The night of the possum. I was getting ready to deliver Bellamy's cookies, but then—*poof!*—the closet delivered me here. I left the cookies and then ran into you downstairs."

"My door was unlocked when I came back up," he says, his eyes still looking at something—anything, it seems—other than me.

"I didn't have a way to lock it. You believe me?" I ask, sounding as desperate and needy as I feel.

Archer finally meets my gaze, his gray eyes all steel. "I ..." He pauses and studies my face. Not with the kind, doting looks I've grown used to, but like he's a scientist and I'm a virus under a microscope. "I'm trying to reconcile this ... *explanation* with the person I knew."

It's the past tense that does it for me. "Right. My explanation. You mean my *lie*."

He doesn't say anything.

He doesn't have to.

I know he doesn't believe me. And you know what? I wouldn't believe me either. I wouldn't if I hadn't had it happen to me. I'm not Sophie, who loves the idea of the building being magical, of it throwing Archer and me together.

So much for that idea.

I can't be mad at Archer because I understand. But that doesn't stop me from being deeply, *deeply* hurt.

I open the door before he can. I need to feel like I'm the one walking out, not like I'm being kicked out.

Even if I can feel the force of a boot right in my sternum.

"I better go." There are other words I want to say.

Call me.

Let me know if you need anything.

I'm sorry.

I'm telling the truth.

I love you.

I say nothing else. Neither does Archer.

And then I walk away down the hall, down four flights of stairs. By the time I reach my apartment, I'm a sobbing, snotty mess.

Chapter Twenty
Archer

RETURNING to New York is like trying to squeeze into the suit I wore to my first board meeting when I was fifteen.

I grew eight inches over the following two years, in case anyone's curious about the fit.

Everything is too loud. Too bright. Too dirty. Strangers brush past me and their shoulders bump mine. Everyone is on a phone—not talking, but looking down at a screen.

"You are a porcupine-poked bear," Bellamy says, leaning against the back wall of the elevator. I refuse to look directly at him, but there are mirrored surfaces everywhere in here, so avoiding his gaze is like trying to roller skate through a minefield.

"A *what?*"

"You know how people talk about poking the bear? That's you. But instead of being poked with whatever people poke bears with, you've been poked with—"

"A porcupine. I got it." I press a finger between my brows, knowing full well it's not removing the crease that feels like it might be permanent.

"Rough night?" Bellamy asks. "Or rough morning?"

That's one way to put it. Traveling to the city from Serendipity Springs isn't the easiest, but today, my private car had a driver who wanted to talk. Then there was a delayed flight out of Boston, and the woman seated next to me in business class had a tiny dog in a travel bag who growled at me the entire flight. Almost enough to make me miss Archibald.

Which reminded me of Willa.

Not that it takes much to make me think of her. But right now, those thoughts are unwelcome. Because I can't think of Willa without remembering the sincerity in her face when she told me that her closet magically transported her into my apartment.

Why was I surprised by this? Willa is the same woman who swore that's how she first got into my apartment the night we met. My initial assessment—aside from recognizing something alluring about her—was that Willa was either lying or had some kind of break with reality. Because in no world do I believe in magical *anything*.

Given our first meeting, Willa's insistence last night shouldn't have been a shock. My first impression served as a warning—one I let myself forget.

I let other things cloud my judgment. I let myself get caught up in her beauty and the lightness she added to my life and—

"Are you planning to use the elevator as an office today?"

I open my eyes. We're at our floor, and Bellamy is holding open the door. From the tone of his voice, I expect he's been holding it open for quite some time. Still refusing to look at him, I exit and storm toward my office, ignoring the stares. I'm sure there are whispers too but all I can hear is blood rushing in my ears.

The rest of the day goes much like this. My day is bookended by two other terrible days. Yesterday: the conversation with Willa. Tomorrow: my father's trial.

Bellamy wasn't wrong about my mood, even if I don't love his animal analogy. My skin feels itchy, and my head won't stop pounding. Every conversation leaves me irrationally angry, and when I find a tin of mints in my drawer, I have a momentary sense of calm. Until I have two in my mouth.

They *do* taste like spicy dirt.

I'm spitting them into a wastebasket when Bellamy walks into my office without knocking. He closes the door behind him and sits down, wearing a grim expression.

"Would you like to talk about it?" But even as I open my mouth, he leans forward and speaks again. "Scratch that. I'm not asking. I'm telling. Talk to me, Archer. This seems like it's much larger than your father's trial. What happened after I left? Something with Willa?"

I don't answer.

"You're going to make me guess? We're playing mood charades now? Okay, let's see ..." Bellamy rubs his chin with the kind of dramatic thoughtfulness that makes me wish his chair was on wheels so I could shove him out of my office and send him careening down the hallway. "Four words. Film. *How to Lose a Girl in Ten Days*? No, wait. That's not the right title. Hm. I've got it! *She's Just Not That into You*."

I try not to rise to his teasing. I try. "Why do you assume it's my fault?"

"Ah, so there is an *it*. It, as in breakup? Or fight?"

I drag a hand over my face. "I don't know. Both? Neither?"

Bellamy waits. And after a moment, I lean forward.

"How would you respond if someone you love lies to you?"

I only realize what I've said after the brief flash of shock Bellamy quickly hides. Love. I love Willa. Not past tense but present.

Which only makes the feeling of betrayal worse.

"Did Willa lie to you?" Bellamy's tone is measured, as carefully constructed as the brutal expression he wears. But I can still sense his shock.

He and Willa have grown fairly close as well—I blame the cookies.

"Yes, she lied." I wince, picturing Willa's face as she told me about transporting into my closet. She was nervous, afraid to tell me. "No. I think she believes what she said."

"And you don't?"

"It's impossible. It can't be true."

"Do you think Willa's delusional, then?" he asks slowly. Each word sinks like a stone in my gut.

"No."

After a moment in which Bellamy clearly hopes I'll elaborate and I clearly am not about to, he stands.

"Well, I'll leave you to it," Bellamy says, pausing at the door. "I guess you need to think about which is more impossible: whatever thing Willa told you or the idea that she lied to you about it."

I'm pacing my apartment later that night when my phone blows up with a series of notifications. All the bells and chimes and vibrations tell me something newsworthy has happened. And because I'm receiving phone calls and texts from Bellamy, whatever it is has to do with me.

I leave my phone on the kitchen counter face down. In my experience, which has been far too frequent the past eighteen months, this won't be good news. Did my father find a way to ditch his ankle monitor and leave the country? Or maybe he found some new, devious way to pin it all on me.

Whatever it is, I have more important things on my mind. Specifically, a more important person.

Bellamy's words clanged around in my head the rest of the day, almost like he was standing inside my head beating a gong.

Which is more likely—Willa lying to me? Or the existence of a magical closet?

If anyone had posed the question to me as a hypothetical, there is no question. I'd believe the person making claims about a magical closet to be a liar.

But it's not a hypothetical person. It's Willa. And the moment Bellamy asked the question, I knew the answer.

She's not lying.

And I also don't believe she's delusional. Which leaves me caught in a kind of limbo, holding two opposing beliefs in my hands.

Willa wouldn't lie to me.

There's no such thing as a closet—or anything else—that can transport people from one place to another. No technology exists.

Yes, I looked it up.

Neither does magic or the paranormal or whatever category such a thing might fall under.

Magic, most would say—at least given the lore surrounding Serendipity Springs. I looked that up too.

Apparently, Galentine wasn't the only one who believed in some kind of magic in Serendipity Springs. There are almost as many posts and blogs dedicated to the city as there are to the existence of Bigfoot, though I'm not sure that is a point for or against.

In any case, having a lot of people talk about the city's historic good fortune and unsubstantiated claims of some kind of magic from the springs doesn't validate anything. And it doesn't help me with my debate.

I either need to believe Willa. Or not.

And if I do believe her, it means choosing to stand firmly

in that belief and then considering the significance of her actual claims later.

I'm shocked to find myself at peace, finally, with this idea.

I don't believe Willa is a liar.

I may not believe in magic, but I believe in *her*.

Which means I'll worry about the closet thing later because I have bigger things to worry about *now*. Specifically, the way I left things with Willa. The look of crushed hurt on her face has been haunting me, and the need to see her and to make things right pounds like a drumbeat in my mind.

It only takes a few minutes for me to debate the merits of returning to Serendipity Springs tonight when I'm required to appear in court tomorrow.

Worth it, I decide. Even if I can't get back and end up in contempt of court.

I'll have to text Bellamy about a private plane. There's no time to wait for anything else. But texting him means picking up my phone and finally facing the notifications and whatever news I've been ignoring.

Not quite ready to do that, I step inside my closet, wanting to pack a few more things to leave in Serendipity Springs.

But I've taken no more than a step inside my walk-in closet when the overhead light goes out. In fact, all traces of light from my apartment disappear. I stumble forward, hands splayed out and reaching for something familiar, but the only thing I find is a wall as I run face-first into it.

Chapter Twenty-One
Willa

WHEN SOPHIE FINDS ME, I've moved through what I'm calling the five stages of self-destruction. My current level—which I'm labeling a bomb shelter somewhere below rock bottom—involved pulling everything out of my closet. I mean *everything*. I dumped the contents on the floor of my bedroom in a messy pile resembling something between a hoarder's stash and a giant bird nest.

I am now sitting in the center like it's my personal, messy throne. My only loyal subject is the dresser I've dragged in front of the closet door. It's one of those pieces of furniture where the drawer pulls give it the look like a human face, so it's staring back at me in something like horror.

Fitting.

"Oh, honey," Sophie says, crouching down beside a pile topped with a handbag and a few unmatched socks. "This is …"

"It's fine." I sniff. "I have ice cream. See?"

Ice cream was the previous stage, and it's bleeding into this one. After my desperate attempt to leave Serendipity Springs and drive to New York failed miserably, I marched into Spring Foods and bought five different pints of the good stuff that's definitely outside my budget. But not today! Because the ice cream stage coincides nicely with the denial stage where I can pretend buying brand name groceries is in my budget. I also bought a large tub of jimmies, the kind of chocolate sauce that hardens on top, and maraschino cherries, which I've been eating straight from the jar. I can feel the sticky juice in my neck.

Sophie eyes me carefully, blowing a dark curl back from her face. "How much ice cream did you eat?" she asks, and I don't appreciate her tone.

"None of your business—that's how much," I snap, taking another vindictive spoonful. All my normal silverware was dirty, so I'm using a massive plastic serving spoon, which hardly fits inside my mouth. "I'll never tell."

But my eyes betray me, darting to the corner of my room where I've thrown three empty pint containers.

"I see," Sophie says. "And how's your tummy feeling?"

The facade of stubborn strength I'm trying to show crumbles. "B-better than my heart."

It takes a good friend to climb inside your heartbreak with you. And the very best of friends who will climb inside not just your heartbreak but your nest of clothing when you most likely have chocolate on your face and definitely have jimmies in your bra.

But that's Soph.

With careful fingers, she pries the spoon and now-empty carton of ice cream from my hand, tossing them both in the corner with the other carcasses. Then she wraps me up in a giant hug, not even deterred by my stickiness.

"You have chocolate in your ear," she says after a moment. I can tell she's holding back laughter.

When you're in the state I am, only a thin veil separates

laughter from tears. My shaky breath gives way to a giggle. "You *assume* that's chocolate."

"What else would it—*ew*. Never mind! Strike the question from the record. We're going to work from the assumption that it's chocolate. Because you also have it in your hair. On the plus side, you smell downright edible."

"Thank you." I sniff.

"Want to talk about what has you sitting in squalor and barricading your closet?"

"No. I really don't." But I do anyway. Because it's Sophie, and she listens but doesn't judge. Also, I need to talk through this.

So, I tell her about transporting up to Archer's closet, finally coming clean about the other time I didn't tell her about. And that he asked me how I got into his locked apartment, which led to him basically telling me I'm a dirty liar, which led to all the stages of grief, culminating in the clothing pile and the discarded ice cream cartons and the dresser barricade.

When I'm done, I really wish I had the last carton of ice cream, but it's in the freezer, and I don't think I could escape Sophie's tight hug anyway.

"You tried to leave Serendipity Springs?" She sounds impressed.

She shouldn't, considering how far I made it.

"Yeah. Didn't make it much farther than last time. Just past the sign saying you're leaving town. About a mile after that I had to turn around."

My hands went clammy on the wheel first, then my heart started feeling like it was being squeezed by a vise. Stars danced in my field of vision until it was too hard to see the road. I only realized I had been holding my breath when I turned the car around and found myself gasping for air.

The only plus side is that I didn't barf.

"I'm sorry," Sophie says. "But I think you're really brave for trying. Next time, let me come with you. Please?"

"It's embarrassing," I mumble. "I feel so stupid."

"It's brave. You're a warrior. And I'm happy to go alongside you, okay? But I have a question. Archer was being a jerk. Why were you trying to go to him? He should be coming to you. Apologizing. Maybe even groveling."

I don't disagree, and it takes a moment to consider my explanation.

"He really hurt me," I say finally. "But I also understand. I mean, you totally bought into this whole closet thing right away. If our roles had been reversed, I'm not so sure I would have believed you. Not that I would have thought you were lying," I add quickly. "I trust you. But believing in some kind of actual magic? It's ... a lot. And Archer is so *very* practical."

He's a lot of other things too: kind, thoughtful, surprisingly funny when he's comfortable in a situation. Handsome. Tender. I suddenly ache from the force of missing him.

"The man's middle name should be Logic," I joke, needing to ease the tightness coiling in my chest.

"Do you know his actual middle name?" Sophie asks.

This silly question pushes me back into tears. I *hate* crying. But hating it doesn't stop my body from doing it anyway. Especially as I think about him giving me his monogrammed handkerchief.

"Oliver. It's Oliver. But I don't know so many other things. But I thought I knew him. I want to know those things. I want ... all of it." Sophie rocks me a little as a shuddery breath escapes me. "I'm hurt and maybe a little mad, even though I do understand his reaction. Anyway, I wanted to go to New York because I know he's got his father's trial tomorrow. Maybe he wouldn't want me to be there, even before the whole closet thing. But I *wanted* to be there. He's a good man, and he deserves to have someone by his side."

The words all come out wobbly through my tears. Sophie just listens and holds onto me like she's auditioning to be my new favorite sweater.

"What about the closet?" she asks, nodding toward the mess in my room and the dresser blocking the door. "What happened there?"

"I got mad at it," I say. "I got inside and begged and pleaded for it to just transport me to New York wherever Archer is. I figured it might work. Maybe the key isn't Archer's closet as much as Archer himself. But it didn't work. Stupid closet." I kick at a bedroom slipper, which bounces off the dresser and lands harmlessly on the floor.

"Aw, sweetie. We don't know how the magic works, but I guess we can definitively say it's not like a genie granting wishes."

"If it were, I'd wish I never met Archer Gaines."

"You don't mean that."

No, I don't. Not even a little bit.

But I do hate this ugly, dark feeling spreading through my chest. It's worse than anything I ever felt after Trey and I broke up. Which feels impossible. Maybe your first heartbreak is just a way to prep you for the real one that's a million times worse.

"I shouldn't feel this way after a few w-weeks," I tell Sophie through a broken sob. "It's not like I'm in love with him."

"You're not?"

"No! I can't be. It's too soon," I say, even though I sound like I'm trying to convince myself. Or convince us both. It's not working on either count.

Sophie hands me a tissue. I'm not sure where it came from, and I don't really care. I wipe my eyes and blow my nose.

"I'm just not sure love works on a specific timeline," she

says. "Days, weeks, years. I think it pretty much does whatever it wants. Like your closet."

"Then I hate love too."

Sophie gives me a tight squeeze, rocking me back and forth. "Don't say that. Because you know what? I have a feeling Archer is just as miserable as you are. Maybe more. And I bet any minute now, he's going to walk right through your door and—"

Sophie is interrupted by a loud thump. The dresser blocking the closet rattles like something hit the door from the other side.

We both freeze.

"What was that?" I whisper.

"I don't know," Sophie replies in the same soft but urgent tone.

Another thud and what sounds like a muffled groan. Then the door handle twists. It should feel like we're watching a horror movie.

Except ... the tiniest kernel of hope is opening in my chest.

I get to my feet, staring at the knob. Someone on the other side tries to push the door open, but the dresser blocks it. Sophie hooks an arm around my leg and holds on tight, cowering.

But I'm not afraid. Maybe I should be, but I have a gut feeling about this.

"Hello?" I call, hesitant but hopeful. "Who's there?"

"Willa?"

At the sound of Archer's voice, something moves through me. A warm liquid unfurls and spreads through my limbs until my hands are shaking. But my steps are firm as I extricate myself from Sophie's grip and step in front of the dresser.

He must not have left, after all. He's been upstairs this

whole time, and now The Serendipity must have decided it was time for Archer to experience the closet transport.

"I'm here," I say. "You're in my closet. Give me a sec. I need to unblock the door."

"Why is the door blocked?" he asks, and the question makes me grin.

Because he's not asking other questions like *Why am I in your closet?* Or *How I did get here?*

Sophie grabs the other side of the dresser, and together, we make easy work of dragging it back to its rightful spot. Then I stop and stare at the closet door, my hands still trembling.

"I'm going to go," Sophie whispers, giving my shoulder a quick squeeze. "But you'd better find me later and fill me in. And make him grovel."

I nod but don't watch her go. Because slowly, the knob turns and the closet door pushes open, revealing a disheveled Archer. His eyes are wide and panicked, though they settle a little when they land on me. He has an angry red bump on his forehead where it looks like he hit his head.

I reach out to touch it, then remember the last time we talked and take a small step back instead. His expression shifts, first falling and then gathering into something a little fierce, mouth a firm line and gray-blue eyes sparking with electric intensity.

I'm not sure how I know, but this is Archer in a boardroom, in the middle of a hostile takeover or dropping some big business bomb. Or ... whatever one does in a boardroom. Basically, this is Archer elite, and it's aimed directly my way.

I already feel myself crumbling.

Make him grovel, Sophie said. And though I'm much more a person who forgives easily, I straighten my shoulders and lift my chin. Archer did hurt my feelings. He didn't believe me— even if I was telling him a story that was admittedly wild.

Now, he's experienced the truth of the magic himself, and I feel vindicated. So, yeah. I can let him grovel a bit.

"I thought you were going to New York," I say, crossing my arms over my chest for a little extra bolstering.

But this reminds me of my sticky hands and maraschino cherry skin. Oh, how I wish I was freshly showered instead of wearing yoga pants and remnants of ice cream. Because this version of Archer—intensely focused, serious, and, as always, in an impeccable suit, feels way out of my league.

"I did go," Archer says.

Frowning, I glance at the open closet behind him. "But ... you're in my closet. You didn't come from your closet?"

"I came from New York," Archer says, and my mouth drops open.

"How is that possible?" I whisper. Moving inside the building is one thing but Archer somehow got sucked here from New York? Now, I'm the one struggling to believe.

"How is *any* of it possible?" he says. Then shakes his head. "Willa, I'm so sorry I doubted you. That I didn't trust you."

"So ... you're sorry now that you know I wasn't lying?"

Archer takes a step forward. When I don't back away, he takes another until we're inches apart and I have to tilt my head a little to hold eye contact.

"No," he says.

"No *what*?"

"I had already decided I was wrong for not believing you. Even if I didn't quite buy into the idea of magic or understand how this closet thing could be true, I know *you*. That is all that matters, and I was wrong for not seeing that before."

Archer reaches out, one big hand cupping my cheek with such gentleness that a whole-body sigh moves through me.

"I was making plans to come back when I stepped into my closet," he continues. "And now, I'm here. It makes no sense. It defies logic. Honestly, it's a little terrifying. But I'm so glad. Because even a private plane wouldn't have been fast enough."

"You were going to take a private plane?"

"I needed to be here now." Archer's thumb brushes over my cheek, I realize he's brushing away a tear. "Don't cry, Willa the Person," he says. "I'm so sorry for leaving the way I did. And for not trusting you. Will you forgive me?"

This certainly seems like enough groveling to me. Throwing my arms around him, I press myself into Archer. One of his hands cups the back of my head and the other spans my lower back, tugging me closer. His warmth, his scent, even the softness of his expensive suit all feel like home. Sliding my hands underneath his jacket, I bunch his shirt in my fists.

"I tried to come to New York," I confess. "Even though I was hurt. I wanted to be there for you."

His arms squeeze me tighter. "Willa. You didn't need to do that. The last thing I wanted to do was put you in that position."

"You didn't! I wanted to be there for you. I even begged the closet to take me. When it didn't, I got mad."

"That's why everything is on the floor and your dresser was blocking the door?" I can hear the smile in his voice.

"There might have also been ice cream involved. In fact, I'm probably getting chocolate on you," I tell him. "Or cherry juice."

"Cherry juice?"

"It's a long story."

"I'd love to hear it."

I pull back, craning my neck so I can meet his gaze. "Is that really what you want to talk about right now?"

His steely eyes become fire. "Not even a little bit."

And then his mouth finds mine. From the look in his eyes, I expect to be hurtled into a passionate kiss, but Archer is full of restraint. Tender. As though he's easing his way back to me. A restart, or at least a fresh one. His lips brush mine as though taking stock of every millimeter of my skin.

I'm dizzy and kiss-drunk, and it only makes me desperate for more. I release his shirt to link my hands behind his neck, tugging him closer until Archer's careful restraint unravels and we're locked in an embrace that feels as much like some kind of battle of wills as a declaration of something.

Love. This is love.

I might have denied it to Sophie—and myself—but I know. Not from the kiss, but from everything. It's just ... Archer.

The insistent ringing of a phone has us pulling apart, panting. Archer reaches in his pocket then frowns. "I think my phone is still in New York."

"It's mine," I say, pressing my mouth to his neck. "We can ignore it."

But it doesn't stop. And it's hard to maintain the mood when I recently changed my ringtone to "9 to 5." Dolly Parton is great in most situations, but maybe not this one.

"Let me just check," I say, reluctantly pulling away to find my phone under a pile of T-shirts. "It's Bellamy. Hello?"

"Is Archer with you?" Bellamy sounds panicked, and I wonder if he was there when Archer disappeared. Did Archer ever tell him about the closets?

I put it on speakerphone so Archer can hear. "He's right here with me."

"Hello, Bellamy," Archer says.

"Oh, good, you came to New York," Bellamy says. "I hope you brought cookies."

"Not exactly."

"You didn't exactly bring cookies? I think it's a yes or no question."

"I'm ... not exactly in New York," I say.

"We're in Serendipity Springs." Archer and I wait for Bellamy's response. It takes a long moment.

Another long silence. "I'm sorry," Bellamy finally says. "But I'm processing and have a lot of questions. First, how in the world did you get there so quickly? You were just here."

"That is a long story, perhaps better told in person," Archer says. "Can you send a plane? I need to be back for the trial."

"I can, but that's the other reason I'm calling. I tried to reach you earlier, but you wouldn't answer your phone."

"It's in New York still."

"You left your phone?"

"Again, part of the long story. What's the other reason you're calling?" Archer sounds suddenly impatient, and, with his fingertips tracing the curve of my waist, I feel the same way.

"Your father decided to take the plea deal. You don't need to testify because there is no trial."

The relief moving through Archer is palpable, and once again, I lean in to hug him. One armed this time, as I'm still holding my phone in my other hand.

"He sent a certified letter through his lawyer, and I'm not sure if you want to read it."

"Did you read it?" Archer asks.

"Maybe."

"Do you think I want to read it?"

"Not right now," Bellamy says. "It's sort of half of an apology and half justification and all very, very typical of your father."

"Leave it on my desk. I'll get it when I come back."

"And when will that be?" Bellamy asks. "Do I still need to send a plane?"

Archer's smile makes my whole body feel fizzy and light. "Can you keep things running there?"

Bellamy scoffs. "I'm the CEO, Archer. The only reason you're as involved as you are is because you don't like giving up control."

"Well, consider this me giving up. At least for a while. I foresee a very, very busy schedule in my future." His voice is dropping lower with each syllable, and I'm tempted to just chuck the phone in the corner with the empty ice cream cartons.

"You've got big plans, hm?" Bellamy sounds amused.

"The biggest," Archer answers, plucking the phone from my hand. "I plan to spend a significant portion of time showing Willa exactly how much I love her."

He ends the call on Bellamy's laughter and then drops the phone into a soft pile of sweaters. I blink up at him, stunned and delighted.

"What?" he asks, lips curling up in the kind of smirk I never could have pictured on his face when I first met him. I trace the line of his mouth.

"Is that how you're going to tell me you love me for the first time—on a phone call to Bellamy?"

"It wasn't how I planned it, no. But then, Willa, you've been frustrating my plans from the moment I met you."

"I'm sorry," I whisper, distracted by his mouth as he leans closer.

"I'm not," Archer murmurs, his breath fanning my cheek. "I love that about you. I love your lightheartedness and your free spiritedness and how your apartment can be such a mess but your cookies are so detailed and perfect. You are a wonderfully beautiful contradiction I never knew I needed, and I love you. I love you, Willa."

"I love you too, Archer. And as much as I want to tell you all the reasons and list them out, right now, I think I'd rather kiss you."

"That can be arranged." This last word is said with his lips against mine, and then he's pulling me up in his arms, carrying me toward my apartment door while kissing me frantically.

"Where are we going?" I ask, giggling as he kisses me again.

"I may love your chaos, but I cannot keep kissing you in the middle of this mess. We're going to my apartment."

"Should we just see if the closet will take us?" I ask, and Archer freezes.

He pulls back a little to look at me, the love and care clearly written in his gray-blue eyes. "As grateful as I am for the outcome, I would very much like to avoid closets for a long, long time."

Epilogue
Willa

"Are you sure you'll be okay?" I ask Bellamy.

His sigh is dramatic, even over the phone. "I'm not an invalid. Or an octogenarian—yet. I'll be perfectly fine without the two of you. I *know* you don't want me joining you for your honeymoon."

Archer, who is seated next to me and leaning close enough to hear every word, plucks the phone from my hand. "No, we most certainly don't."

"And you promise to take good care of Miss McKitty Face?"

One of the presents Archer surprised me with after our wedding was a little orange fluffball of a kitten. She's a little bit of a nightmare between the shredding of the furniture and her insistence on using people's shoulders as her personal perch, but we are both obsessed.

And I'm not sure I've seen anything hotter than Archer walking around the apartment with a tiny orange kitten on his shoulder. It's my new phone wallpaper. I'm thinking about creating my own calendar where every month of the year is just Archer and McKitty Face.

"Yes, but I promise you I *won't* be calling her that," Bellamy says. "Her name is Vivian. A perfectly distinguished name for a—ow! Remove your talons from my trousers, Vivian! I am not a trellis!"

"Good McKitty," I coo, even though I doubt she can hear me. I catch Archer smiling. "Very distinguished."

Bellamy grunts. "Anything else besides your adorably evil kitten? Any quirks to the apartment I should know about?"

Archer and I exchange a look. We never did tell Bellamy about the closet. Not because we didn't think he'd believe us —Bellamy definitely seems like he would be all-in on the idea of magic in the building. But now, it feels like something that's just more private. Something special just for Archer and me to share.

"Nope," Archer says.

"But maybe ... stay out of the closet," I add quickly.

"Ah, is that where you're hiding my Christmas presents?" Bellamy asks, sounding excited.

"It's July," Archer says drily. "Anyway, thank you for watching McKitty and goodbye." He ends the call abruptly, then turns my phone off before handing it back. "There. That's better."

"What if I wanted to make another call?"

Archer raises a dark brow. "You already called your parents —twice—and Sophie. Do you really need to call anyone else?"

"Maybe."

"Fine." Archer leans back, crossing his arms. But there's the tiniest quirk in his lips. "Make your call."

I power my phone back on and turn the screen away so he can't see it. "Fine. I will. But I need some privacy for this one."

Archer looks ready to stop me as I get up, but he quickly gets distracted. I take advantage as he reaches in his pocket for his phone and duck around the corner and out of sight.

"Hello?"

Even over the phone, his low, rumbly voice has an impact on me. "Hello, Mr. Gaines."

A pause. "Willow. What a lovely and unexpected surprise."

I'm grinning like a fool. After he decided Willa the Person was too long of a nickname for me, Archer started calling me Willow. I like it a lot—something I never would have imagined the night we met. But it reminds me of how far we've come.

I couldn't have imagined any of what followed. Honestly, had you asked me beforehand what was more believable, me falling in love with a grumpy billionaire or The Serendipity actually being magical, I probably would have gone with the magic building. The closet transports ended after Archer was transported from New York, though I'm still a little wary any time I enter Archer's—now, *our*—closet.

I have no desire to appear in some other person's closet again. I've got my person. And I can't help but wonder if The Serendipity really somehow did shove us—literally and magically—together.

"Where are you right now?" Archer asks. A slight shift in background noise tells me he's on the move.

We are at the airport. That's right—the *airport*. La Guardia, to be exact.

This is maybe the only thing that could have surprised me more than falling in love with Archer *or* the magic closet: finally making progress with my agoraphobia. I scaled back Serendipitous Sweets, supplying cookies to a few local bakeries rather than taking custom orders. For almost a year, I've focused on regular therapy with Judith and cognitive behavioral therapy with someone she recommended. As of a few months ago, I can leave Serendipity Springs without incident and without the overwhelming anxiety.

Okay, not entirely true. I feel anxious about getting

anxious. It will be a while before I can leave town without wondering if I'm going to have an anxiety attack. Every time I go, there's a sense of worry leading up to it. But then ... my heart doesn't race, my lungs don't stop working, and—best of all—I don't barf.

I am *free*.

Free to leave Serendipity Springs. Free to stay. Just ... *free*.

And now that Archer and I got married last month, we are making the most of it. It might have taken us weeks to leave for our honeymoon because of some kind of big deal Archer had to be in New York for, but now we've got a full three weeks away. Bellamy is taking a break and staying at our place, and we are going ... somewhere. Archer refused to tell me our destination. He even asked to pack for me, which was an ultimate test of trust on my part.

I waver between excitement for the surprise and feeling like I'm going to lose it if I don't know details *now*. I leaned heavily toward the latter as this trip approached. I tried to make Bellamy tell me by threatening to cut off his cookie supply, but not even that could get him to tell me. Archer, unsurprisingly, never wavered with all my begging and bargaining and threatening. The man doesn't crack.

"Wouldn't you like to know where I am?" I tell Archer now, ducking behind a potted tree. "You'll have to find me. If you can."

We aren't just in the regular airport part of La Guardia. We're in some kind of fancy lounge. It's two full stories with a big, curved staircase and balcony overlooking everything. The décor is slick and modern but comfortable with plush couches and tables around a circular bar. The alcove where we were just sitting had a marble-topped coffee table with actual hardbacks on it. Real books! In an airport!

It's what my mom would call hoity toity, a.k.a., meant for

wealthy people. Which, technically, now that I've married Archer, I *am*.

We mostly don't live like it, still inhabiting Archer's apartment in The Serendipity since our wedding. It suits us just fine until we decide what we want to do long term. Now that I'm not trapped in Serendipity Springs, we could go to New York or somewhere else altogether. I suspect, however, we'll stay. Especially now that Archer and my dad meet several times a week in the basement to do train stuff.

That was definitely not on my bingo card, but it's really adorable. And it's been so good for both my dad and Archer. Bellamy even joins them occasionally, and the three of them have a whole bromance thing going on.

"I *will* find you," Archer says, and I catch sight of his back as he walks around a corner. He's looking out toward the bar, and I see several women checking him out.

I almost give up the game, ready to go claim my man, but his gaze skates right over the women. Disappointed, they turn back to their drinks. Triumphant, I grin. Then quickly duck behind a wall and scurry toward the stairs as he nearly spots me.

"You can try," I whisper ducking and walking behind a small group of people to give me cover. I catch sight of a blur of black suit headed away from me that I *think* is Archer. Hard to tell since the people I'm using as cover also block my view.

I get a few strange looks but ignore them and manage to duck into a private suite bathroom. Which is probably cheating somehow in this game we're making the rules for as we go along.

In all honesty? I *want* to be found.

No, I'm not usually a make out in public bathrooms kind of woman. But I'm on my honeymoon. And if you can't make out in a fancy airport lounge's fancy bathroom, then what even is the point of paying for access to this place?

"Give me a hint," Archer practically growls into the phone. The sound makes my toes curl.

"What will you offer me in exchange for a hint?" I ask, opening the door a crack to peek out.

"I'll tell you one of the stops on our trip."

Oooh, the man knows how to get me. "*One* of the stops? How many are there?"

"Give me a hint," he repeats.

I'm dying to know. As much as I love surprises, the not knowing makes me feel like I'm about to explode. Are we headed somewhere warm or somewhere cold? Somewhere in the United States or somewhere outside of it? Archer insisted I get a passport once I was able to leave town, and it's feasible he packed it for me. He did all the work to check us in for our flight ahead of time, so there have been no clues at all once we got through security and came to the lounge.

"Fine. Think about where we had our first kiss," I tell him.

Almost immediately, I catch sight of him striding this way. Before he can see me, I slam the door and press my back up against the wall next to it. The cool marble sends a pleasant shiver down my spine. Or maybe that's just anticipation.

The door flies open a moment later and then Archer towers over me. He ends the call and slides the phone into his pocket. Then he slowly and deliberately reaches out a hand and locks the door.

Me? I'm still standing here with a phone pressed to my ear.

"You found me," I whisper, dropping my phone into the crossbody bag I bought for this trip.

"I did."

I expect him to move toward me, to touch me or kiss me,

but he just keeps ... standing there. Looking tall and impossibly handsome and very kissable in his suit.

"So, where are we going? You promised to tell me one of our stops."

Archer's blue-gray eyes burn into me. "A promise is a promise. Do you want to know the first, last, or one of the middle stops?"

My mouth drops open a little. "How many stops are there?"

Archer shrugs in such a casual way that I feel sure there are far too many stops for a reasonable vacation. While it's true that we don't live like most people who have his net worth, he does find unique and absolutely outlandish ways to spoil me.

"A few."

"You promised not to go overboard!" I give him a light shove. "How. Many?"

"Would you like to know one of the stops, or would you like to know how many? You only get one answer," he says. The man is infuriating. Impossible to crack.

Correction—*almost* impossible to crack.

I step closer and tiptoe my fingers up his chest, finally reaching the bare skin above his collar. I slide my fingers around to the back of his neck and into his hair. "What if I throw in a kiss to sweeten the deal? Will you tell me how many stops *and* give me the first one?"

Archer sways toward me. I can tell he's trying to hold it together, but he's about to break. Stretching up, I place a kiss on his neck, just below his jawbone, and hear his sharp intake of breath.

With my lips still against his skin, I whisper, "Well?"

There's no warning. He spins me so my back is to the wall again, surrounded by Archer. His hands bracket my head and his cheek brushes mine. Usually he keeps his face clean-shaven, but he decided he was going to try growing a beard while on our honeymoon. After asking my opinion of course.

I'm not sure how I'll feel through all the itchy stages of it, but right now, the scratch of his stubble is really working for me.

"For one kiss from you right now, I would give up any secret. Reveal any thought. I'd trade the world for you, Willa. Don't tempt me."

I'm the one who's tempted here. Or maybe we both are in equal amounts, which seems like the best foundation for a relationship.

Until the doorknob rattles and then there's a loud knocking on the door. Archer sighs and his breath stirs my hair against my neck.

"Later," he murmurs against my ear, a rough but tender promise, and I can hardly wait as he takes my hand and leads me out of the bathroom.

Not just for the *later* where he'll probably pull me into a quiet corner of the lounge and kiss me or the plane ride to follow or wherever our destinations are, but the *later* of weeks and months and years to come.

I spend a lot of time thinking about our future, caught up in a constant state of anticipation.

When Sophie tried to tell me to stop wishing my life away, I couldn't find a way to articulate why that's *not* what I'm doing. I'm definitely enjoying the now. It's just that for the first time since before Trey and before my agoraphobia, I have hope.

It's not something I consciously realized I lost. But now, with Archer in my life and the ability to leave Serendipity Springs, I feel the hope expanding from where it had atrophied for so many years without me even realizing it.

When I look and think ahead, I'm simply exercising my hope muscles. Hope fills my current life with more meaning, more joy, more everything. I'm practically bursting at the seams to make room for all of it.

So, *later* is my new favorite word.

"Hey." I pull Archer to a stop near an unoccupied seating area in the corner.

His eyes are immediately on mine. Attentive. Focused. Curious. "Are you okay?"

I nod, biting my lip, like that can do anything to hold back my smile. "I'm great," I tell him.

"Then why are you smiling while you also look like you're about to cry?" His concern is so endearing, and it only makes all the emotion bubble up out of me more.

"I'm happy," I say, my voice wobbling.

Archer pulls me into his arms, a tight, strong hug. "Please don't cry, Willow."

"They're happy tears. Promise. I'm just ..."

He waits, and after a moment, gently urges, "You just what?"

"I'm just really, really happy."

Archer cups my face with both hands and presses a soft kiss to my lips. The sweetness of it makes me ache.

"Are you ready for your answer?" Archer asks. "It's only fair now that I've kissed you."

But I shake my head. "No. I've changed my mind. I don't want you to tell me anything. I want everything to be a surprise. I like the anticipation and the wonder. All I need to know is that wherever it is we're going, Archer, I'm with you."

Want to know what happens when Bellamy apartment-sits for Archer and Willa?

Hint: it involves the closet, a kitten, and an unexpected meeting.

Read ONLY BELLAMY IN THE BUILDING, a companion bonus scene, when you sign up for Emma's email list.
https://emmastclair.com/mmb

(Unsubscribe at any time. But I'll do my best to make you want to stay.)

Only Magic in the Building
a whimsical romance series

The Serendipity
Emma St. Clair

The Cupid Chronicles
Courtney Walsh

Petals and Plot Twists
Jenny Proctor

Misfortune and Mr. Right
Savannah Scott

Clean Out of Luck
Carina Taylor

Off the Wall
Julie Christianson

Signed, Sealed, and Smitten
Melanie Jacobson

The Escape Plan
Katie Bailey

A Note from Emma

Dear readers,

I am so thankful you're here!!! Because if you're here, I'm guessing you didn't just skip ahead to read the author note (wait—does anyone do that?), but you're here because you just finished *The Serendipity* and then kept turning the page.

I hope you loved this fun, whimsical love story. I will never, ever get tired of the grumpy sunshine dynamic—you've been warned.

It was so refreshing to do something a little different with this book and this series. The planning and the preparation and all the behind-the-scenes work has been going on for well over a year, and I'm honestly proud of our work, but PROUDER that we somehow managed to keep our mouths shut. These group projects are so much work but also so rewarding, and I'm so glad to be part of this group.

I was a little nervous about Willa's anxiety and how that would land with readers. I didn't realize agoraphobia could be something beyond being unable to leave your home, but it is an anxiety disorder that can manifest in many ways. I have a friend who has struggled with leaving their city at all, which partially inspired Willa's story. If you or someone you know struggles with anxiety or agoraphobia, it can be crippling—but there is also hope!

(Probably NOT in the way of a portal closet, though.)

I had a lot of fun writing Willa's parents. My family used to play with the telemarketers (not QUITE as much as Willa's dad) and my uncle Mason had a huge train set in his basement.

Once, when I was six, I asked if he would leave it to me in his will. I had just learned about wills, and no one explained that this was rude. (Spoiler alert: he did NOT leave it to me in his will.) I have very fond memories of sitting on a stool while he made the extensive and intricate train set run. Sometimes he even let me push the buttons and make the horns blow. It was really fun to remember him and to write these memories into the story.

If you'd like to read a little bonus scene featuring Bellamy while he's apartment-sitting, you can download that at emmastclair.com/mmb. (The MMB stands for Magical Matchmaking Building, which is what I called this series while we worked on it.) It's not a FULL story, but more of a cute little bonus snippet about Bellamy's time in the magic building.

If you want to connect, you can find me on Instagram (@kikimojo) or join my community of readers at emmastlcair.com/community.

Thank you so much for reading! I hope you enjoy the rest of the Only Magic in the Building stories!

-e

Acknowledgments

Every book is made with care AND with the support of so many readers and support people who help.

A giant thank you to the following people who read early copies and caught the sneaky typos that really wanted to stay in the book: Jordan, Rita. Bethany, Shannon, Abby, Kimberley, Carole, Cristi, Mandi, Priscilla, Alicia, Marti, Marilee, Micah, Jody, Lindsay, Ruth. If I missed anyone who sent them, I'm so sorry!

Thanks also to Emily of Midnight Owl Editing and to Jenny Proctor for always being the BEST.

A giant thanks to all the other Only Magic in the Building author, especially Courtney, for keeping me stable (ish). Jenny, Savannah, Julie, Carina, Melanie, Christina—you guys rock.

And a huge thanks to Melody Jeffries for making the most amazing covers EVER.

What to Read Next

The Appies

Just Don't Fall- Emma St. Clair

Absolutely Not in Love- Jenny Proctor

A Groom of One's Own- Emma St. Clair

Romancing the Grump- Jenny Proctor

Runaway Bride and Prejudice- Emma St. Clair

Love Stories in Sheet Cake

The Buy-In

The Bluff

The Pocket Pair

Sweet Royal Romcoms

Royally Rearranged

Royal Gone Rogue

Love Clichés

Falling for Your Best Friend's Twin

Falling for Your Boss

Falling for Your Fake Fiancé

The Twelve Holidates

Falling for Your Brother's Best Friend

Falling for Your Best Friend

Falling for Your Enemy

Oakley Island (with Jenny Proctor)

Eloise and the Grump Next Door

Merritt and Her Childhood Crush

Sadie and the Bad Boy Billionaire

Izzy and Her Off Limits Love

About the Author

Emma St. Clair is a *USA Today* bestselling author of over thirty books and has her MFA in Fiction. She lives in Katy, Texas with her husband, five kids, and a Great Dane who doesn't make a very good babysitter. Her romcoms have humor, heart, and nothing that's going to make you need to hide your Kindle from the kids. ;)

You can find out more at http://emmastclair.com or join her reader group at https://www.facebook.com/groups/emmastclair/

Emma is represented by Kimberly Whalen, The Whalen Agency.